PRAIS

THE ELIZABET

# THE TWYLIGHT TOWER

"An exciting mystery . . . What makes *The Twylight Tower* comparable to the fine works of Alison Weir is the strong wr    f       thor, interweaving historical tidbits into a po        ne." —THE MIDWEST BOOK REVIEW

"H        fine touch. . . . Both her fictional and histori- cal        s breathe and provide the reader with spirited ent        ent. So do her plots, perhaps as complicated as the rea        of Elizabeth's court. Join the Queen's Privy Plot Co      and sleuth along with the best."

—MYSTERY NEWS

"H      r's Elizabeth is a brilliant and willful young wo      . . . . Conspiracies and lies take the story through tw      nd turns. . . ." —BOOKLIST

## THE POYSON GARDEN

"A        ing cross between a swashbuckling historical ro        mystery novel. The heroine is spunky, the co        e and truckle, capes swirl, daggers flash, and ho        —PORTLAND OREGONIAN

"P        ss, betrayal, sibling rivalry, and a mass mu        ievably made the       of El      ethan tin        he pe        NAL

"I        and he        MES

# THE TIDAL POOLE

"Harper's facility with historical figures such as William Cecil, Robert Dudley, and the treacherous Duchess of Suffolk is extraordinary." —Los Angeles Times

"A nice mix of historical and fictional characters, deft twists and a plucky, engaging young heroine enhance this welcome sequel to *The Poyson Garden*." —Publishers Weekly

"Peopled with historical figures and bounding with intrigue and mystery, *The Tidal Poole* is a triumphant read. Harper does a masterful job at re-creating the era, and her portrait of the young queen is brilliant. The intricate plot will immediately carry readers away to Elizabethan times."

—Romantic Times

"Harper delivers high drama and deadly intrigue. . . . [She] masterfully captures the Elizabethan tone in both language and setting and gives life to fascinating historical figures. . . . Elizabethan history has never been this appealing."

—Newsday

"Rollicking good action, wicked doings, and lively characters." —Colorado Springs Gazette

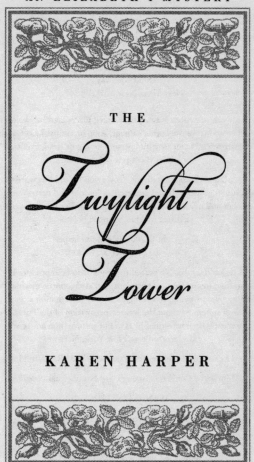

THE

*Twylight*

*Tower*

KAREN HARPER

A DELL BOOK

Published by
Dell Publishing
a division of
Random House, Inc.
1540 Broadway
New York, New York 10036

Library of Congress Catalog Card Number: 00-064470

ISBN: 0-440-23592-8

Reprinted by arrangement with Delacorte Press

Printed in the United States of America

Published simultaneously in Canada

February 2002

10   9   8   7   6   5   4   3   2

OPM

*For Sharon and Nancy,
who shared a lovely trip to
England with us.*

*Also my gratitude to
my far-flung sister Elizabethan experts
and fellow Anglophiles:*

*Susan Watkins, who first suggested Dr. John Dee
as a fascinating character. Susan's* THE PUBLIC
AND PRIVATE WORLDS OF ELIZABETH I
*has helped me set many a scene.*

*to author Eloisa James for pointing
me toward and lending me* THE ARUNDEL
HARINGTON POETRY *manuscripts.*

*to author and researcher Dorothy Auchter.*

*Best wishes for his continued stellar career
to my former British literature student, and the
world's best living lutenist, Paul O'Dette.*

*And, as ever, to Don,
for living so many years with a wife who spends
much of her time in the 1500s.*

# *Elizabeth* I

1533 Henry VIII marries Anne Boleyn, January 25. Elizabeth born September 7.

1536 Anne Boleyn executed. Elizabeth disinherited from crown. Henry weds Jane Seymour.

1537 Prince Edward born. Queen Jane dies of childbed fever.

1543 Henry VIII weds sixth wife, Katherine Parr, who brings Elizabeth to court.

1544 Act of succession and Henry VIII's will establish Mary and Elizabeth in line of succession.

1547 Henry VIII dies. Edward VI crowned; Edward Seymour, Duke of Somerset, his uncle, becomes his protector. Thomas Seymour, King Edward's younger uncle, weds Henry's widow, Queen Dowager Katherine Parr, in secret. John Harington enters Thomas Seymour's service. Seymour tries to seduce Elizabeth in Parr's household; Elizabeth is sent away.

1548 Katherine Parr dies in childbirth. Thomas Seymour tries to court Elizabeth and Jane Grey; fails in attempt to gain control of King Edward.

1549 Thomas Seymour arrested for treason. John Harington accompanies Seymour to Tower. Elizabeth denies complicity in Seymour plot. Thomas Seymour beheaded; Harington released. Edward Seymour ousted from power as Lord Protector by John Dudley, Duke of Northumberland, father of Robert Dudley.

1550 Robert Dudley, age seventeen, weds Amy Robsart.

1552 Edward Seymour executed.

1553 Lady Jane Grey forced to wed Guildford Dudley. King Edward dies. Mary Tudor overthrows Northumberland's attempt to put Protestant "Queen" Jane Grey and her husband, Guildford Dudley, Northumberland's son, on the throne. Robert Dudley sent to Tower for his part in rebellion. Queen Mary I crowned. Northumberland executed. Queen Mary weds Prince Philip of Spain by proxy; he arrives in England in 1554. Queen Mary begins to force England back to Catholicism.

1554 John Harington weds Elizabeth's friend Lady Isabella Markham. Protestant Wyatt Rebellion fails, but Elizabeth implicated. Jane Grey, Guildford Dudley, and Henry Grey, Duke of Suffolk ("Queen" Jane's father) beheaded. Elizabeth sent to Tower for two months, accompanied by Kat Ashley, John and Isabella Harington.

1555- Elizabeth lives mostly in
1558 rural exile as queen sickens.

1558 Mary dies; Elizabeth succeeds to throne, November 17. Elizabeth appoints William Cecil Secretary of State. Robert Dudley made Master of the Queen's Horse.

1559 Elizabeth crowned in Westminster Abbey, January 15. Parliament urges the queen to marry; she resists, February 4. Bishop Alvaro de Quadra becomes Spanish ambassador in England, May. Mary Queen of Scots becomes Queen of France at accession of her young husband, Francis II, July.

1560 English army defeats the French in Scotland, January. Cecil achieves Treaty of Edinburgh in Scotland to get France out of Scotland and make Scotland a Protestant nation, July.

1561 Now widowed and not permitted to pass through English territory, Mary Queen of Scots returns to Scotland, August 19.

*House of Lancaster*    *House of York*

**Henry VII**   m.   Elizabeth of York
r. 1485-1509

## HOUSE OF TUDOR

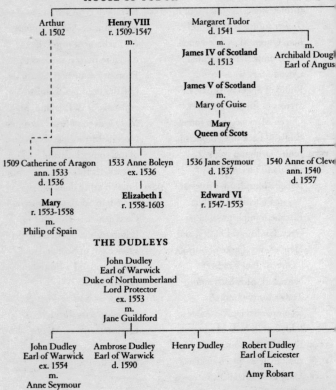

Arthur
d. 1502

**Henry VIII**
r. 1509-1547
m.

Margaret Tudor
d. 1541 —————————

m.
**James IV of Scotland**
d. 1513

m.
Archibald Doug
Earl of Angus

**James V of Scotland**
m.
Mary of Guise

**Mary
Queen of Scots**

1509 Catherine of Aragon
ann. 1533
d. 1536

**Mary**
r. 1553-1558
m.
Philip of Spain

1533 Anne Boleyn
ex. 1536

**Elizabeth I**
r. 1558-1603

1536 Jane Seymour
d. 1537

**Edward VI**
r. 1547-1553

1540 Anne of Cleve
ann. 1540
d. 1557

## THE DUDLEYS

John Dudley
Earl of Warwick
Duke of Northumberland
Lord Protector
ex. 1553
m.
Jane Guildford

John Dudley
Earl of Warwick
ex. 1554
m.
Anne Seymour

Ambrose Dudley
Earl of Warwick
d. 1590

Henry Dudley

Robert Dudley
Earl of Leicester
m.
Amy Robsart

Mary Tudor
d. 1533
m.

**Louis XII of France**
d. 1514

m.
Charles Brandon Duke of Suffolk
d. 1545

Frances Brandon
d. 1559
m.
Henry Grey
Duke of Suffolk
ex. 1554

m.
Adrian Stokes

1540 Catherine Howard
ex. 1542

1542 Katherine Parr
d. 1548
m.
Thomas Seymour of Sudeley
Lord High Admiral

Mary Seymour

Jane Grey
Queen 1553
ex. 1554
m.
Guildford Dudley
ex. 1554

Katherine
Grey

Mary
Grey

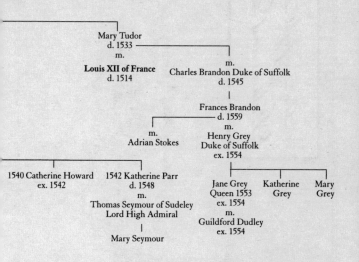

Guildford Dudley
ex. 1554
m.
Jane Grey
Queen 1553
ex. 1554

Jane Dudley
m.
Henry Seymour

Mary Dudley
m.
Henry Sidney

Catherine Dudley
m.
Henry Hastings
Earl of Huntington

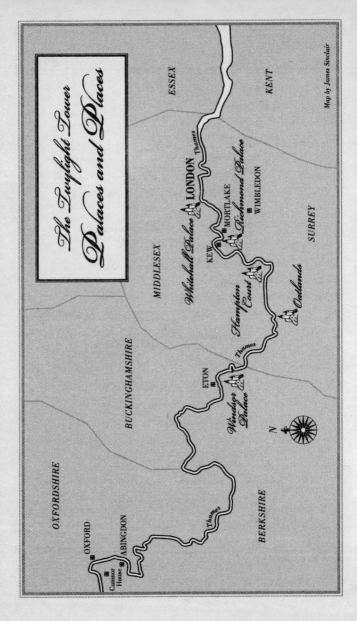

The Twyford Tower Palaces and Places

OXFORDSHIRE
OXFORD
ABINGDON
Cumnor House
BUCKINGHAMSHIRE
BERKSHIRE
ETON
Windsor Palace
Thames
MIDDLESEX
Hampton Court
Thames
Oatlands
KEW
MORTLAKE
Richmond Palace
WIMBLEDON
SURREY
Whitehall Palace
LONDON
Thames
ESSEX
KENT

N

Map by James Sinclair

THE

# The Twylight Tower

# The Prologue

*Venomous thorns that are so sharp and keen*
*Bear flowers full freely and fair of hue:*
*Poison is also put in medicine.*
*And unto man his health doth oft renew.*
*I trust sometime my harm will be my health.*
*Since every woe is joined with some wealth.*

— SIR THOMAS WYATT, *the Elder*

MAY 30, 1560

WHITEHALL PALACE, LONDON

THE QUEEN KNEW A STORM WAS COMING, but it wasn't going to halt her necessary duty.

"I cannot fathom this large a crowd could form so quickly with bad weather threatening," Elizabeth observed as her chief adviser, Lord William Cecil, and her Horse Master, Robert Dudley, escorted her from the palace toward the public street. Other counselors and courtiers trailed after her as the crimson-clad yeoman guards used their halberds horizontally to hold back the press of people.

"It is hardly popular fervor to see Cecil off to Scotland to negotiate a dry, nitpicking treaty, Your Grace," Robert put in before Cecil could say aught. "This public thoroughfare through the palace grounds is always this crowded on market day. Your subjects are heading for Cheapside or the public barge landing—ah, but they are thrilled, of course, for the opportunity to see their queen," he added, evidently realizing his banter could be construed to insult not only Cecil.

"Though they may also be here," Cecil muttered, "to see you, Lord Robert. As usual, you are dressed as gaudily as—"

"You were not going to say as our queen, my lord?" Robert interrupted, his voice mockingly abashed.

"Hardly. As a peacock. Her Grace's taste is matchless."

The queen saw Cecil bite back the rest of his comment and merely roll his eyes. He had, no doubt, wanted to remark that her taste was matchless in all things except choosing intimate friends.

It was true that her dear Robert—she ever called him Robin—wore only the finest fig at court, as if he dared rival her royal selection of fabrics and styles, though the man had no fortune but that which she had bestowed. She had granted him the right to export wool without a license and awarded him twelve thousand pounds to cover his court costs, else he'd never have been so finely arrayed, not after the treasonous tumbles his family had taken more than once. But she did indeed—whatever Cecil and other courtiers thought of him—trust Robin.

Amidst the swelling crowd noise, the horses of Cecil's waiting retinue stamped and snorted. Or mayhap the big beasts sensed the coming storm. At least, she noted, for she had a keen eye for horseflesh, the steeds and their trappings had been selected to match the occasion. Her Robin might think Cecil a stern stick-in-the-mud, but he knew to prepare a fine show for a queen's man heading out to do his duty.

On her accession, Elizabeth had made Robin her Master of the Horse, later a garter knight and Lieutenant of Windsor Castle. The position was no sinecure, for it made him one of her closest advisers. In addition, Robin oversaw the royal stables and the purchasing and training of the 275 household horses there. He rode directly behind her in all ceremonial occasions. She felt safe from everyone when she was with him, except sometimes from herself, since he held such manly appeal for her. Cecil feared that too, though he should know she was, above all, master of her own heart.

"I shall not have you two sniping at each other like schoolboys," she scolded. "Worsening weather or not, I want a public departure, not only to assure my people all is well after our brief, victorious war with the French in Scotland, but"—she lowered her bell-clear voice so only the two of them could hear—"because I want the whoreson, poxy French and Spanish spies to tell their masters of my people's affection for their queen."

"Then my leave-taking is best done in the open air, even if 'tis chill and wet, Your Majesty," Cecil agreed, hunching his narrow shoulders. "As you imply, your palaces are oft infested with self-serving ears and eyes that lurk above a smiling mouth."

The queen saw him glare at Robert again, but other conversation was thwarted by huzzahs from the crowd when they caught their first glimpse of their queen emerging from the shelter of rose-hued, brick Whitehall. She smiled and gave a stiff-armed wave, but was sore annoyed to see that the late-morning sky looked like twilight and already spit rain.

"Should we go back inside, Your Grace?" Robert asked, sweeping off his bronze-hued satin cloak and slanting it aloft to shield her.

"The queen of England had best not be shaken by a bit of rain," she retorted as they hurried toward the protection of the triple-arched King's Gate. Connected to the palace yet spanning the public street, it was three stories topped by twin turreted towers of gray stone with protruding cornices and busts of Roman rulers. Some courtiers not in her immediate retinue crowded its narrow second-floor mullioned windows. Trumpets blared, sounding as if they had something stuck in their brassy throats. No turning back now, though it rained harder and thunder rattled the cobbles underfoot as if cannonballs rolled along them.

About twenty feet away the lead horse Cecil would mount whinnied and shied. Though a groom seized the reins, Robin handed his cloak to her women Kat Ashley and his sister Mary. "By your leave, Your Grace," he said before he darted over to comfort the big beast. Suddenly, for no reason, Elizabeth felt as skittish as that horse. She sensed something amiss, someone . . .

As Robin reached the horse, a full-fledged rose hit her hair from above, then skidded down her face to scratch her forehead and nose before plopping at her feet. When she cursed and squinted skyward another sodden flower smacked her, its thorns snagging her hair before it fell off her shoulder. Through raindrops, she saw numerous heads and arms leaning out windows above her but no one heaving flowers.

"Hell's teeth!" Cecil cried, seeing her plight. "Your Grace, your face is bleeding from a thin scratch. . . ."

"It's nothing," she insisted. "Some overzealous dolt is throwing Tudor roses instead of simply petals. Jenks," she called to one of Lord Robert's men who was also dear to her, "go up there and see the bouquets from heaven cease!"

Though slow to grasp what she meant until another rose pelted down between her and Cecil, Jenks ran back into the palace to access the upper tower.

After Kat Ashley dabbed at Elizabeth's forehead with a damp handkerchief, Elizabeth nodded to the crowd but glanced again at Robin calming the horses with those big, steady hands. They were thicker than hers, but also long fingered, skilled at the pursuits of riding, hunting, and dancing that she excelled in. And he was doubly skilled in the art of making a woman feel tenderly touched, wanted, and beloved.

Sometimes Robin almost seemed her other self, though his hair was a more muted chestnut while hers gleamed red-gold. Neither had milky English complexions. Hers was olive-hued, a heritage from her mother, while Robin's was more burnished. His nose was classically long like hers, and his eyes dark too. "The gypsy" some courtiers called him behind his back, and she almost believed he could put a spell on her. Tall, perfectly proportioned, and poised with an athletic body both powerful and graceful, he was also the queen's masculine ideal of wit and charm. They were of an age, and both had suffered much to survive in turbulent times, binding them even closer.

When Robin rejoined her, she stood on the square of carpet someone had originally put down for her but refused the canopy of his cloak. Nor did she move under the shelter of the tower, for then her courtiers above could not see or hear. She cleared her throat and nearly shouted her words.

"My Lord Cecil, your queen charges you with the honored task of riding to our northern neighbor Scotland and seeing that the French we have defeated are expelled forthwith by lawful treaty."

As raindrops thudded harder, Elizabeth watched Robin's finery go from speckled to blotched to sodden, and knew Cecil would not get far on muddy roads in this deluge. He would have to put everyone in his train up at his city house and set out on the morrow, but she wanted to maintain the illusion he could charge off at her bequest the moment she commanded.

Elizabeth admitted to herself she wanted him to go. He didn't approve of the time she spent in Robin's company, though it was none of his damned business. Under her full brocade gown, she stamped her foot.

"And so farewell and godspeed for the betterment of our righteous realm!" she shouted, and cut her carefully planned speech short as Cecil knelt before her.

"Rise, my lord," she said, her voice softer. "I am certain, despite this wretched beginning for your trip, the sun will smile upon you in this great endeavor."

"I pray so—for the sake of queen and kingdom," he said to her alone as he rose and replaced his cap on his slick head. "Your Grace, I also pray you'll not heed seductive Siren voices while I am away—"

Thunder made him look like a mute mouthing words. No one waited until he and his men were mounted. When the queen made it back inside and wiped the rain from her face, her palm showed smeared crimson.

"Vile thorns. Jenks," she called when she saw him at the fringe of the soaked crowd, "did you find who tossed those roses?"

"Probably," Kat Ashley, her First Lady of the Bedchamber, put in, "the same person who sneaked in and hacked them from your privy garden during the night. Least that's what your herb girl said."

"These were up on the top windowsill," Jenks said, and extended a handful of wilted roses. "Nearly up to the roof—see?"

"But who threw them so carelessly, or did the wind just sail them amiss?" Elizabeth demanded.

"Don't know," he said, frowning and shrugging. "No one was there."

"It was, no doubt," Robin said in the awkward silence, "some secret admirer so driven by passion he did not heed the proper way to give flowers to the queen of his heart."

"Then I shall have music to soothe the savage

beast," Elizabeth retorted despite her annoyance and unease. "Someone fetch my master lutenist for a song about a sunny day!" she ordered, and clapped her hands as everyone scattered to fall into line behind her again. Except, that is, for Robin, who walked backward up the broad staircase, holding her hand and leading the way.

# Chapter the First

*Pastime with good company*
*I love and shall until I die.*
*Grudge who will but none deny*
*May God be pleased, thus live will I*
*For my pastance, hunt, sing, and dance*
*My heart is set on goodly sport*
*For my comfort, who shall me let?*

— KING HENRY VIII

JULY 28, 1560

 WILLIAM CECIL STRODE RAPIDLY FROM HIS hired barge through the edge of town to Richmond Palace. Though but forty years old, the pounding ride from Edinburgh had made mincemeat of his muscles, so he'd managed to come the last few miles on the Thames. Usually he was glad to see the tower-topped silhouette of Richmond, the queen's favorite summer home, but today he wasn't so sure.

Rumors the queen was besotted with Robert Dudley were rampant, even in the northern shires, and he could tell from afar she was letting her royal duties slide. Did she think the business of her kingdom could go on a holiday at her whim? He'd been away from court two months, and that was two months too long.

Cecil stopped and stared at the looming palace.

Situated eight miles outside London with thick orchards and a game-filled park embracing it, Richmond offered all sorts of pleasant diversions and escapes, though this visit promised neither. As he gripped the leather satchel with his important papers close to his chest, hoping something would calm him, his eyes skimmed the balanced beauty of the place.

Unlike jumbled Whitehall, the queen's principal palace in London, the main structure here had been laid out in a planned and orderly fashion. It was a place after his own heart, he thought as he trudged across the outer quadrangle. The first Tudor ruler, the queen's grandfather, King Henry VII, a stern and disciplined man, had overseen Richmond's construction. Ironic, Cecil mused, that his heir, Henry VIII, was of the opposite disposition, all passion, appetites, and swagger. And their heir Elizabeth? Somehow she was both personalities at war with each other.

"Good for you, Lord Secretary, settling the Scots war with profit for our England!" someone called to him from a cluster of courtiers as he entered the gate to the middle court. He lifted his free arm in reply, but kept going toward the entrance to the state apartments, a series of rooms with the finest views in the vast place. Out one set of windows was the great hall in all its Gothic splendor, and in the opposite direction, the stunning chapel royal. Glancing up, one saw various of the fourteen towers of the palace proper with their bright banners and gilded weather vanes, not to mention the eastward river view over lush gardens and orchards.

Human traffic thickened the closer Cecil got to the queen through the presence chamber, then the gallery to the privy chamber. He recognized most courtiers; a few gave him good day, but he kept going at a swift clip so as not to be drawn into conversations. Still, more than once he was sure he heard the sibilant whispers of the words *Scots* and *Cecil*, interspersed with the duller, drumlike thud of *Dudley, Dudley*.

Beyond the next closed set of double doors lay the royal withdrawing room, bedroom, bathroom, and library, among other privy chambers, but still he saw no queen to greet him. With each step he became more annoyed. He'd specifically instructed the two messengers he'd sent ahead yesterday to request that he see Her Majesty privily before they faced her council together about this treaty he'd sweated and nitpicked over to get her the most advantageous terms from the rough Scots and prideful French. Not only was no one prepared to welcome him, but not even to receive him.

So as not to seem as frustrated as he felt, Cecil slowed his steps through the privy chamber. The queen's ladies of the bedchamber and maids of honor sat about on cushions, chatting and embroidering, playing with lapdogs and an azure parrot that kept squawking, "Yes, Your Grace! Yes, Your Grace!" Why had these women not been sent out? And where was the queen herself in this giggling coterie? He'd insist the First Lady of the Bedchamber, Katherine Ashley, whom he saw looking out the open oriel window, dispatch these women forthwith.

As if he'd called her name, the dignified, silver-

haired Lady Kat Ashley turned to him. Looking relieved, she smiled and picked her way toward him
through the puddles of brocade and taffeta skirts. Kat
had been Elizabeth's governess years ago and had
stuck with her through tough times before Queen
Mary died and Elizabeth finally inherited her throne.
In fact, Kat was the closest Her Majesty had ever
known to a mother, as her own, Queen Anne Boleyn,
had been beheaded when Elizabeth was but three.

"My Lady Ashley," Cecil intoned as he swept off his
cap and inclined his head. "Would you please request
Her Majesty see me—in private?"

"I've been keeping an eye out for you, my Lord Secretary. Thank God you're back safely, as you know my
steadying hand on Her Grace has not been heeded of
late, and it's been worse since you left."

"What's amiss?" he demanded as they huddled
closer. The chatter and giggles muted and, without
looking, he knew everyone was watching them. "Will
you bid Her Majesty come out to see me now and clear
this . . . gaggle of pretty geese?" he went on, keeping
his voice low.

"She's not here," Kat whispered, lifting her gray
eyebrows conspiratorially. "That is, not within, though
everyone out here believes so. You'll have to go to her,
I fear."

*I fear.* Those words snagged in Cecil's mind. What
was Kat not telling him? What had he not sniffed out
from his allies at court who should have kept him better informed?

"You don't mean," he said, nearly mouthing his

words, his back to the women, "she's covertly gone off on her own somewhere on secret business when she promised us she would not? I repeat, what is amiss?"

Twice Elizabeth Tudor had probed and solved crimes that threatened her person, enlisting the aid of several of her most loyal servants as well as Kat, Cecil, and her cousin Henry Carey, Baron Hunsdon. But, praise God, there had been no such threat since her coronation one and a half years ago. Cecil had been hoping that Her Majesty would not so endanger herself again.

"No, not solving some dire crime again," Kat clipped out, forgetting to whisper. "Come in with me, and I'll explain."

She nodded to the liveried yeomen guards who swept open the doors, then shut them in everyone's faces when she and Cecil were inside. The elegantly appointed withdrawing room was empty too.

"The only mystery afoot," Kat muttered with a shake of her head, "is how the queen can carry on as she has." She kept nervously twisting the cord to the hanging scented pomander that dangled from her ample waist.

"Aha. Dudley still?" Cecil asked.

"Still and more than ever," Kat declared, a frown furrowing her high brow. "She's gone out with him now, walking in the orchards, but she said you might come out and find them by the Turtle Cage. Obviously they didn't want everyone with them this time."

Cecil felt deflated, angry, and alarmed. *I fear,* his own thoughts echoed Kat's words. Once, it had not been like Elizabeth of England to evade the business of her realm. Once, she had relied on his judgments and advice. And was he expected to brief her on a treaty that ended a bloody war with archenemies France and Scotland amidst cooing turtledoves in an orchard?

"Are the two of them out there unescorted?" Cecil demanded, forgoing *sotto voce* now.

"But for three servants, none of whom will say a peep to her courtiers, who think she's in here. Her Grace has Ned Topside with her, reciting love sonnets, I warrant. Meg Milligrew is supposedly picking posies for garlands, and Her Majesty's favorite lutenist, Geoffrey Hammet, playing pretty tunes." Kat's voice, usually sweet and conciliatory, was bitter and mocking.

"Hell's gates," Cecil said. "Not one proper companion? Has she taken leave of her senses?"

Kat snorted and edged toward the window to look out toward the orchards again, her fingers now tying knots in her pomander cord. "Her Grace tells me," Kat said, shaking her head, "that her senses are more alive than they've ever been. But her cheeks are a hectic hue, and she hasn't been sleeping worth a fig. She makes no bones about boasting of her care for her Robin and he for her. Devil take that jackanapes popinjay!" she cried, turning back to Cecil.

"We must keep calm," Cecil urged, still holding his distance from the window as if that would help him stay objective about this mess.

"I cannot. I only hope and pray, my lord, that Her Grace will listen to you about the Scots war—about something sobering. She and her Robin even go to each other's bedchambers for visits, though if I try to scold her for that, she insists they are never really alone, with courtiers, servants, or me about. She's always been willful, of course, but she's just not herself!"

He went over to pat Kat's shoulder as his own anger grew. He still held his leather satchel with the treaty and other papers of international import for the queen to sign. Dudley was not to be trusted; his family had twice turned traitor to the crown. And he'd been ten years married, for heaven's sake, so how dare he play the gallant lover?

"Will you come out with me to find and face her down, Kat?" he asked, keeping his temper and voice on a tight rein.

"That I will," she said, squaring her plump shoulders. "Though she told me to stay here, you do need a guide to find the Turtle Cage in all those trees, don't you?"

"Yes, let's go together," he said, though he knew full well where to find the secluded place.

"No, not that way, my lord," Kat cried, gesturing as he made for the double doors. "Let's take the privy staircase down and walk the covered passageways, just as she and Lord Robert did to ditch them all."

MEG MILLIGREW HAD NEVER BEEN HAPPIER. SHE WAS working with her beloved herbs and flowers, fashioning blossom necklaces for her dear queen and, better

yet, for handsome Lord Robin. She was with the
queen's principal player and sometimes fool, Ned Topside. Since she'd known him, she had secretly adored
Ned, though the handsome actor was so stuck on himself he hadn't the slightest notion she felt that way.
While he flirted with many a household maid, the
wretch treated Meg only as a companion or pupil,
since he'd taught her to talk and walk to resemble Her
Majesty—and urged her to be her bumpkin self for
contrast the rest of the time. But what Meg liked best
about the day was that she was still out of London,
where her husband no one knew about could not find
and claim her and make her leave the queen.

A little distance off, Meg's royal mistress strolled
hand-in-hand with Lord Robin around the large,
wide-netted dovecote. Meg and Ned's friend Geoffrey
Hammet sat in the low crotch of a pear tree and played
one ballad or madrigal after another on his lute, including ones the queen's own father and courtiers had
written. Unfortunately, Geoffrey did like his sack and
got Ned to drink too much, but both looked sober
enough right now. They sounded good too, sometimes
singing sweet duets while Meg kept plaiting strands of
gillyflowers and sweet william.

Her heart began to thud when Ned ambled over
and sat down on the turf where she worked. A pox on
the man, she thought as she nervously spilled the
flower chain off her lap. Ned's black curly hair and
green eyes, not to mention his rugged face and well-
turned legs, always affected her like that.

"You look as smitten by him as our queen," Ned observed.

"Mm," she said, trying not to look into his eyes. She was relieved he thought it was Lord Robin who turned her into a clumsy, stuttering dolt. "What woman wouldn't, breathing Lord Robin's air, even a mere lass dubbed Strewing Herb Mistress of the Privy Chamber?"

"Though our queen mislikes to hear it, just remember the man is married," Ned said, aping exactly the way Lord Robin talked, "though neither of them acts it sometimes."

"Acts it? You would say that," Meg muttered, gathering her scattered flowers from the ground. "But you were wonderful as the king of Rome in that play scene last night," she admitted with a sigh.

"As Caesar, Meg," he corrected her, resetting his cap as if he still wore the laurel wreath she'd sewed for him of bay leaves. "Yes, I believe my forte is depicting great leaders—"

"God save us," Meg interrupted. "Here comes my Lord Cecil with Kat, and neither looking happy."

Ned craned his neck. "I haven't the vaguest notion why," he said wryly, back to his own voice now. "Cecil and Robert Dudley always get on about as well as the English and the Frenchies."

Geoffrey saw them coming too and left off the plaintive song he had just begun. But he strummed three quick chords, which Meg figured would have to do for trumpet fanfare out here.

The reunion of the queen and her chief minister started well enough, Meg noted, with proper greetings and a thanks to Cecil for what he'd done. But things didn't stay so nice and quiet.

"I would like to speak with you alone, Your Majesty," Secretary Cecil said with a pointed glance at Lord Robin, "about the treaty and the unfortunately still-defiant French attitude, even in defeat."

"Say on, my Lord Cecil," the queen urged, starting to walk around the large, dome-topped cage of cooing birds with Lord Robin still at her side.

"For your ears only, Your Gracious Majesty, until we present this to the Privy Council, of which, of course, Lord Robert is a part," Cecil prompted, standing his ground in more ways than one.

The queen swung back to face him so fast, her bright blue skirts belled out. Meg knew that look on her face. It was usually her sign to find a way quickly out of Her Majesty's presence.

"Lord Robert is privy to my business and to be fully trusted," Elizabeth informed Cecil, her voice cold and clear. Cecil stared her down one moment, then wisely complied.

"The treaty terms were the best I could get and mean we now have a triple blessing in the French defeat, Your Grace. The French are out of our northern neighbor's lands for good. Better yet, Scotland will be Protestant now, and thirdly, the Papist French have realized what a power you and England can be, so—"

"But not enough of a power to get Calais back?" Lord Robin interrupted. "An area right across the

English Channel, long held by us, forfeited by Her Grace's sister, Queen Mary, in an ill-advised Spanish war for her husband's sake and—"

"Don't lecture me about Calais, Lord Robert," Cecil interrupted this time. "But I see you are now elevated to a height to criticize kings and queens, a Tudor queen included. And evidently you are making foreign policy in my absence, not to mention oth—"

"I do wish," the queen said to Secretary Cecil when Meg almost thought Lord Robin would dare to strike him, "you had pushed them for Calais. Mary Stuart and her husband, King Francis, have no just claim to it. Robin is right."

Cecil, who Meg knew could hide his real feelings as well as a clever actor like Ned, gaped for air like a beached fish before he recovered. "You must realize, Your Gracious Majesty," Cecil said, "that Queen Mary and her royal husband are neither cowed by you in war nor friendly in peace. As a matter of fact, I have word here," he went on, indicating his satchel, "that she is telling everyone in her court that you plan to make a way to wed your married Master of the Horse, something she found most amus—"

"The slandering, lying witch!" the queen shouted. Meg would have wagered she'd scream some more, but she only said, "Leave off, Cecil. And leave your documents, which I will sign when I can. I am certain you have missed your Mildred more than you have missed your queen. And you have come here with a stiff neck and tawdry rumors from that court of frogs!"

Meg almost snickered at that picture. The English often called the effete French that because they actually ate such things as frog legs and snails instead of hearty fare like good English roast beef. She could tell the queen was dismissing Cecil now, so didn't he catch on, being such a brilliant lawyer?

"I appreciate," Cecil said, backing up carefully and bowing at the same time the way only courtiers could do, "your kind thoughts and concern, Your Majesty, for how much my wife must be missing me, living in the country as she is, deprived of my presence and care while I attend you at court."

Meg saw Lord Robin jerk and stare, like he'd been hit over the head with that clever insult. Everyone knew his wife, Amy, was a country mouse who never came to court and was seldom seen by her husband. Meg watched, wide-eyed, holding her breath for one of the queen's raving fits, while Kat curtsied, looking as upset as the rest of them, and left with Lord Cecil.

" 'S blood," Elizabeth cried to Robin, and followed with a string of curses. She banged a fist against the birdcage, and turtledoves fluttered and flew, only to stay trapped inside. "Do those two," the queen went on, pointing stiff-armed after them, "whom I have trusted and favored, presume to glare and lecture their queen like parents with a wayward child? What you and I do in our friendship, Robin, we do in the broad light of day with others in attendance."

With that, she darted a sharp glance in Meg's direction. Meg quickly plunged back to stringing flowers. Ned, she could tell, was just leaning back against the tree, staring off into the distance, so that the queen probably thought they couldn't hear a word she said.

"Cecil has too much authority," Lord Robin said softly, but his voice still carried on the mounting breeze. "You need someone you can trust as a counterbalance to his power and pomposity."

Meg could not believe it when the queen nodded, took his arm, and gazed into his eyes. It was evident even to an herb girl that the queen of England was caught deep in love's snares, just like in the words to a song Geoffrey often sang.

THE SUMMER DAYS BLURRED BY FOR THE QUEEN AS FAST AS did the other couples dancing around her and Robin two weeks later. "Another gay galliard!" she commanded her musicians in the raised gallery. "No more slow pavans. Wait—instead I shall have *la volta*!"

Cornets and sackbuts wailed at a faster pace while recorders, timpani, viols, lutes, and citterns picked up the romping beat. Robin partnered Elizabeth again, whirling her about between the set-piece intricate steps, then—during the women's leap—throwing her into the air and catching her. Women squealed and men shouted in their exertion and excitement.

Elizabeth laughed and urged on the others. They ought to be grateful, she thought, that unlike in slower movements, she had no time to correct dancers who didn't know their footwork. She was relieved she hadn't eaten much of the huge meal, but then, she never did. If courtiers and servants ate as she, the eighteen kitchens of Richmond would hardly have to turn out the vast tables of food each day.

As Robert spun her again, Elizabeth realized these had been the most wonderful months of her life, even if she did miss her dear friends Bella and John Harington, whom she had sent into rural exile for lying to her. She doubly regretted having to do that, for their daughter had run away on top of all their other troubles. They'd been gone for over a year now and she intended to summon them back soon. A precedent about being able to trust one's friends must be set.

Elizabeth sighed, even in the midst of a strenuous swing step. Bella had been such a fine sportswoman and dancer that Elizabeth would love to have her here to vie with for the highest *volta* leaps. Now she was stuck with the likes of simpering, snide Katherine Grey, a cousin with Catholic leanings whom she feared the Papists would champion behind the queen's back. At least, Elizabeth thought as she nearly tripped on the redheaded chit, she had Katherine where she wanted her, among her ladies under watch and— curse the woman—underfoot.

"Faster, dear Robin, faster," Elizabeth cried as he spun her just before the final vault and catch. Aha! She was certain she had flown higher than her ladies. Everyone laughed and gasped for breath, looking to see what their queen would command next.

But again, as increasingly of late, Elizabeth felt someone staring, someone hostile. Quickly, carefully, she skimmed the crowd, then scrutinized her musicians' faces. The men, her ensemble—professional musicians were always male, of course—were leaning forward from their gallery above, waiting for her next selection. No face seemed out of place, nor a single countenance threatening. The same among the courtiers, though Elizabeth would like to smack Katherine Grey's smug face.

"You've quite exhausted everyone with hunting this morn and now such dancing," Robin said, no doubt put up to hinting she end the evening. Realizing it must be nearly midnight, she turned to face him with a smile. She knew that more and more, as people saw he was the favorite, however much some of them still resented the parvenu, upstart Dudleys, they went to him with bribes and requests much greater than this one for her ear alone.

"Have I worn you out?" she countered, trying to keep from appearing to be so out of breath.

"Never." He leaned closer, whispering in her ear so hotly his breath made her earring bob. "Summon me or visit me alone tonight, and I will show you I am still up for whatever you would like."

"Why, my lord, I believe you're being bawdy. But in truth, I am exhausted. It's Cecil's fault, moping around here day after day since his return, and Kat's taken to giving me her long looks again."

She made a dour face at him, and he laughed as he escorted her back toward the table. "But I believe I shall take pity on you all and have you escort me to my chamber. Master lutenist, music!" she called with a sharp look at Ned Topside, who nodded and went to fetch his friend Geoffrey Hammet from the gallery for some privy playing.

Robert Dudley bowed, and others followed suit as Elizabeth left the great hall. He escorted her properly—if a bit dramatically—to her bedchamber door and bent to kiss her hand. Though she warranted few could tell, he always turned it up before planting a warm, sometimes wet kiss on her palm instead of the mere proper brush of the lips between her knuckles and wrist. Had any other man tried that she'd have knocked him silly.

In return, she merely cupped his bearded cheek with her other hand and disappeared inside, trailed by her ladies of the bedchamber. Best to keep even Robin guessing what was coming next, she thought. He had mocked the Scots for their hide-and-seek warfare where they'd disappear into a mist or duck into one of their glens, then jump out later to fight again. She had not said so, but that was a well-tried Tudor tactic too.

Her ladies divested her of gown and petticoats, unlaced her stays, and helped her don her gold brocade robe, a gift from Robin. "Out, out, but Kat and Mary Sidney sleeping in the trundle beds this night," the queen commanded with a narrow-eyed look at Katherine Grey for dawdling. Elizabeth had never given the girl the honor of sleeping in here at night, for she dared not close her eyes on her.

Though Kat would no doubt snore and Mary muttered in her dreams, those were the two Elizabeth preferred to have with her. She didn't sleep well of late and would sometimes rather be alone, but especially now with people so unreasonable about her friendship with Robin, she needed the chaperones. Ah, if only she had her friend Bella back or at least had been able to locate her and John's runaway daughter for them. But she'd had servants, including Ned Topside, loose in London in various guises for days last year who never so much as came up with the scent of the runaway Hester Harington. Most of all, she'd like her lutenist in here, but she could hardly keep a male, servant and musician or not, in her bedchamber at night.

At least, as was usual when the court was at Richmond and it was temperate weather, Geoffrey would play the lute, sitting in a deep notch between two crenelations at the top of the tower parapet opposite her windows. Yet despite the tunes drifting in, Elizabeth thrashed her sheets to waves around her.

Geoffrey, even when he was dog drunk with his beloved sack, could play circles around anyone she'd ever heard. His straight blond hair, sky-blue eyes, and boyish face made him look like an angel, but he could drink like the very devil. She could use a stiff drink now to relax this taut coil inside her.

The queen pounded her pillows flatter behind her head as Kat did indeed begin to snore, seemingly in rhythm with Geoffrey's ballad, one about lost love. Mary seemed to breathe evenly in sleep. Elizabeth edged out of her high bed and found the velvet mounting stool with a bare foot, climbed down, and tiptoed over to the window casement, set ajar to catch both river breeze and tunes. Some said night air was unhealthsome, but she felt she had proved that untrue. Sometimes it was simply sitting on the pinnacle of the realm, day or night, that could do one in.

But foolish superstitions like the night air must have no place in her kingdom, she'd see to that, she vowed silently. She believed in scientific thinking, like Robin, who had learned it from his friend Dr. Dee, whose home was not far from here. Mayhap tomorrow she should agree to ride with Robin to see the brilliant man's instruments and show him the Flemish-made astrolabe Robin had given her.

The queen sank on the cushioned window seat. When Geoffrey paused between tunes, she heard that other music she loved here, the eerie humming of wind blowing through the tower vanes like heavenly lutes.

As her eyes adjusted to the shapes of walls and towers outside, she fancied she could pick out her lutenist's silhouette on the parapet against the night sky, but perhaps that was only because she could pinpoint his music.

Elizabeth started when she heard a wooden thud from the tower, then a muffled cry that faded and stopped. Something in the courtyard below, perhaps, echoing off the walls. Now silence, but for the wind playing the vanes. Had Geoffrey dared to drop that imported Italian lute she'd given him on the Twelfth Day of Christmas? Surely not over the edge. Why didn't he begin to play again?

And then he did, a sweet, slow madrigal, curling on

the breeze into her window and her heart. The seductive tone seemed more mellow, sadder.

Elizabeth stretched, then poked her head out. The music had stopped or else merged flawlessly with the music of the dark towers. She had just pulled back inside when a man's shout echoed from the stone courtyard below.

"Help ho! I think he's dead!"

# Chapter the Second

*My lute, awake! Perform the last*
*Labor that thou and I shall hast,*
*And end that I have now begun;*
*For when this song is sung and past,*
*My lute, be still, for I have done.*

— THE EARL OF ROCHFORD

 "KAT! MARY! SOMETHING DREADFUL HAS happened outside! Get up, up!"

Yanking on her robe and shoving her feet in her woolen mules, Elizabeth did not await her ladies. That voice had surely been Ned's, but who did he think was dead?

The queen's first impulse was to go to the privy staircase that led to both the roof and garden, but if foul play were afoot, that could be dangerous. As the startled Kat and Mary scrambled into robes behind her, Elizabeth ran through the empty withdrawing room and banged a fist on the double doors to the gallery. Her yeoman guards, halberds still crossed, swept it open and gaped to see her.

"Someone's hurt in the courtyard below," she told them, shoving through. "Bring lanterns."

Both hulking men fell in behind her. With them, Kat, Mary, several of her other women, and the night porter strung out behind her, the queen hurried down the lantern-lit staircase. She gestured to more startled guards to unbolt the front door, and she burst out into the courtyard.

"Ned?" she cried. Her little entourage halted behind her. A fine falling mist muted sounds and sights, but she could swear she still heard the weird wind music from the towers. "Ned Topside!"

"Here, Your Grace," he answered, his voice breaking. She saw him huddled over a fallen form directly under the tower opposite her window. "It's Geoffrey," Ned choked out, "fallen to his death."

She traversed the slick paving stones and bent next to the kneeling Ned. Her lutenist sprawled facedown, his blond hair fanned out, his arms and legs spread as if he'd tried to fly. His face was turned to the side, the angle of his neck askew. A trickle of blood from his ear puddled on the pavement.

"I—I didn't turn him over," Ned whispered. "That's the way he landed, but I felt for the pulse at his neck. He's gone."

"Yes," she said, "poor player."

Ned glanced up at her, evidently unsure if she meant her lutenist or her favorite actor himself. Kat and Mary clung to Elizabeth as if to pull her back, but she shook them off. Doors slammed and feet came running amidst random cries in the courtyard.

"Oh," the queen said, fanning the air before her face as she straightened. "No wonder the man lost his balance. I smell strong drink on him. Let that be a lesson to you all," she said, addressing the growing circle of courtiers and servants. "Geoffrey Hammet was a fine musician who loved his lute but also loved his drink overmuch, and it must have cost him his life."

Meg's teary face appeared next to Ned's stunned one. Elizabeth knew the two of them had been fast friends with Geoffrey. "We will all mourn his loss," the queen continued, her voice gentler. "Geoffrey was dear to me and to others too."

"Including his poor wife," Meg blurted out.

"Wife?" Elizabeth cried. "The man told me plain when I took him on he was unwed."

Meg's mouth went to an O, and even in the push of people to glimpse the corpse, Elizabeth saw Ned elbow the girl. "Ned, is this true?" the queen demanded, glaring at him. "Speak up, man."

"An early marriage," Ned said, his voice hushed. He seemed to speak to his feet rather than to an audience for once. Someone tried to quiet the others so they could hear. "There is one child, yet of toddling years," Ned whispered, clearing his throat. "And a babe."

"I see," Elizabeth pronounced. "Then I can only hope that others who serve their queen intimately do not keep such secrets from her, for whatever reasons."

At that, Meg looked sorely stricken that she had given her friend's secret away. As the fine mist turned to raindrops, she began to cry, but Elizabeth had no time for such indulgences. "My lord," she said to Robin, who had appeared looking sleepy and disheveled, "have some of your men find a coffin for my musician. We shall bury him on the morrow and mourn his and his music's loss."

As Robin pulled three men forward, including her former guard Jenks, Elizabeth almost stopped them. She could send for young Gil Sharpe, her court artist in training, who always traveled in her retinue of servants when she was on progress. The boy was skilled at sketching people and scenes. But no—there would be no examination of a corpse or investigation of a scene for a drunken fall.

The queen stepped back as the men turned Geoffrey over. She noted well two things, neither suspicious. He had an abraded, bloodied bruise on his head and a splotch of blood—no, it looked more like wine—on his shirt. Her musician must have filched a great deal of drink to make himself dizzy *and* to spill that much. A thief as well as a liar, she thought sadly, but she would not speak ill of the dead. She motioned with her hand, and the men lifted the body.

Elizabeth returned the lantern and started away, then turned back. "Where is his lute?" she inquired. "Did it not fall with him? But I heard him playing it even after . . ." Despite the heavier rain, she paused, frowning. That music she had heard after the thud and muffled cry, which must have been Geoffrey going over the edge, could have been the sounds made by the wind on those humming old weather vanes.

"Meg, to me," she called to her herb girl. The slumped, pale-faced redhead sniffled and wiped her nose on her sleeve. However much Meg resembled her sovereign physically, Elizabeth thought, Meg Milligrew was hard-pressed to emulate queenly carriage and control.

"Your Grace," Meg began, "I regret I didn't tell you about his wife, but he begged me not t—"

"Not that. I want you to go up with Ned on the parapet where Geoffrey played across from my window and fetch his lute out of the rain. Dry it off and bring to it me tomorrow, as it was my gift to him. And I shall send coin to his widow, so do not fret for that. I am not some heartless harpy, though your face seems to say so."

"Oh, it's not that, Your Majesty. I mean, I don't ever think that of you. It's just"—she lowered her voice and glanced around—"when do you want to call a covert meeting of those of us who helped you solve the murders before? You know," she pursued when Elizabeth looked past her to see if Robin was coming this way, "to find out who killed him."

Elizabeth looked back at the girl. "Who killed him? I said the man got literally tipsy and killed himself with a tragic and careless fall. Look at the proofs, if you must. It was an accident."

"But that's not sack spilled on him, and that's all he ever drank. It smells like malmsey, your own favorite. . . ."

"My father's favorite," Elizabeth muttered. "It did indeed smell like sweet malmsey. If Geoffrey's been into my stores of wine, that's another strike against him. Now fetch Ned and find that lute."

Robin joined the queen and her women as Meg scurried off. "Things are cared for as you ordered," he told her, taking her arm and escorting her back into the palace. "A sad business, the sudden death of one so young, skilled, and promising. It could not be suicide, I take it?"

Elizabeth sighed heavily. "I believe not and did not summon servants or counselors alike out into this dark and rain to create rumor or myth about the poor wretch's accident."

"Ah. Well, at least this gives me the opportunity to see how fetching you look in that robe."

"Not tonight, Robin. The man's loss is a loss to me."

"If you grieve for him, he is blessed. Will you grieve for me if I leave tomorrow for Cumnor for a few days? You know Amy hasn't seen me in weeks, and I worry for her health. Or will you tell me again," he said, and she saw his gaze catch lantern light to glitter over her, "that you cannot spare your Robin, your eyes?" Elizabeth had more than one pet name for him, but the latter had always amused him. He'd taken to signing notes or letters to her with two dots inside circles to show he served as an observer for her, a second vision of the court and country, as it were.

"Tomorrow?" she said. "I thought you wanted me to ride to Mortlake with you to meet your brilliant Dr. Dee."

"But you said you had business since Cecil has returned to crack his whip," he countered quickly.

"*I* am the only one who cracks the whip here," she declared. She pulled her elbow free from his hand as she started up the stairs toward the royal apartments with Kat and Mary still in tow. "You may, of course, go to Cumnor to visit—after we make our own visit to Dr. Dee."

"As you wish, my queen," he said, catching up with her.

" 'S blood, I need something to cheer and divert myself tomorrow, as the other lutenists have ham hocks for hands compared to Geoffrey's fine ones," she went on, gesturing broadly. "I'll never find a decent replacement for him until we're back in London this autumn. Though it appears at the last Geoffrey was a sneak and scoundrel, I shall miss the man. Robin," she added, seizing his wrists, whispering now, "don't you ever turn sneak and scoundrel. Don't ever make me learn things I mislike about you."

"Then there is naught you mislike about me now?" he challenged with a taut smile. "But, my beloved queen, if you'd allow me, I'd make a new sort of music between us to fill your life with joy."

"With joy—you already do," she said, and turned away at the door to her royal apartments. "But then, always before," she whispered to herself as she walked away from him, "with that looms loss and pain."

"WHAT WERE YOU DOING IN THE COURTYARD SO LATE TO discover Geoffrey's body anyway?" Meg asked as she and Ned climbed the narrow, curved watchman's stairs inside the tower near where their friend had fallen.

"After I sent him to his nightly post, I realized I was starved and knew there would be at least one venison haunch left in the royal kitchen."

"Not to see that kitchen girl, Sally?" she demanded,

keeping close on the steps, as Ned had the only lantern and it was pitch dark in the tower.

"Hellfire, Meg, can't you stow it even tonight? What would I want with the likes of her, reeking of tallow, grease, and smoke? You smell a hundred times finer with your herbs and flowers, and I'm not chasing after you."

Meg just shook her head sadly. Another of his back-handed compliments that stole as much as they bestowed. She couldn't count the many times Geoffrey had defended her when Ned ranted at her. She'd miss the lutenist sore, and not just for his music.

"But now that you ask," Ned muttered as he passed the lantern back to her so he could lift the heavy latch to the narrow wooden door, "I'd best get my story straight before Her Majesty starts questioning everyone tomorrow."

"She won't," Meg muttered.

"I realize she trusts me, but she always demands to know ev—"

"She's decreed Geoffrey's fall mere happenstance and she, or we, won't be looking into it. Besides," Meg explained as Ned opened the door into the bucking wind, "she's much too busy with Lord Robin."

"Do I hear resentment?" he challenged as they stepped out onto the narrow walkway that linked the towers. Rain swirled around them. "I thought you adored the man as much as she does—albeit more privily, of course."

"Don't you mock me or Her Grace. I just think Lord Cecil may be partly right about her listening to

Lord Robin too much, that's all. I don't see the lute," she said, lifting the sputtering lantern higher and scanning the area. "If Geoffrey was sitting in his usual place and didn't have it when he went over, wherever is it?"

As they moved, wind-whipped, along the parapet, their light caught the familiar polished sounding board of the pear-shaped, stringed instrument, leaning against the low wall, about ten paces from where Geoffrey always sat. The lute's intricately carved sound hole, the rose, stared at them like a single, doleful eye. The neck and pegboard were laid against the wall to balance the instrument perfectly.

"He put it down that way as he accidently fell over?" Ned whispered.

"And in a thickening mist? You know he worried the damp air would warp the wood and stretch those gut strings he was always tuning. You don't think . . . he put it down deliberately . . . and killed himself?"

"No. The man loved his life and his calling at court. And if he didn't just fall, that leaves one alternative," he declared, lifting and cradling the lute to him, just as Geoffrey would have. "If the queen's not going to call a meeting of her Privy Plot Council to investigate a possible murder, I am."

BECAUSE OF HEAVY RAIN, IT WAS THREE DAYS BEFORE the queen, Lord Robert Dudley, four of her ladies, and a contingent of guards rode out from Richmond toward Mortlake several miles upriver to see the learned Dr. John Dee, Robin's former tutor, though the man was but six years Robin's elder. Robin still saw much of the man, because the queen had given her favorite a house at Kew not far from Mortlake. Now the royal retinue cantered down the muddy, rutted river lane past occasional thatched houses with their gardens sprawled to water gates on the Thames.

"You know people say the man's a magician," the queen observed to Robin.

"All rumor," he countered quickly, turning slightly toward her in his saddle. "People slander him when they claim he dabbles in wizardry. Besides their petty jealousy of a brilliant man of a mere thirty-three years, I think it's because when he studied at Cambridge he found a nearly invisible way to make people seem to fly to the heavens in the plays they put on there."

"Really?" Elizabeth said with a little laugh. "Ned Topside would like that. Invisible strings of some sort?"

"Wires and pulleys. At any rate, that reputation, which he's never been able to shake, was one reason he was put in prison and charged with casting spells on your sister when she was queen. But he was soon released and ended up helping his gaoler cross-question others on *their* crimes against the crown. Actually, people call him doctor because he is so learned, though he did study medicine abroad."

"I'm already intrigued by the man, I must admit." They slowed as the Dees' little house, courtyard, and Thames-side gardens came into view. "Anyone who loves learning and books as he does," Elizabeth declared, "is a man after my own heart, not to mention he could be my eyes and ears on the Continent with his many travels."

"So you are not coming here just to humor me or to show him the astrolabe?" Robin said, seemingly as much to himself as her. "I knew you had an ulterior motive for accepting this visit at last. And if Dr. Dee ever gathers foreign political information for you, I could be his intermediary instead of Cecil."

Suddenly something compelled Elizabeth to glance into the thick trees along the riverbank. Since her lutenist had fallen to his death, more than ever she'd felt she was being watched, even through her bedroom windows, as if someone stalked that fatal parapet and could peer closely in. She'd put a guard up there two nights, but she didn't like the idea of him seeing in the windows either and had revoked that order. It was simply too warm this time of year to pull all the draperies.

Dr. Dee and his elderly mother hurried out their garden gate to greet them. Robin had sent Stephen Jenks ahead to tell them of the visit, though Jenks had disappeared somewhere and annoyed Robin by not joining their entourage. Elizabeth studied their hosts. The old lady was frail, and Dr. Dee, tall and slender, handsome but somber, dressed all in black as if he were a cleric. Yet for some reason Elizabeth liked the man instinctively.

"Dr. Dee, Lord Robert has told me so much about you," she greeted the smiling man as he swept her a low bow. They exchanged courtesies as they strolled into the small, square courtyard of his house, actually his widowed mother's place, he said, since he often went abroad. He mentioned Antwerp and Paris, and it struck the queen that these were places she would never see with her own eyes.

"I brought something to show you, sir," she announced, feeling like a child who could barely keep from displaying a new gift. She nodded to Mary Sidney, who removed the astrolabe from a velvet sack and unwrapped it.

"Robert gave me this," Elizabeth explained, "but I haven't yet learned all its possibilities."

"Ah," Dr. Dee said in obvious delight as he took it in his long-fingered hands, "you can navigate by the stars with such a fine astrolabe, and I shall show you how. Come, Your Majesty, step inside, and I will demonstrate my quadrant, prisms, and mirrors."

"Mirrors, sir? I did not take you for a vain man," Elizabeth said with a smile. Her courtiers knew to laugh, but Dr. Dee only nodded. Leaving everyone except Robin in the courtyard partaking of raisin cakes and ale with the doctor's mother, Elizabeth preceded Dr. Dee inside as he indicated.

"I hope to experiment with mirrors as signaling glasses across rivers or from ship to ship, Your Majesty," he explained, his voice becoming even more animated. "I am also fascinated by numerical codes and all sorts of secretive devices of intelligence, you see."

She didn't precisely follow him, but said, "A man with so many ideas can be of much import to his monarch and country."

"Robert told me you were wise in all ways," Dr. Dee said as he nodded to indicate a room with several shelves of books. "I'd gladly beggar myself for books," he admitted, while he kept moving his hands together as if he were washing them. "I sense we have a great deal in common, though I am the commoner here," he added in a quiet voice.

Unsure if he had made a jest, she nodded and walked over to a table with mirrors and prisms and an open book full of scribbles she, who knew Greek, Latin, French, Italian, and Spanish, could not read. "So all of this—your life," she said, "is to gain outside knowledge, but not to look within." She held up a strange, concave mirror that made her distorted image lunge at her.

"We must all look within, Your Majesty," Dee said solemnly, "even when we don't think we recognize ourselves there."

"Robin—Lord Robert—tells me you can make people appear to fly," she said, and put the glass down with a slight shudder. The stupid, curved thing had made her look ugly, as if some darker self were watching her. "Could you make me fly, Dr. Dee?" she asked.

"Only if we have some sort of high ceiling, and if you're not afraid to fall if something goes awry," he replied, and glanced at Robin instead of her. The queen thought of poor Geoffrey again and moved toward the window, where more instruments were displayed.

"Her Majesty is born under the sign of Virgo, the spinster, doctor," Robin said behind her, "and you know Virgos have their feet planted firmly on the ground."

John Dee glanced from Robin to her, then back to his former student again. "This, Your Majesty, is a *radius astronomicus*," Dee said as if to change the subject. He hastened toward the window to join her. "Besides peering up at the stars, one can see miles away on earth with it as if one were close-up. I call it my observation cylinder."

Elizabeth studied the odd thing, a long tube hanging in a leather sling, its larger of two glass end-pieces aimed out the window. For one moment she wondered if Dr. Dee had been watching her approach with it, but that would hardly explain her odd feelings other times and places of late.

"Look through here, Your Majesty," he told her as Robin came closer. "There!" Dee said triumphantly when she gasped at how trees across the river leaped at her. "See how close and clear everything becomes?"

"Invisible wires and signal mirrors and magic glasses," the queen marveled as she squinted to fix her gaze again. "A thousand ideas and possibilities. Dr. Dee, I believe I shall visit you again or send for you some day to come to court."

* * *

MEG THOUGHT KAT ASHLEY LOOKED LIKE SHE WAS SITTING on pins and needles instead of a bale of straw. They'd talked her into joining them on the sly, since she'd seen Geoffrey Hammet play for courtiers on numerous occasions where they had not and might have something to contribute. If Her Majesty wouldn't look into poor Geoffrey's death, Ned, Jenks, and Meg intended to.

They'd even included the twelve-year-old, angelic-faced Gil Sharpe, the queen's favorite artist, who had helped them investigate a previous murder. No worry Gil would ever talk about their doings, as the boy was a mute. So the servants of the queen's Privy Plot Council gathered while Her Majesty rode to Mortlake. Jenks claimed this would be the safest place, even if the queen suddenly returned, since she hated how the stables stank.

Actually, Meg did too. She'd known only one other who was more fretted by bad scents than the queen and her—Gil's mother, Bett Sharpe, who'd been left back in London. Since Gil couldn't talk, Bett had taught her boy a signal language of sorts, and after two years everyone sitting here was pretty good at it, though never as clever as the queen and Gil, who would rattle on with face and hand signs so quickly no one could keep up.

"The perfect positioning of his lute and the fact he would never steal—and didn't like to drink that malmsey spilled on him—points to someone else's hand in this," Ned finally concluded his lengthy opening statement, grand gestures and all, as if they were an audience.

You might know, Meg thought, the queen's so-called fool and principal player had taken over this meeting just the way the queen herself did when she called her council to order. Of course, they were missing William Cecil and Her Grace's Boleyn cousin Lord Henry Carey, now called Baron Hunsdon. But Meg didn't doubt Ned would try to run things with the lofty likes of them here too.

"What worries me," Ned went on, "is why Her Majesty—Bess, I mean," he added, using the name Elizabeth insisted on in meetings when they had solved the earlier crimes, "is so taken with Lord Robert, she's ignoring facts and proofs about Geoffrey's death."

"Mayhap," Meg put in with a shake of her head, "the queen will only solve crimes where the victim is of the nobility or she herself is threatened, like in the earlier investigations."

Gil bobbed up and began signaling madly about how the queen had helped save his mother from hanging. He rolled his eyes and stuck out his tongue as he mimicked a noose tightening about his own neck. "True," Ned said. "I know she cares for all of us just as she does our betters, but let's not get off the subject here, and that is Geoffrey's demise."

Jenks frowned and shifted, and Ned kept quiet for a moment as Gil sat back down. It was finally Kat who spoke. "I have found that Her Grace cares dearly for all her people," she insisted. "I'm sure when you inform her—carefully—of the evidence about the malmsey and stress again the placement of the lute, as well as anything else you can turn up..." She frowned. "Mayhap Geoffrey's wife was disgruntled he'd been gone so much and sent someone to insist he come home, and push came to shove up there on that tower walk, or—"

"You mean that someone breached Richmond's security, stumbled on him playing on the parapet in the middle of the night, and did him in?" Ned countered, his voice incredulous.

"No," Kat said, angry now, "it would have to be someone clever hired to follow him about who knew his every move and blended in."

"Oh, pish," Ned insisted. "If spouses sent hired persons to kill their mates for being at court without them, we'd have a bloodbath here, starting with Lord Robert Dudley."

Kat rose and brushed straw off her skirt. "You just let me know what you decide to do next. I've got the queen's ladies and wardrobe to oversee, and today or tomorrow my Lord Cecil's bringing Bishop de Quadra, the Spanish ambassador, to court," she added. She peered out the half-open stable door like a felon, then darted away.

Ned stood and started to pace as if, Meg thought, he would plunge into another long soliloquy. "Let's remember that Bess and Cecil—I mean Will," he said, using the man's nickname during the queen's privy investigations, "always stress that the motive to the crime is the key to finding the criminal. *Sui bono*, who profits? Marital desertion aside, why would someone want to kill Geoffrey? What could he have possibly had that they want?"

Suddenly Ned held up his hand and tipped his head. Meg heard it too, the queen's bell-clear laugh. Close. Too close. And then Lord Robin's voice just outside the half-open door.

"Wait until you see this new chestnut Barbary foal, my queen. We'll have to leave it behind when you move the court to Windsor, but I'll have him sent to London before the winter roads become impassable."

"Talk about murder," Meg whispered. "She'll *kill* us for going behind her back."

Jenks, who usually reasoned at the speed horses did, leaped up and grabbed Ned by one arm and Meg by the other. Gil, always quick on his feet, darted after them. Jenks yanked them down the walkway between stalls to an open area and shoved them both up against the railing there. Meg's breasts bounced so hard against a board she whoofed out a breath; Ned banged his nose and muttered a curse. Meg was considering throwing herself flat on the ground and covering herself with straw until her betters passed, but she saw that stupid Jenks had hauled them right to the place the queen was coming. A mare and obviously new foal stared at them through the widely spaced rails.

"Oh, Lord Robert!" Jenks blurted, sounding very surprised, when Meg was afraid to so much as turn around. "And Your Majesty! I thought maybe Gil could sketch it—the new colt—and I just wanted to show it off, my lord."

"My thought exactly," Lord Robin said, staring at the four of them.

"A fine—ah, little stallion," Ned choked out with a quick look at the colt's privates as they made their obeisance to the queen. Meg punched Gil in the shoulder to remind him to bow, as he was madly signing something to the queen, who was nodding.

"A fine stallion, but destined to be a gelding," Lord Robin muttered ominously, staring at Jenks, not the horses.

"We didn't hurt it." Ned stammered, "Jenks said that we shouldn't pet it or anything like that."

"Meg," the queen said, frowning, "I don't believe you'll find many strewing herbs out here. Unless you've taken to gathering horse apples, you'd best—all of you—get back to business, though Gil may return to draw the mare and foal. I'd rather fancy that as a gift for you, Robin."

"And where were you, lad," Lord Robin asked Jenks, "when I wanted you in the escort to Mortlake?"

"Didn't know I was to do more than take the message to Dr. Dee," Jenks said smoothly, getting on much better, Meg thought, than the honey-tongued queen's player. Even Gil was doing better than Ned. But Meg could tell, even though the queen had a perfumed glove stuck in front of her nose and mouth, she was not smiling. Meg dropped another crooked curtsy and beat both her confederates out the door.

# Chapter the Third

*My mother said I never should*
*Play with gypsies in the wood.*
*If I should, she would say,*
*"Naughty girl to disobey."*
*I wish my mother would*
*Hold her tongue.*
*She played in woods*
*When she was young.*

— ANONYMOUS
FROM A CHILD'S SONG

 WILLIAM CECIL ENTERED THE PRESENCE chamber at Richmond Palace, accompanying Alvaro de Quadra, the elegantly black-clad Catholic bishop, who served as ambassador from the court of King Philip of Spain. He could only pray that the royal rudeness to state business and his own person would not extend to a foreign diplomat. Not that he intended to abet de Quadra's dedication to coercing the queen to wed a Catholic suitor such as Charles, Archduke of Austria, now that she'd turned down her former brother-in-law, King Philip of Spain. But decorum was decorum and Elizabeth at least used to know it.

True, Cecil trusted de Quadra about as far as he could throw a Spanish galleon, so the man had to be watched. Cecil knew full well that once the bishop

ferreted out the queen's disinclination toward a
Catholic match, he could turn to more dangerous
scheming. The man might try to place her pliable
cousin Katherine Grey on her throne, or perhaps even
champion Mary, Queen of Scots and France.

"Her Majesty will be with us soon, Secretary Cecil,
Bishop de Quadra," Robert Dudley told them as he
emerged from the gallery that led to the queen's
rooms. The man almost glittered in his peacock blue
and silver-slashed doublet with amethyst buttons and
emerald silk stockings that emphasized his muscular
legs. "She decided at the last minute to have her teeth
scaled," Dudley added, picking his own with a silver
toothpick.

Somehow Cecil managed to hold his tongue; de
Quadra slanted one silver eyebrow while a tiny gri-
mace twitched the corner of his mouth. The Spanish
ambassador was short and compact, but seemed to ex-
ude the presence of a far taller, larger man. Though his
words were heavily accented, his English vocabulary
was broad. Cecil liked his dry wit, though he'd heard
through informants that of late the bishop had been
sharpening it on the Queen of England's reputation.
Cecil's sources said that de Quadra had given credence
to the lies that the queen was with child by Dudley,
however reed-thin she remained. A damned sheep in
wolf's clothing, Cecil groused silently—and that described Dudley as well as de Quadra.

"Her teeth scaled? It sounds, Lord Robert," the
bishop observed, straight-faced, "as if Her Grace has
been eating far too many fish."

"Her teeth are being cleaned," Dudley explained as if they were both imbeciles, "by my barber, to be precise." He motioned them toward two padded stools facing the vacant throne across the vast chamber. "Too many sweets and suckets," he went on. "Her Majesty adores them, but they're not really good for her."

*"Santa Maria,"* de Quadra whispered to Cecil as they dropped back to follow Dudley slowly, "the wretch describes himself. They call him 'the gypsy' with that swarthy skin, you know, and I fear he could steal her blind of all she holds dear. You must warn her, Cecil."

"She refuses to credit the rumors flying here and abroad," Cecil admitted, suddenly wishing he dared unburden his fears to de Quadra. "If you know from whom such rubbish emanates, please let me know, bishop," he added pointedly. De Quadra didn't so much as blink. "Said lady has a mind and heart of her own," Cecil explained, "and said lady is the queen, her father's daughter."

"Lusty and in love with love, you mean," de Quadra said, speaking quietly and quickly. "Cecil, you and I may not agree on much thus far, but we both know this woman must marry. And not to that freebooter," the bishop added with a slight flaring of his nostrils. Ahead of them Dudley took the third stool on the other side of—but much closer to—the royal dais than their seats.

"Is there no way to discredit him in her eyes or make her pull back?" de Quadra whispered. *"Santa Maria*, the man is her Horse Master, a traitor's son, and married at that."

"And his wife is ailing, I hear," Cecil said, "of a tumor in her breast. You know, bishop, I have a strong-minded, clever wife, but that has hardly readied me to deal with Elizabeth Tudor. Perhaps, bishop, each in our own way, we can only pray."

"Ah, Cecil, I have not been on these shores long, but already I know you better than that. Men like us pray, perhaps, but also always act."

THE NEXT AFTERNOON, ELIZABETH OF ENGLAND GIGGLED as blowing rose petals caught in her hair and bodice. Meg Milligrew was strewing them in the satin-swagged royal barge as the queen's party put out into the Thames for an afternoon ride and repast. The petals' light perfume drifted on the river breeze, far preferable, Her Majesty thought, to that oily perfume burned to cover the reek of the Thames during the warm months in London. The twenty oarsmen bent to their easy task, heading downriver toward a favorite meadow spot. It wasn't far and they could have ridden, but the day was hot and the barge a place to stretch out in repose. The queen already felt giddy.

She had gone against her instincts and invited Cecil and de Quadra along. Perhaps, she had thought, she could mix business with bliss. Yet both of them glanced at her far too often, and she soon felt she was being watched again. Perhaps one or both had spies at court to see what she and Robin were doing. If so, she was throwing down the gauntlet.

"Dear bishop and my Lord Cecil, since both of you

wish me to marry, I have a lovely surprise for you," she called to them and summoned them to her pillowed seat.

"Of course you must wed, for England as well as for your own happiness and an heir," Cecil said, looking as wary as Bishop de Quadra looked hopeful. Elizabeth noted that her ladies, and even the servants, hushed to listen.

"And your thoughts, bishop?" she inquired with a smile.

"It would be my greatest joy to see such a brilliant queen ally herself with the countries of Europe and build a greater—"

"Catholic countries, Catholic husbands, of course," she interrupted.

"Your father was once named Defender of the True Faith by the Holy Father, Your Grace," de Quadra parried.

"Ah, yes, before we found the true Protestant faith here and he became Supreme Head of the Church of England, as I am." De Quadra was a formidable adversary; he barely blanched at all that. "But I was thinking then, bishop," she plunged on, "you as a churchman could perform a marriage ceremony for Robin—Robert—and me this very moment and then report back to your master, King Philip, that you have achieved at least half your mission. And half is better than most get, is that not true, my Lord Secretary Cecil?"

Robin got in the act by going down on one knee and kissing her hand. Meg threw more rose petals, and

Ned began a lilting love song about swimming in love's pulling tide. Everyone knew they were all just playing, so the queen hoped de Quadra and Cecil would lighten their moods too. Though she'd have favored a romping tune today, she had refused to bring her other lutenists in remembrance of Geoffrey's demise. No player could soar to his heights anyway.

"Put in here in the shade of these woods instead of in the far meadow," Elizabeth ordered her barge captain, and watched as her oarsmen pulled the craft to the sedgy bank. Amidst servants scurrying off to open blankets and carting off baskets full of food, the laughing queen let Robin carry her to shore over the narrow gangway.

"Though you but jest of wedding me," Robin whispered to her as her voluminous skirts nearly muffled and blinded him, "yet I carry you over the threshold of our future." The rogue bounced her once as if he'd drop her. She squealed while others roared with humor or dismay, but her Robin was sure-footed and strong-armed. She was quite out of breath when he plopped her down on the largest blanket in the thick shade and someone offered her a goblet of malmsey— and then she remembered Geoffrey again. Because . . . because . . . was that lute music on the breeze she heard now or just birdsongs and the ripple of the river?

Elizabeth hushed everyone and strained to hear. Had they played a trick on her and smuggled aboard some strange musician to cheer her? It was none of her own men. She could tell that flat out, for the fingering was delicate, fast, and sure. Though lute music was always soft, she was certain the deliberate grace notes would have put Geoffrey to shame. She feared for one moment she was so exhausted or emotional that she was imagining it all, mayhap as she had imagined such melody when she had heard nothing but wind music after Geoffrey fell.

"Where in heaven's name is that coming from?" Robin asked, helping allay her fears she was hallucinating. Everyone fanned out looking, and soon Ned produced a slender lad, still playing, dressed in a worn, loose-fitting forest green doublet, smudged gray trunk hose, and baggy-kneed stockings. His face was so pale and delicate that Elizabeth startled, as if Geoffrey had come back from the dead. But this one's flat, straight hair was brown and his eyes dark. A country lad, left-handed, and his lute most plain and scuffed—and creating quite the most lovely sound she had ever heard.

"Bring him to me," she commanded when the song was over, and everyone stood so hushed she knew the boy was a stranger to them all. Though his playing had been controlled, he seemed quite out of breath with shoulders heaving. When he tripped lightly, almost eagerly, forward, she added, "Your name, lad?"

"Franklin Dove, Majesty."

His voice was reedy, without manly tones yet.

"Master Dove of the lute," she dubbed him with a smile, as if she were giving him a knighthood. For one moment she wondered if Robin had arranged this as another gift for her, but he seemed surprised too. "Your age and home?"

"Nigh on fifteen, Majesty, and walked all the way to Richmond from Dover to offer my services, though folks said I was crazed as Tom O'Bedlam to think the queen would e'en hear me play. So forgive me, Majesty, but I used a bit of stealth, running from Richmond along the river path behind you, hoping you'd put in."

"The people were wrong, and the queen will hear you, Franklin. See that he is given food and beer," she ordered, "and then he shall play for us. Who taught you music so well in seafaring Dover, lad?" she added.

"At first my father, a sailor who learned in Calais and practiced at sea, Majesty. And then, somehow, when I surpassed him, forgive my boasting, I just taught myself."

"Ah," she said, instantly intrigued. "Well said." She had learned much from her father too but hoped to surpass him in the memory of her people.

Even as the servants set a half of partridge, a peach, bread, cheese, and beer before the boy, he began to play again. As well as being a charming, stylish lutenist, he seemed to sense her need for levity and romped through verse after verse of "The Crafty Miss of London," which everyone was soon singing:

> A friar was walking in Exeter-street
> Dressed up in his garb like a gentleman neat;
> He there with a wanton young lady did meet
> And freely did offer and earnestly proffer
> To give her a bottle of wine.

*His glittering guinnies soon dazzle'd her eyes,*
*That privately straight she began to devise*
*By what means she might get his rich golden prize;*
*Two is a trifle, his purse I will rifle;*
*I hope to have all now or none.*

"Will you take a guinny or two to come play with my musicians at Richmond and elsewhere?" the queen asked the flushed lad, a genius of his craft, she was sure now. She intended to surround herself with such brilliance in all arts during the years of her reign: in music with this boy; in science with men like Dr. Dee; in theater with actors like Ned Topside and his ilk.

" 'Tis my life's dream," Franklin Dove said, interrupting her thoughts. "Someday will I go to London too?"

"If I can keep you from falling into the clutches of some lecherous friar on Exeter Street," the queen said with a laugh and a sharp look at Bishop de Quadra.

Everyone—even Cecil and de Quadra—laughed while Franklin turned teary-eyed with joy.

"I SHALL MISS YOU SORELY, ROBIN," ELIZABETH TOLD HIM two days later as he took his leave to head forty-five miles to Cumnor in Oxfordshire to see his wife. "Late last night, I regretted I did not have my imp of an artist sketch your face so I at least have that with me. You know I need you here in many ways, my eyes."

"Give the command, and I'll never leave you," he

vowed, stepping closer in the courtyard, where his saddled horse and those of his two companions blocked other courtiers and gawkers from seeing them. His boot toes touched her slippers, shoving her voluminous skirts behind her.

"No, it is right that you should go," she insisted, though she was tempted to try to keep him here again. "You must give Amy my best hopes for speedy recovery from her bodily ailment. If you find her more ill than you surmise, I shall send a physician."

"But not Dr. Dee," Robin said with a little smile as he pressed Elizabeth's clasped hands to his leather-clad chest. "Amy's not much for learning or the learned."

"What is she for then?" Elizabeth asked, though they seldom talked of Amy, almost as if she didn't really exist.

"Baubles, trinkets, gifts, pretty tunes."

"She's not getting my new Dove of the lute."

"And," he added, almost as if he hadn't heard her, "quiet, rural charms with no complications."

"Mm. No wonder she abhors court life. And if she yearns for your face—to see your eyes—as much as I, I pity her indeed."

"I believe, my beloved queen, that is the sweetest thing yet you have said to me. You haven't let me kiss you half enough, but—"

He didn't get the words out before she leaned close and kissed him quickly, almost pertly. "Be off now, Robin, and safe journey."

He held her wrists tighter as she tried to step away. "Your lips were so lovely, but unexpected, my queen.

Let me kiss you back when I know what bounty will befall me, and you'll see. . . ."

"Go, you braggart, for I have another now to keep me company."

"If you mean anyone but that beardless boy, I'll run the blackguard through!"

She laughed at his bravado, however much it thrilled her. "Besides the horses, that's the other reason I keep you about, my lord," she told him, and stepped away so he could mount. "I need an overly passionate swordsman to counterbalance my overly rational scrivener Cecil."

AFTER ROBIN RODE AWAY ELIZABETH DRIFTED DREAMILY into her bedchamber, feeling suddenly aimless. Writs awaited her signature, and she could call a Privy Council meeting to tend to swelling business, but she needed Robin there to—as she said—keep a leash on Cecil's urging this and that. Three days. Three days without Robin. And he would be with Amy and no doubt bed her, the queen thought and hit her fist against the windowsill. Cecil had told her once that Robert Dudley and Amy Robsart had been a love match, a lust match at least, but surely his ardor for Amy had cooled. He'd said it, sworn it!

"There you are," Kat said, coming in and closing the door firmly behind her as if to keep Elizabeth's other ladies out. "For one moment, I feared you'd hop on pillion and ride off with him."

Elizabeth hadn't heard that strident, scolding tone

from Kat since she'd been a child and only then when she'd done something very naughty. The Tudor tactic of the best defense being a loud offense would most suit this impertinence.

"Where were you when I bid Robin a privy farewell?" Elizabeth demanded, her fists propped on her waist above the swell of her skirts.

"On the parapet from which Geoffrey took his tumble, if you must know. I could look almost straight down on that kiss. He wanted more, and I'll warrant he'll get it if he hasn't already and at great price to you."

"*If* he hasn't already?" Elizabeth exploded, throwing out her arms. "If you don't know I'm chaste yet, where have you been?"

"I know you are chaste, lovey, but others don't, and they're hardly listening to me. It's the way things *look* that's being bandied about far and wide. Cecil said the Queen of Scots and her French husband are even calling themselves the king and queen of England, wagering this will bring you down."

"Devil take Mary Stuart, and Cecil too for spreading such tripe here. And, Kat, you'll not lecture me as if I were some green girl or tavern doxy—"

To her amazement, Kat went down on both knees on the tall bed's mounting stool, as if she knelt at a prie-dieu.

"Kat, get up. Your old knees don't need—"

"I've invested my life in you, Elizabeth Tudor," Kat plunged on, gripping her hands before her as if she were praying. "You are on the cusp of your destiny, and I'll not have you sullied and sneered at by—"

"They dare not!" Elizabeth protested. "Cecil has put you up to this."

"He has not. Do you think Cecil is the only one around you with half a brain, after all we've been through together? And that includes Ned, Meg, even Jenks."

"Then de Quadra's poisons have been spreading here, and you've given ear to them. I know the man has slandered Robert Dudley for his own purposes."

"No, I have not heard one vile thing de Quadra's said, though I can imagine," Kat countered with a little shake of her head.

"You—all of you closest to me," Elizabeth said, "against my express wishes, have been investigating Geoffrey Hammet's death behind my back, have you not? That's why you were up on the parapet, besides watching Robin's farewell. I knew someone's been spying on me!"

"If you want to speak of Geoffrey, it wasn't white Canary Island sack on him but sweet, red Madeira malmsey," Kat countered. "And his lute was placed up on the parapet so carefully, Ned and Meg told me, and I saw the very place."

" 'S blood, you are saying there is some foul murderer afoot up in the towers? Against Geoffrey? Against me? Some conspiracy?"

"You are becoming frenzied, lovey. I have worried so that you are burning the candle at both ends over wanting Robert Dudley but keeping him at bay. I came not to discuss Geoffrey Hammet, and it is you who have adroitly changed the subject. The foulness afoot, a conspiracy, yes, could topple you off your throne just as, we fear, someone could have pushed Geoffrey over th—"

"Kat, I have not given Robert Dudley but kisses and my time. And bestowments, of course, but then I've given those to several who were loyal to me. I've made cousin Carey Baron Hunsdon, given him an old royal hunt lodge, and named him Master of the Queen's Hawks. I am virgin and unsullied, or I would not be fearless in showing the court and country—and those vile wolves baying for my blood on the Continent—that Robin and I are friends, just dearest friends. I let him go to his Amy, you see. I encouraged it."

"Oh, my lovey, remember how your own mother's enemies pulled her down to destruction along with married men accused of adultery with her so—"

"Stop it!" she screeched. "This is nothing like that. *I* rule here, not de Quadra, not Mary Stuart, not Cecil, not gossipmongers, and not you! But I tell you now, if I had the will—or found pleasure in such a dishonorable life as you imply, from which God preserve me— I do not know of anyone on earth who could forbid me, including you!"

Elizabeth turned and banged out of the room, striding through her presence chambers where her ladies and Franklin Dove—their new pet in place of lapdogs and parrots—scrambled to fall in behind her. She did not slow until she reached the gardens overlooking the river. Under a bower of white roses, she sat on a turf bench and summoned Franklin with a flick of her wrist.

"Play something that suits," she commanded. "Something about fickle friends will do."

Elizabeth ignored the fact that Katherine Grey snickered and Mary Sidney shook her head. The queen closed her eyes and felt the river breeze cool her flushed cheeks and neck as Franklin began,

> *Right true it is, and said full years ago:*
> *Take heed of him, that by the back thee claweth.*
> *For none is worse, than is a friendly foe.*
>
> *Though he seem good,*
> *All things that thee delighteth,*
> *Yet know it well, that in thy bosom creepeth....*

# Chapter the Fourth

*Prince Robert wedded a gay lady,*
*He wedded her with a ring;*
*Prince Robert wedded a gay lady,*
*But he dare not bring her home. . . .*

*Oh where is now my wedded lord,*
*And where now can he be?*
*Oh where is now my wedded lord?*
*For him I cannot see.*

—ANONYMOUS

 AMY DUDLEY WAS OUT OF BREATH FROM HER climb up the steps of the monastery's skeletal bell tower. Even the double flight of stairs in the manor house hadn't prepared her for this. But now she could see down the road Robert must ride to Cumnor. He'd sent one of his men ahead to tell of his coming. Without even asking, Amy knew his visit would be short. She propped her elbows on the remnant of the windowsill to watch, then put them down at her sides when the lump in her breast hurt again.

Petite but buxom and childless after ten years of marriage, Amy Robsart Dudley couldn't abide living with her brother's or half-brother's families. She used to visit, but they were always fussing at her, always saying she should go to court, as if Robert wanted her there, as if some wives were even allowed there if they didn't directly serve the queen. Right now her sisters-in-law would be fretting over her ailment and accusing her of moping. It was better to be here.

Robert had housed her on old monastery lands King Henry VIII had given to his physician Dr. Owen, whose son now owned it and whose widow still lived in part of the manor house. Anthony Forster, Robert's steward, and his family also leased here to oversee the farm and Robert's interests in the nearby fields he owned. Amy and her waiting woman, Mrs. Pirto, had some rooms of their own on the second floor and ate noonday dinner with the others, but it wasn't like really living in a family.

Amy wondered what people thought about the twenty-eight-year-old country wife of the queen's Lord Robert, if they thought of her at all. Did they know he had a house at Kew and fine apartments within beck and call of their queen, while Amy was still a paying guest in other people's houses?

Yet Cumnor was a pretty place. It had a park, terraced walks shaded by elms and oaks, and a pond with flashing fish. Fine farmlands stretched to the wild downs. If one wanted shops, it was six miles to the market village of Abingdon and four to the university town of Oxford.

Still, she always thought about the abbots who used to hold this country seat and were buried beside this tower. Sometimes she fancied she heard their mournful voices, singing, praying. She often walked among their graves, and if she was alone, laid flat on the ground and stared up at the sky. Then she heard them chanting right through the turf. After all, Cumnor had been ripped from the abbots when Queen Elizabeth's father ruined the holy church. If he could do that, what couldn't his royal daughter take from anyone she pleased?

Amy sucked in a breath when she saw three riders on the road. Her heart beat fast, and she began to perspire. She shouldn't have worn her best gown. Picking her way down the stairs, she waited in the garden amid tall hollyhocks and bright roses. Years ago she and Robert had coupled on the grass in a bower of roses. Robert had watched her face and said she blushed so prettily. She pinched her cheeks to make some roses now.

Her belly fluttered as she watched her husband ride closer. How fine and proud he looked, even dust- and mud-spattered. She always forgot how tall and robust he was when they were apart. But now he rode next to his thin-as-a-rake favorite groom, Fletcher, so maybe that made him look ever bigger.

"Amy, love," he said, all smiles, dismounting and unstrapping a saddlepack. "I'm heartened to see you outside instead of keeping to the house."

Fletcher was the only one of his companions she recognized. The other was a burly queen's man, she supposed. While they went to stable the horses, Robert pecked a kiss on her mouth, then hugged her hard. That hurt her breast, and she flinched, but he didn't seem to notice. He threw an arm around her shoulders and walked her toward the house, the pack in his other hand. Anthony Forster, who would do anything to please Robert, came out to greet him. They started talking rents and crop yield, but not for long.

"I'll speak with you later," Robert told Anthony as he took her hand. "See to my companions, will you? I've brought gifts for my lady, and she'll make mincemeat of me if she doesn't have them forthwith."

"As if I'd ever gainsay or order you about," she protested gently as they climbed the stairs to her suite of four rooms. Mrs. Pirto bobbed him a curtsy at the door and went out, God bless her.

"Amy," he said, and sat in her favorite chair by the empty hearth and pulled her onto his lap, "I am sorry to see you paler and thinner. You must eat better, my pet, keep up your strength."

Amy had gone over many things she'd say to him. She wanted to scold him and insist he had no right to court the queen, that's what all the rumors were saying. Rumors he might ask for a divorce to wed the beautiful, young Elizabeth. He deserved his wife's scorn and spite, but Amy loved him yet.

If these gifts in his saddlepack were bribes, she told herself, she didn't want them. Still, she watched as his sun-browned hands drew them out: an alabaster jar with sweet-smelling something in it, a new ruff, an embroidered sky-blue silk scarf with bouncing fringe, a porcelain pomander for herbs and perfumed petals, and so much more.

"I can't bear it," she blurted, and burst into tears.

"Are you in pain?" he asked, seizing her shoulders and trying to study her face while she sobbed. "You miss me, don't you? Are you well treated here? Do you need another physician?"

Sniffling, she nodded at his first three questions and shook her head at the last. He offered her his fine handkerchief, and she snatched it to hide her face.

"Amy, Amy," he said, sounding like her father, "we have already discussed that this is my—our—great moment in time, our moment of destiny. To have the goodwill of the monarch after the two great falls the Dudleys have taken, after my own father and brother were executed for the rebellion, is a blessing to us all."

Amy tried to listen, but his words blurred. Sometimes Robert's reasonings came out all twisted together. She blew her nose and dabbed at her eyes.

"But now, my pet," he went on, "we have the opportunity to regain some of our lost lands and ruined wealth from those disasters. . . ."

*Disasters,* she understood that, all right. She squirmed off his lap, though she would have loved to cling to him, more fool she.

"Monarch, you called her," Amy said, blowing her nose again. "As if she is not a flesh-and-blood woman to you, as if she could be a man just as well."

"She intends to rule like a man, mayhap without a man, so she needs advisers who—"

"You think she needs you as a man, as *her* man!" she exploded. She wanted to break the porcelain pomander over his head, to gag or strangle him with that new scarf.

"Amy, don't you turn on me too," he said, rising and coming to pull her gently to him. His voice was silky smooth. She tried not to cling, but she turned her head and rested her wet cheek on his leather doublet. Through its thickness, she fancied she could hear his heart beating right over the sound of the abbots' songs.

"Who else dares to bear you ill will if she is your friend?" Amy choked out.

"Ah, to know so little of how the world works. Many resent that I fly high and fast and they yet hate my father for taking the badge of the earls of Warwick. Some cannot abide he named himself Duke of Northumberland, the first subject unconnected with royal blood to hold the ducal rank."

Amy lifted her head as his voice rose. She saw his neck veins throb. "They are all hellfire, raving jealous, and I must show them they need me," he went on, glaring into space. "Sometimes, I almost think, all but her—and you—hate me. My beloved, I can still count on you?" he asked, and held her at arm's length and bent down to look straight into her eyes.

Amy sighed, and nodded. What little strength she'd summoned flowed from her, and she sagged against him. He lifted and carried her to the bed and sat perched on it, holding her hand as daylight fled the room. Soon she fell asleep and when she woke, Mrs. Pirto was sitting by the hearth in lamplight, and Amy could hear Robert's voice somewhere below ... entwined with his steward's ... if the voices weren't the monks' singing their sad chants from their graves out back again.

· · ·

"DEAR HARRY, I AM GLAD TO SEE YOU!" ELIZABETH TOLD
her Boleyn cousin Henry Carey, now Baron Hunsdon,
as he bowed before her in her withdrawing room.
Harry had been gone just over a week and, in truth,
she'd hardly noticed, even if he was the captain of her
personal guards, the Gentlemen Pensioners. Robert
had been away only one day and night, and she missed
him like the very devil.

"How did you find your lady wife and the children,
my lord?"

"Good news, Your Grace, as Anne is with child so
soon again."

He looked as proud as he did pleasant, the queen
thought. The thirty-four-year-old son of her mother's
sister was a bluff, forthright man, but one who also ap-
preciated fine things in life. Harry was russet haired,
but with that and his prominent nose, the family re-
semblance stopped. He was stocky, broad faced with
wide-set eyes, blunt fingers, and a deliberate, stiff
walk. But he was stalwart in tournaments and would
serve well in war, God forbid, she thought.

"Harry, I share your joy and will be honored to
stand godmother to the babe. And how did you find
your lands at Hunsdon?" She rose, indicating they
should stroll toward the gallery. It was then she noted
another man, a stranger to her, in the shadows across
the room, mayhap waiting for Harry. She shivered as
if someone were spying on her again, or as supersti-
tious folk used to say, someone had walked on her
grave.

"And who have you brought to court this time, my lord?" she inquired, for Harry was always mentoring young men of talent. This one would have done for one of her guards or porters with his height and clean, good looks were he not already attired in the new buff-and-brown Hunsdon colors.

"Your Grace," Harry said, "may I present my new man, Anne's second cousin, Luke Morgan."

She offered her beringed hand for the young man to kiss, which he did quite smoothly for one new-come to court. "He is more than a body servant and less than a bodyguard, I take it, Harry? Come along then, Luke," she added, savoring the familiar blush she could bring to a man's cheek with sudden attention or displeasure—except for Robin, who thought he ruled her, the wretch.

Her ladies quickly fell in behind them. Elizabeth had been trying to give her courtiers more of her time since Robert was away. At least Harry's arrival cheered her. They shared a love of music and drama, and bestowing lands and titles on him was her way of elevating her once-slandered mother's family in everyone's eyes and diverting attention from the gifts and preferments she showered on Robert. Because she'd named Robin Master of the Queen's Horse, she'd named Harry Master of the Queen's Hawks.

"Oh, I nearly forgot, I have a surprise for you," she said, turning to her entourage. "Mary," she said to Robin's sister, "will you fetch Franklin Dove? Baron Hunsdon will like to hear him."

"And who, pray tell, is Franklin Dove?" Harry asked as they descended the steps to walk outside in the shade of the covered passages.

"Geoffrey Hammet fell to his death last week," she explained, her voice catching. "I recall he was another young man you had taken under your wing once. Someone surprising came along to replace him, and I had to *carpe diem*. And don't you be trying to lure this one away with promises of patronage or more than I pay him, my lord."

"Then, Your Grace, you in turn will not try to filch Luke from under my aegis. Besides, no one could lure anyone from you, nor can a mere youth tempt me to try to displeasure Your Gracious Majesty. But—Geoffrey fell to his death, you say?"

As she explained the details of Geoffrey's demise, she noted Harry's deepening frown. Unlike many at court, her cousin's emotions were writ plain on his countenance. She was expecting him to question her or ask what he could do to help probe the death, for he had served her twice thusly before. But as they sat in the shaded courtyard by the fountain and Franklin perched on its stone lip, playing, and Luke stood in the shadows as if he were guarding them all, Elizabeth would have wagered Harry forgot all about Geoffrey Hammet.

"Remarkable!" he said, looking astounded and awestruck at Franklin's performance. "Exquisite! Such alacrity and delicacy of fingering, but such robustness in interpretation too. The seething passion held within, I cannot fathom. Your Majesty, as tragic as is Geoffrey's loss, this lad stands far above him. But fifteen years of age, you say?" he asked, squinting at the boy.

"And I also said you'll not pirate him."

"Ah, no, but I shall sue for just one favor."

"Which is, my lord?"

He lowered his voice and leaned closer. "I can tell you are determined to put Geoffrey's loss behind you, Your Grace, so will you not allow me to go up on the parapet where he played for you and portray what could have happened? You could meanwhile sit in your window and watch for what we both might discern. You have done such before in like matters."

"I fear, cousin," she whispered, "you have been talking to the others of my Privy Plot Council, Kat perhaps, Meg or Ned."

"No, but will this not set all minds at rest if they are uneasy? And you, no doubt, are far too busy with the kingdom's business to pursue such investigations anymore. Just allow me to borrow Franklin to play the part of Geoffrey, though I swear to you on my life, I'll not let him fall."

"Aha," she said, rising, "my Master of the Queen's Hawks wants to seize my Dove after all. But, yes, Harry, I think that is a worthy idea. We'll do that tonight to put all suspicions of suicide or murder to rest once and for all. For," she added, staring at him pointedly, "I believe Geoffrey's demise was naught but sad mischance."

*    *    *

"SHOULD THE LAD SING AS WELL AS PLAY, YOUR GRACE?" Harry's voice boomed across to her that evening.

Sitting in her darkened bedchamber window, Elizabeth shook her head and rolled her eyes. She had sent everyone but Kat from the room to keep this secret, and Harry was shouting from the tower. Did he not know other windows opened onto this courtyard?

" 'S blood," she hissed across the short distance to him, "melody, my lord, just melody. Something sweet and soothing merging to a tune more dissonant, I cannot recall exactly what."

Franklin's lute knew what she wanted, even if Harry did not. But Elizabeth could tell that Harry had Franklin sitting too far over, no doubt not even above the fatal spot in the courtyard. The wind was picking up again, playing its haunting music, blending with the night. Then, devil take him too, her lute lad began to play that tune about fickle friends again.

"I'm going out there myself," the queen told Kat.

"But your ladies and guards will all know if you go out—"

"Out the back stairs. Come if you will," she added, snatching and lighting a fat beeswax candle before Kat could lay her cloak about her.

Going out the small back door and down a short hallway, Elizabeth climbed the curving stairs inside the tower's thick stone skin. At least Harry had left torches at regular intervals, for, as on the night of Geoffrey's death, no lights lit the parapet. Not waiting for Kat, whom she could hear laboring on the stairs behind her, Elizabeth banged the wooden door open against the wall as she joined the others. Her candle sputtered out, but she could see better here.

"Ah," she said, looking up into the vast heavens, "the stars are out."

Luke Morgan, standing closest, swept her a bow. "It takes the dark to make some things clear," he said, like some sage philosopher. She thrust her candle at him and pushed past on the narrow walkway toward Harry and Franklin.

"Sit at least two more niches that way," she ordered her lutenist, pointing. "Harry, where you stand was, so I hear, the place the lute was leaned on this low wall."

"These natural seats are so deep here," Franklin put in, doing as she bid, "and have such a solid backrest, I cannot fathom anyone just toppling over from lost balance."

"He had been drinking heavily," the queen countered, though she realized he'd had little time to do so between playing for the dancing and starting his music up here. Had she just been so angry with him for falling and for smelling of strong drink that she'd blamed him unfairly for his own death? Or had she not wanted anything dire to interrupt her fine summer with Robert and resented Geoffrey for that?

"At least, Your Grace," Harry's voice broke into her agonizing, "Geoffrey carefully preserved that lute you gave him, honoring mayhap both his music and you before he—he must have fallen or leaped, as you say."

"It could have been thus," she put in as she pictured it all. "He had recklessly mixed his sack and my malmsey and knew he would puke. Wanting to protect the lute, he put it carefully down a bit away from him," she explained, pacing and mimicking motions, "then leaned over the edge to throw up—and simply toppled."

"Whatever we can deduce, one thing is sure," Harry said when she stood gazing overlong into the night. "Though it was no doubt as black as this, you must be the only eyewitness. How much time elapsed between the moment he ceased to play and when you heard Ned Topside shout from below? How much could you really see?"

Harry was cleverly playing on her guilty conscience, but it was hardly her fault that the man died, she thought, growing more frustrated and furious each moment Harry kept meddling. In each of the other two murders she had solved, she owed a debt to the deceased or was at risk herself. But she could not—would not—go willy-nilly about her realm solving the deaths, however dubious, of anyone she knew, liked, or admired.

"I cannot say!" she protested, smacking her hands on her skirts. "The timing of the sounds were a blur, and as for seeing—take a look yourself. I hardly had some magnifying scope like Dr. Dee's, and it can't pierce the darkness either," she added sarcastically. She turned away from their stares. If only Geoffrey had worn Dee's flying harness and soared safely to the ground, her little band would not keep looking for high-flying solutions.

"Harry, I cannot be sure about the timing between

sounds," she admitted, her voice more controlled. "I may have heard a thud and muted shout *as* he went over, but I cannot be certain *when* he stopped playing because I could have heard the wind in these vanes."

Frozen like statues, they all listened to the eerie hum above their heads. Then Franklin began to strum a melody that blended perfectly with the vanes.

Wrapping her arms around herself in a sudden chill, the queen said, "Yes, you see? That's why I cannot be certain of things."

"Your Majesty," Franklin put in with a thump of his thumb on the hollow lute, "could this have been the thud you heard? Mayhap Geoffrey added a finger beat accompaniment to what he played."

"I just don't know! But I heard no clear voice before Ned's below, no one calling out in surprise or fear. Without other proofs, I cannot but judge that poor Geoffrey fell either by accident or by intent."

Franklin stopped playing and asked, "Majesty, where is that fine lute you gave him?"

"Safe, and I shall let you try it out tomorrow, my Dove," she said, and started wearily away. Kat, who had waited near the steps, fell in behind her, then Harry and Franklin, but Luke stepped close to hold the door for her.

"A word about your lutenist," Luke whispered.

"Geoffrey?"

"That one," he said, nodding surreptitiously at Franklin.

"One moment," she told the others, and let only Kat

into the tower with them. "Well?" she asked the avid man when she faced him in flickering torchlight at the top of the turret.

"I was in the jakes when the lad was, and I fear he's misled Your Gracious Majesty," he said in a rush.

He did not waver under her withering frown. The jakes? What could the palace's public latrine have to do with this? "Say on, man," she ordered.

"He is much older than fifteen years and, Your Majesty, I am certain Franklin Dove is a eunuch."

She gasped. "A castrato? That would make sense, for he seemed older to me too, and that high voice . . . I need no lutenist—no one—who misleads his queen. Still, I understand his reluctance to be gawked at. We English do not favor such barbarian practices like the Italians and French do, at least not but in our gelded horses. Luke Morgan, I shall remember your honesty to your queen. Have you told Lord Hunsdon this?"

"I was going to tell him so that he might broach it with you, but when I saw the opportunity to warn you . . ."

"Warn me? This will suit me well, for no one will blink an eye if the queen keeps such a lutenist close in her bedchamber. I've had enough of music coming through windows."

She nodded at Kat to open the door behind them again. Harry looked a thundercloud and Franklin white-faced with fear. Could he have realized what Luke just told her?

"I made the mistake of looking over the edge of the parapet, Majesty," the lad explained. "I never knew I had a fear of heights before, but I feel sick enough to puke, and dizzy too."

"Then let your heights be only with your art," the queen declared, thinking that same malady could have suddenly afflicted Geoffrey. But if Geoffrey had been queasy on heights, would he not have protested playing on the parapet long ago?

She turned to Harry but nodded toward Luke Morgan. "Lord Hunsdon, you have a fine new man here. And I have a fine new lutenist to play for me. Franklin, come along. I'll let you try out Geoffrey's lute, playing not from the tower through a window but from the next room to me through an open door. And we have much else to discuss."

WHEN AMY WOKE, IT ALL CAME TUMBLING BACK TO HER. Robert was here. He had finally come to bed with her, though he had only held her hand. Now his side of the sheets was as cold as if he'd not been there at all. It was pitch black, but she was sure she heard men's voices like last night, not the monks' singing this time, just quiet talk.

She cracked the hanging bed curtains to see where he had gone, annoyed he'd closed them on her in the warm house. Though daylight dusted the horizon, Robert had lit a lamp on the table in the corner of the room.

Amy rose when she realized Robert was talking to Anthony, mayhap in the hall or on the stairs. His words came clear when she cracked the door. "Wake Fletcher for me to take a missive to Richmond Palace today," Robert told his steward.

"Straightaway, my lord. You still want to ride out to survey the fields this morn? Your lady won't mind?"

"We'll do it early so I still have time for her. And send for that Oxford physician to visit her again after I leave."

As Anthony started to detail the things they should see on the farm, Amy glanced down at the table where Robert had evidently been writing. She wondered what message he would have to send the queen so soon. That he was safely arrived? That his wife was weaker, sicker?

She bent over the letter he had obviously just written and sanded. He had dumped the gritty stuff on the floor, where she could feel it under her bare feet. Amy was slow at letters and reading. She did little more with pen and ink than sign her name and add simple numbers. But she studied the first line to know how Robert would address the queen and saw it wasn't written to her at all. It was for someone named Franklin Dove, a lut—lut-en-i-s-t. And there was something about a song—the words were here, but so many of them. Moving her lips to sound them out, she tried to read the letters. The first three words, mayhap the name of the song, she could not get at all, so she forced herself to try to decipher the others:

CHI AMA CREDE

*Though she be glittering and wise*
*With flaming hair and sparkling eyes,*
*Excelling in each art she tries*
*Are her vows she loves me lies?*
*For* chi ama crede.

*Day by day great grows my need,*
*And hers seems also to indeed,*
*Yet my plea she does not heed*
*And my hopes begin to bleed,*
*For* chi ama crede.

"To bleed?" Amy repeated. *Hopes bleed,* she tried to puzzle out. She did know one thing though. The first few lines meant the poem was never destined to be sung to or for Amy Robsart Dudley, abandoned wife.

She scurried back to bed when she heard Robert coming. Perhaps seeing the curtains were agape, he came and stood over her, but she pretended to sleep. He went to the table and folded the letter. She watched, squinting, as he sealed it with wax and his signet ring, then went out.

Since her rooms looked over the back gardens and the old tower, she pulled on a wrapper and hurried barefoot to the end of the hall with its window fronting the road. This corridor connected her suite of rooms and those of Dr. Owens's elderly widow. She got around only with a walking stick, but her mind was still sharp. She was always talking about cures as if she'd been trained in the medical arts too, and Amy felt jealous of the fact the deceased doctor had shared so much of his life and knowledge with his wife.

Amy glanced out to see Robert hand the letter to his man Fletcher, already mounted on his brown-and-white horse. The man carried the letter not in his pouch but on his person. Robert also handed him a small coin purse. Amy could hear the bell-like ringing of those coins vying with the chants of the abbots and monks.

"Oh, good morning, Lady Dudley." Amy jumped at the Widow Owens's scratchy voice. She at least should have heard the clunk, clunk of her walking stick. The old woman did not see well, but her hearing was still sharp.

"Good morning, Mrs. Owens," Amy said, stepping back from the window as if the widow would report her spying.

"Feeling a bit better with his lordship here?" Mrs. Owens asked. The old woman had actually given her medical advice from time to time, but Amy preferred the Oxford doctor Robert paid to treat her.

"Oh, of course," she lied. "But—could I ask you what some words mean, if you know? And please don't tell Robert, because I don't want him to think I didn't know what he—he said."

When the old woman nodded, Amy blurted, "I cannot really spell or say them."

"Just repeat however he pronounced them," Mrs. Owens urged.

"Chi ama crayda or creeda." Amy did her best to sound out what she had read, praying Robert took his time coming back upstairs.

"Hmm," the widow said, nodding sagely, as if she'd been asked to diagnose some dire illness. "You know, I think he slipped in an Italian phrase on you. Yes, I warrant that's Italian for 'Whoever loves trusts' or mayhap, 'Who loves must trust.' "

"Oh, right, that's it," Amy said, and made for her rooms. "Thank you, Mrs. Owens," she called back before she closed the door behind her and, crumpled against it, broke into smothered sobs. She still loved Robert Dudley, but how could she trust him now?

"I SHALL SPEAK TO MY LUTENIST ALONE," ELIZABETH told Kat when the three of them returned to her bedchamber from the roof. Kat nodded jerkily and went out into the withdrawing room, leaving the door slightly ajar. Franklin, who had been obviously surprised to see a secret back way into the queen's rooms from the roof, held his lute before him like a shield.

"Sometimes, Franklin, leaving something unsaid is as bad as lying," Elizabeth began. "Luke Morgan has told me the truth of your—of your sex—and you should have trusted your queen to tell her yourself."

Her glib, clever lad stammered like a deaf and dumb man, eyes darting, mouth opening, then closing again. "B-but, Your Majesty," he finally choked out, "I can explain, but . . . Luke Morgan told you?"

"You feared I would cast you off, thinking you not a

man? Rather you are an angel with your heavenly
melodies and sweet voice, and the Bible says angels are
neither male nor female nor married, so do not fret.
Castratos have long made fine musicians."

"I—yes, I'm relieved—that you know. I hated to
keep such from you, but knew people would whisper
and point, spread rumors if they knew how this state
befell me—castration, you mean, is that not it?
Majesty, drunken louts did it to me in France several
years ago"—the words spilled from him when she
nodded—"when they caught me playing and singing
for a man's wife, though I myself was not the lover, but
the messenger. . . ."

"I need not the dreadful details. Years ago, becoming a castrato was a gift one gave to the church, to
God's music, you know. Perhaps He meant your sacri-
fice as a gift to me. And, Franklin," she said, stepping
closer and patting his shoulder, "I understand your
fear of people talking because you are different, because you do not fit the pattern that we should marry
and multiply. . . .

"Then too," she went on as she paced to her window and glanced toward where Robin's bedchamber
would be blazing with lights if he were here, "there is
another blessing in it. You see, if you are alone with
me—say, here in my privy chamber—naught can be
amiss, since you are but a eunuch. You know what I
mean," she added hastily.

But even after bucking him up—actually, Franklin
looked quite smug about it now—the queen shuddered. When her father had let his vile henchman,

Thomas Cromwell, bring her mother down, they had made Anne Boleyn's favorite lutenist, Mark Smeaton, no eunuch, tell all he knew of the queen's private life behind closed doors. They had tortured him to make him say what they wanted, including that he too had committed adultery with the queen. Though unwilling, the lutenist had been their spy in the ruination of the queen's reputation.

But, Elizabeth told herself, striding to the door to let Franklin out and Kat back in, her safety did not hang by a thread on any man's goodwill. She was queen in her own right and had naught to fear.

# Chapter the Fifth

*In thine array, after a pleasant guise,*
*When her loose gown did from her shoulders fall,*
*And she me caught in her arms long and small,*
*And therewithal so sweetly did me kiss,*
*And softly said: dear heart, how like you this?*

— SIR THOMAS WYATT, *the Elder*

 ON THE ROYAL BED, KAT ASHLEY CAREFULLY laid out the garments the queen would wear to welcome Robert Dudley formally back to court that afternoon. She even checked the points at which the ribbons and eyelet holes would lace together the separate pieces of bodice, sleeves, and skirts. And then Kat realized the ninnies had not brought the right farthingale. This one had bell-shaped whalebone ribs knit by canvas strips, and the huge, black-and-silver skirts draped over them would drag. The new-fledged style of the fuller, wheel-shaped underpinnings was needed for this gown.

"God save us, but the fan's the wrong one too," Kat muttered. "Nary a tinsel ribbon on it."

She was horrified to realize the slip-up might be her own. But that would never do. Furious, she did not bother to send someone to fetch the right ones, but went herself, hauling the farthingale and fan, however out of breath she felt, down the gallery toward the three rooms that housed Elizabeth's modest traveling wardrobe.

Kat was not only First Lady of the Bedchamber but also Mistress of the Robes, so she oversaw the staff that cared for the queen's garments. In London for the long winter, an entire suite and additional storage building were used to house the royal array, but on summer progress they had to make do.

Kat didn't begrudge the young queen's passion for clothes, not after all the years the princess had been out of favor and sometimes even declared bastard. Exiled from court, the poor, thin thing had been clad in out-moded or overworn clothes. And after the nearly disastrous scandal with that smooth seducer, Thomas Seymour, Elizabeth had purposefully dressed in plain, dark garb. Now Kat only prayed that the queen's dazzling rainbow of fabrics and fashions with which she adorned her slim body was not to seduce Lord Robert Dudley.

" 'Tis Mistress Ashley!" she called out to the keeper of the keys, and rapped her knuckles on the door that led to the wardrobe rooms. "Let me in this instant, or I'll have your thick heads on a platter!"

The door swept open, and Kat swept in. "You sent the small farthingale and the French fan," Kat told the guard and two girls who were rubbing crushed laven-der—the queen's favorite summer scent—on the rows of heavy, hanging garments. Bodices hung separate from sleeves; petticoats from kirtles. Smocked, em-broidered, and patterned undergarments, which the queen changed daily, were rotated to take their weekly turns at the vast royal laundry down by the main kitchen block.

"*This* fan, you lackbrains," Kat said, snatching the one she wanted from the clothes press shelf. "And fetch that biggest wheel farthingale forthwith!"

When the wardrobe girl hesitated, Kat stepped forward to unhook the disjointed, skeletal thing herself, but she nearly tripped over a basket of lavender.

"Oh, sorry, milady," the girl gushed, and bent to scrape the sweet-scented flower heads back in. "The queen's strewing mistress just been up with these fresh from the gardens and coming back, she is."

Kat glanced down at the tipped basket and saw amidst the pale purple bounty a man's shirt. "Men's clothes in here?" she demanded. "Surely that shirt is not Meg Milligrew's."

As the girl shrugged, then spread the shirt out on her knees, Kat knew from whence it came. Meg had been hiding or hoarding the shirt Geoffrey Hammet died in. Its red malmsey stain was clearly etched as if it were faded blood, right over where the man's heart would be. And the shoulder where the poor wretch hit the pavement was filth-smudged.

Kat gathered the clattering whalebone farthingale to her. Perhaps her leaving the meeting in the stables early last week had made Meg and the others decide not to keep her apprised of their investigation. Or was the shirt a mere keepsake for the girl? Had she stubbornly wanted to make it smell sweet instead of reek with drink?

"Give me that shirt and open the door," Kat ordered gruffly. She cut a huge swath down the hall, the loose-boned farthingale swaying, the fan in one hand and poor Geoffrey's shirt over her arm.

But just when she was certain nothing else could go amiss, she nearly bumped into that smug chit Katherine Grey, coming full speed around the corner. "Best heed where you are going, my lady," Kat said, her voice sharp. She hoped the girl took that as a warning against attracting a Catholic rebellion to her as well as against charging about the palace like a knight at a tilt rail.

"Oh, dear," Katherine said, a little grin twisting her saucy lips. "Now Her Grace has you fetching and carrying for her too."

She was off like an arrow but not before Kat saw full well that Edward Seymour, whom Katherine had been told to steer clear of, waited down the hall. Not only did the queen keep an eye on who her ladies tarried with, but Katherine's ties to royalty would eventually make her marriage an affair of state—or if forbidden, treason.

"The only one worse than Edward Seymour she could be rushing to would be that Spanish ambassador so they could hatch a plot together," Kat muttered as she managed to open Elizabeth's bedchamber door without calling a guard. Most of the ladies were outside attending the queen on her morning stroll, thank God, so Elizabeth would never know the truth that Kat had forgotten to specify which pieces of wardrobe she wanted, then blamed the staff for it.

Still fretting, Kat surveyed again the pieces of garments on the bed. The clothing was slightly mussed. Someone had dared not only to move them, but perhaps to try them on, or at the very least, to hold them up, mayhap in front of the mirror. Katherine, the snippet, surely it was she.

As Kat laid the farthingale down and began to rearrange and smooth out the garments, she saw she still held Geoffrey's death shirt. Tucking it up under her own voluminous skirts, she vowed to discuss it with Meg Milligrew later. Just like these garments waiting to be mixed and mated, the clues to Geoffrey's death had endless possibilities.

THOUGH ELIZABETH WAS ARRAYED TO OUTGLITTER ANY earthly queen, she awaited Robert's arrival in a rustic setting, the apple orchard hard by the Thames. Amy Dudley liked uncomplicated country matters, did she? Elizabeth fumed. She would show Robin her version of that. And she wanted him to realize the gulf between them, for it frightened her how much thinking of him with Amy, especially in bed at night, had tormented her.

So she sat on a pile of ivory silken cushions, eating an apple with only Kat and Mary Sidney in attendance, though her other ladies and guards were spread along the covered walkway Robert must traverse. Meg had strewn rose petals everywhere, and Franklin provided the music.

Elizabeth Tudor's heart beat hard and she almost

choked on the fruit as Robin strode straight to her and went down on one knee, head bowed. Yet, devil take the man, he seemed not a bit awed or humbled. And despite her orders that he join her here forthwith, he had obviously bathed and changed his riding garb to jade green and sapphire garments that made him glitter like a rare gem.

"My Lord Robert."

"Here I am," he said, looking up boldly despite her intentional use of his formal name, "looking for the queen of England and queen of my heart, and I find Eve with an apple in the garden. And I would take that seducing bite should it cast me out of paradise forever—were it offered me."

Despite herself, she gaped at him, then as if mesmerized, extended the half-eaten apple to him. He smiled and stepped closer to kneel again, his knees nearly in her skirts. He reached for her wrist and turned it just so and took a huge chomp from the fruit.

"I am glad you are back," she admitted, not saying what she had intended. She had wanted to make him suffer a bit, to wait for her goodwill.

Robin chewed and swallowed his bite of fruit with gusto. "Time drags into eternity when we are parted, but I have a gift for you, my queen, so you realize my thoughts were ever with you."

To her surprise, he turned to Franklin and flicked his wrist. The lutenist nodded and came closer, going down on one knee. "I am bid to tell you, Most Gracious Majesty," Franklin's high, melodious voice recited, "that the words to this song come from the heart of him who wrote it and sent it to me for you. I ne'er learned to write myself, you see, and concoct my own verses in my head—but I can read well enough to learn Sir Robert's beauteous lines."

Franklin played and sang a song called "Chi Ama Crede," He—or She—Who Loves Trusts. It was achingly beautiful and swept her defenses down and away. Surely, *surely*, of all the men that ever were, she could trust this one, her Robin.

ELIZABETH AND ROBIN STROLLED THE CONVOLUTED, covered passages of Richmond, dined together, then stood in the huge oriel window of the royal rooms to watch the sun sink.

"There is one thing that is business, my lord, I would speak of," she murmured.

He held her hand tighter. "I would go to the far reaches of Araby or the frozen plains of Muscovy for you, business, pleasure, anything."

"Dear heart, this only entails seeking out Bishop de Quadra in London and telling him you think Katherine Grey would make a good heir for me."

He muttered a string of curses and turned to her so their shadows merged and shut out those who stood behind them. "You're going to name her as your—"

"Hardly," she said, placing three fingers on his lips to still his protest. "Kat tells me she's been not only flippant but perhaps lurking some places where she should not be of late, and I know she will do anything to vex me. I said merely *tell* him you favor Katherine. I want to see how readily he goes for that bait. The man bears watching."

"Of course, I'll do it, though I'd rather be watching you."

Elizabeth smiled. If she did love and therefore must trust Robin, why did she still feel some dark, creeping unease? The sensation that someone was spying on her had been just as sharp when he was away as now. She squinted into the bloodred sun, balanced on the horizon like a ball on a table, before it was sucked into oblivion.

IT WAS LATER THAT NIGHT, WHILE KAT WATCHED THE opening of the dancing with the stately processional of the pavan—her memory no doubt tweaked by the sway of the queen's huge farthingale—that she recalled she wanted to scold Meg Milligrew. She rose unobtrusively, edged around the moving, shifting crowd, and went to locate the girl. She finally found her in her distilling room back by the kitchens, making rose water from plucked petals.

Kat stood in the doorway of the room, watching Meg measure out a peck of salted petals, then one quart of water. Once the first boiling extracted the natural oil, the remaining water was siphoned off, then run through again to make the fragrant double distillation. As steam escaped the hissing pot behind Meg, she seemed some sort of bedraggled witch at a cauldron, for the room was hotter than the hinges of Hades.

"Ouch," the girl cried as she obviously brushed her knuckles against the still.

"Best use some of your own healing salve," Kat said, making Meg jump again.

"Oh, Kat, is Her Grace all right? Has she sent for me?"

"No, but I thought I could save you from that if I came myself." Kat surprised Meg by ruffling up her petticoat, then reaching up under it to pull out Geoffrey's wrinkled, stained shirt. The girl looked so glad to see it, Kat let her have it back.

"Oh, I wondered where I'd lost that—surely not there."

"In your lavender basket in the wardrobe rooms," Kat said. "But saved for a keepsake or a clue?"

Meg sighed and leaned back on the table, dipping her scalded knuckles in the vat of saltwater. "Both, I guess. I just—we—can't let Geoffrey's death go the way the queen evidently can. Ned learned Geoffrey was having dizzy spells, or at least had one. He got that kitchen slut Sally to admit he nearly toppled over after he sneaked to her pallet and lay with her the other night."

"Ned or Geoffrey lay with her?" Kat asked, stepping into the room and closing the door.

"Geoffrey, of course, though I don't dupe myself that Ned probably hasn't enjoyed her wares too, the lying churl."

"Meg," Kat said, her anger ebbing when she saw again how the poor thing cherished the pompous Ned, "a man's getting light-headed and nearly toppling over after enjoying a wench may not mean he's prone to dizzy spells fierce enough to make him fall off a tower height—after putting his lute down."

"But it could mean something. It's a clue, and if Her Grace would only help us, she could figure it out!" Meg wailed.

"Don't wager on our queen solving mysteries ever again," Kat warned. "She can't even understand herself of late, and I'm afraid there's no help for her."

Meg looked so frightened that Kat put her hands on her shoulders, wishing she could comfort Elizabeth like this. The two of them stood unmoving until the pressure in the still began to build and hiss, and Meg turned away to tend to it.

"I AM IN DEEP DESPAIR ABOUT THE QUEEN," WILLIAM Cecil admitted to his wife as they lay abed in their small country house at Wimbledon. Mildred snuggled closer to him, her bottom in his lap as if they were a pair of perfectly matched spoons. At least she had been happy to see him, disrobing sensuously and luring him to bed tonight as if they were new-wed. The queen could hardly abide him in the week Robert Dudley had been back at court, as if her Principal Secretary's mere presence made her feel guilty.

"She ignores her duties," he complained to Mildred, "romping with that man all day and half the night. She makes mockery of official visits by ambassadors. . . ."

"And by her principal adviser who helped save her

from her bloody sister during hard times and loves her dearly."

"It's true," he muttered, "I do love her, but not—never—the way that I do you."

"I know that. Family, duty, queen—that should be the motto emblazed on your escutcheon, my lord."

Cecil turned Mildred to face him in the twist of mussed sheets. "As of now, you are the wisest woman in the kingdom," he told her solemnly. "You have stood by me even as I have stood by Elizabeth, and now I have a favor—a great boon—to ask you."

"You are thinking of resigning, are you not, and want me to understand?"

"I—yes," he said, amazed at her again. "I thought it would be a blow to you after how long and hard I've strived to reach this pinnacle. But I am praying my threat to resign will rattle her into ending this disastrous summer. I have intelligence that says de Quadra has actually been telling other high-placed ambassadors in London that the queen may lie down one night a queen and wake up with herself and her paramour in prison!"

"Surely he does not imply rebellion? Will you tell her that?"

He sat up in bed and put his head in his hands. "When I tried to tell her how dangerous the Mary, Queen of Scots, situation could become—and then there is the threat of others swarming around Katherine Grey—she lost her temper and would not heed me. But I have to try again, my love."

"Of course, you do. We've lived through down times before but—"

"But only because I had great faith our Lord God had destined Elizabeth Tudor to rule and rule well. Only because I had hitched myself to her star and now she—she has tumbled from the sky."

"You'll not take de Quadra with you to face her down?"

"No. I go into the lioness's den alone—if she will take the time to see me."

"My dearest, is there no way you can use Robert Dudley to your benefit, perhaps make some deal to work with him to bridle her?"

"I'd rather die first," he admitted, throwing the covers off and getting up to pace, "but then, indeed, it may come to that."

"Working with Dudley, you mean, not dying, my lord!"

"At least the dungeons of the Tower are a good distance from Richmond," he mused, going over to his desk to try to write down the points he must make to the queen tomorrow. "Though one of Her Grace's musicians fell off a tower at Richmond to his death, and I warrant if I cross her the wrong way, she might give me the heave-ho off that very parapet."

He gave a little laugh but saw that Mildred had begun to cry quietly and went back to comfort her.

IT TOOK CECIL MOST OF THE DAY TO GET TO RICHMOND BY horse and barge and most of the evening to get a privy meeting with the queen. He had decided to face her without his usual sheaf of letters, warrants, and writs, hoping that would convince her he was serious about leaving if she could not give the realm's business her time and attention. But on his way into the presence chamber—he had heard she had pulled herself away from playing cards to receive him—he ran into his nemesis.

"Lord Robert," Cecil said with a mere inclination of his head.

"Secretary Cecil. I can only hope you are not here to counsel Her Majesty to wed some foreigner again. I swear, anyone who urges such advice on her is as good as a traitor and—"

"And you, Horse Master, certainly should be an expert on traitors—entire families of them," Cecil replied, holding his ground when Dudley advanced several steps on him. "I warrant you were just playing cards with her and I tell you, my lord, you are showing your own hand and have wagered entirely too much to win in the end."

"You're sounding desperate, Cecil," Dudley responded with a smirk. "We could work together, you and I, on intelligence gathering, on counsel to Her Gr—"

"Has she appointed you yet?" Cecil interrupted, his choler rising. " 'S blood, man, if you truly cared one whit for her future, you would urge her to stop this midsummer night's madness and get back to business."

"Ah," Robert said, obviously enjoying this, "what are those lines from Proverbs Her Grace quoted to me but the other day? Oh, yes, I have it: *For by wise coun-*

*sel you will wage your own war, and in a multitude of counselors there is safety.* In short, she needs more advisers than the one who always lectures and preaches to her that—"

"Preaches? I believe it is you who just quoted Scripture to me. But," Cecil countered, clenching his fists and hoping his fury did not betray his control, "Proverbs also says that the monarch's heart must be in the hand of the Lord. The *Lord God*, Dudley, not some upstart blackguard who knows how to glitter, cajole, and seduce. . . ."

They might have come to blows if the double doors had not been opened from within. Dudley stepped back into the shadows and was quickly on his way as Cecil turned to face the queen, seated far across the large, lighted room on the slightly raised dais under the swag of drapery emblazoned with the huge, ornate *E R*. He strode quickly to her chair, and as the guards closed the door behind him, he saw they were indeed alone in the chamber.

"Is there some uprising or rebellion that you demand to see your queen the moment you arrive and without summons?" Elizabeth began as soon as he bowed and stood facing her again.

"Indeed, Your Gracious Majesty, a rebellion of sorts. Mine. I cannot serve you in such fashion where I must stand in line with the kingdom's essential business in hand to await the whims of dancing, boating, or gambling at cards, while all the time you gamble with your own future. I honor and admire you far too much to see that happen."

She probably, he noted, would have cut him off, but she looked so shocked, she gasped for words. Good, he thought. He had her full attention at last.

"You—you are resigning?" she choked out. "I'll not allow it! You are but vexed I have for once taken some time to enjoy myself before my return to London."

"London, Your Grace, where people are muttering that you will wed Robert Dudley."

"I cannot wed Robert Dudley!" she shouted, and jumped up to come at him, then swerved to pace before the throne. "The man is married, for heaven's sake, Cecil."

"Your father's being married never stopped him when he desired to wed, that's what your subjects are remembering. And rumors say Amy Dudley is ailing and—"

"Rumors?" she cried, flinging out both arms. "I am indeed doomed if my chief adviser is making his decisions on rumors. Are you demented, my lord?"

He nearly dared to ask her the same. "Your Grace," he said, choosing each word carefully, though he couldn't recall one of his well-rehearsed pleas, "you have said you wish to rule by the goodwill of your people. I am only asking that you hold personal affairs more at arm's length and return to state affairs in London to assure the country and the watching world that you are the ruling queen of England, not only the reigning one."

"I could put you in the Tower for such insolence." She leveled a stiff arm and trembling index finger at him. "You are speaking sedition, if not treason, and I can hardly allow a man who knows so much of the state's business to go about scot-free."

He thrust his wrists forward as if they were in shackles already. "I will gladly go to the Tower to rot there rather than see all my dreams rot here, Your Grace. I told Mildred I had almost feared you might have me cast off one of the towers here, but I just might do it myself."

"Do not jest with that," she said, her voice quiet for the first time. "But no, you may not resign. I will return to London, my lord, but later, after a little while at Windsor. Yes, have you not heard? I've ordered the court to progress to Windsor on the morrow as this place does not please me now."

He saw her eyes dart around the room. He felt instantly protective of her, just as he had for years. "Because of the death of your musician?" he asked, his voice almost a whisper.

She shrugged. "I know not. Something—I feel someone is watching me, wanting to harm me. It's a foolish fancy."

"Or a guilty conscience," he dared.

She stared straight at him, nostrils flared and fists clenched. He was certain she would strike or banish or even order him imprisoned.

"Be on my barge tomorrow and bring your—my— most important papers," she said, and swept from the room.

When he was alone, he realized his legs were shaking so hard he had to lean against the wall behind the throne until he felt steady enough to leave.

* * *

BUT ON THE BARGE, DESPITE CECIL'S HIGH HOPES, THINGS weren't much better. The queen signed papers without reading, half listening to Dudley's chatter and her lutenist's eternal repetition of some song entitled "Chi Ama Crede." She kept up a running patter with her cousin, Lord Hunsdon, who—God bless him—understood Cecil's dilemma and tried to steer Her Grace back to business. And besides seeming to hearken to everyone and everything but state papers, she kept squinting at the passing shoreline as if some enemy was hidden there. She had Gil Sharpe, her mute little lad of an artist, sketching faces and bringing them to her to comment on. More than once she sent Lord Hunsdon's new young protégé—some handsome family cousin named Luke Morgan—on errands to order the bargemen to row faster or put in for a few moments. Cecil ground his teeth.

"Everyone had best hold on," Luke announced to the entire barge when he returned to sit at the queen's feet for the fortieth time. "The barge master says the rain in this area's been bad and the rapids below are up a bit."

Several ladies giggled in anticipation, though Cecil could see no white water ahead. Perhaps it was rocks newly hidden in the swirls that made the danger, for the bottom of the barge bumped and scraped. Cecil saw Dudley immediately seize the queen's arm to steady her. At least, Cecil thought, the blackguard wouldn't let her perish in the water, even if he was willy-nilly drowning her reputation.

A woman screamed. Everyone looked up; some bent over the side.

"It's Dove, your lutenist, Your Grace," Dudley's sister Mary cried. "Perched on the side, he's fallen in!"

"Fetch him out!" Her Majesty shouted, rising to her feet despite the barge tilting on the rock. She shoved several, including Robert, aside to clamber to the back of the barge near where the lad had popped up in the rush of water, still holding his lute. Shivers shook Cecil. Whatever her flaws, the courage of Elizabeth Tudor was magnificent.

Before her oarsmen or guards could reach an oar to help, Luke jumped off and fought his way through coursing currents to the lad. At first they were swept too far to reach the oars, but Luke half dragged, half swam them toward the barge. Oarsmen towed them in, both sputtering and hacking river water.

Men cheered, ladies applauded, and Elizabeth leaned over the side to take the lute from Franklin and clap the sopping Luke on the back. She refused to step back even when the two men were hauled over the side and drenched her skirts.

"I believe, Franklin," Her Majesty said, "I must indeed let you use Geoffrey's lute now, as this one will warp." Mary Sidney threw a swag of satin bunting over the boy and sat him down in the back of the barge. Cecil saw the queen speak to Luke and shuffled closer to hear.

"You are a good man, Luke Morgan," Her Majesty said.

"But Your Grace," Cecil heard him say, out of breath, "I led you wrong about the lad's being a eunuch."

"What?" she asked as the others made their way back to their places to hold on while the oarsmen got the barge off the rocks. "You could tell when your hands were on him? You could feel he's not been gelded?"

"I could feel," he gasped out, "full breasts that were bandaged tight and popped free under that sopping shirt. Majesty, your he—your eunuch—is a she."

# Chapter the Sixth

*I have endured pain and travail,*
*So much grief and misery:*
*What must I do for you*
*To stand in your good grace?*
*With grief my heart is dead*
*If it look not on your face.*

— PIERRE ATTAINGNANT

 AFTER THE ROYAL BARGE SWEPT PAST THE palaces of Hampton Court and Oatlands, Meg saw the gray stone mass of Windsor Castle hove into sight with the little town sprawled around its stony skirts. Though the queen liked her other palaces well enough, the lofty view and fresh air of Windsor always brought her back in late summer. Sometimes Her Grace complained the place itself was like to tumble down about her ears, but she had plans to rebuild it when she got the money.

Peering over the walls sat ornate St. George's Chapel, where the queen had made Lord Robin a Knight of the Garter in a fancy ceremony Meg had only heard about. Rising above the chapel, the hulk of the old Norman Round Tower frowned down on them all, but right now its heavy brooding could not outdo the queen's.

Meg could tell Elizabeth was seething, but she

wasn't sure why. Even when Franklin fell in the river,
Her Majesty had been in a soaring mood, glad to see
him plucked out. It was only his old lute he'd ruined,
but now the queen kept glaring daggers at the bedraggled lad. No, more like it was that the barge had
sprung a leak. Most of the men were bailing with hats
or even boots, and the queen, like the rest of her ladies,
had sopped her skirts and shoes.

"Franklin," Meg heard the queen say in a sharp
voice, "or what must I call you now?"

Meg edged closer as Franklin shuffled through the
four inches of water to the queen and bowed very low.
"In truth, Felicia Dove, Your Gracious Majesty, but I
thought if you knew I was really a—"

"Indeed," the queen cut him off. "Evidently you
deem yourself worthy to do my thinking for me and to
dupe me. When we dock, you are to go with Lord
Hunsdon and Luke Morgan to Eton and return to
court only when I send for you—accompanied by one
or the other of those men."

"If you please, I can explain, Your Maj—"

"I do not please. Go write songs about deceivers for
that wet, warped lute, if you can!"

Baron Hunsdon's man Luke, as if he knew what
the queen was ranting about, stepped forward and
seemed to take the poor lutenist prisoner. *Felicia
Dove?* Meg thought. And then, when Franklin had to
unwrap himself from the satin swag he'd clung to like
a shawl, Meg saw that the lad was indeed a maid. Despite the barrier of the lute, the sodden shirt clung to a
feminine form.

Meg gasped at the wench's trick, crafty as Ned's turning lads to ladies for the stage with wigs, face paint, and padded breasts. Mercy, thought Meg, the queen had gone about as a lad a time or two herself, so why hadn't she discovered that ruse? Though, of course, Meg and Ned hadn't either. Still, she was certain more was expected of queens, and that must be why Her Grace was out of sorts.

Set between town and castle, the royal barge landing was a bit past the bustling public one. Under a grassy bank where Meg tended the queen's rose and herb gardens, the palace's wooden dock soon swarmed with townsfolk who saw the queen's barge. After her betters had disembarked, Meg clambered out. The queen's castle steward, a portly man whose name Meg could not recall, greeted Her Majesty with a low bow. The royal litter with carriers awaited her short ride up to the castle. Though it wasn't far, someone produced horses for Lord Robin and other men to make an escort.

"A difficult journey, I take it, Your Grace," the steward intoned, "but we can no doubt repair the barge."

"Do so, but also send for another back in London," the queen clipped out, settling herself in her litter with Lord Robin's helping hand. "And," she said, speaking loudly enough for everyone on the landing to hear, including the barge crew, "order new oarsmen sent with it who know how to keep me off the rocks, hidden or not."

Meg's insides cartwheeled. Not only were the poor

oarsmen shamed and dismayed, but Felicia Dove was also downcast. Her Grace's command could hurt Meg too. Meg's estranged husband was an oarsman in London, and she'd told the queen not one thing about him—not even that she'd been wed before she lost her memory.

Meg had learned of him in London and seen him too, close-up, the ruffian. So every time new rowers were hired for the royal barges, Meg shuddered to think one might be Ben Wilton, come to work for Her Majesty. He would see Meg, whose name had once been Sarah Scutea, and claim his wayward wife. And what if, like Felicia Dove, Meg thought as she hurried to keep up on foot with the queen's entourage, the queen cast her off for lying? If she ever had to stop being Meg Milligrew and leave Elizabeth Tudor, she'd just as soon throw herself off a tower, maybe like poor Geoffrey'd done.

As Meg hurried through the King Henry VIII gateway of the palace, she glanced up to see fierce gargoyles glaring down at her.

ELIZABETH ORDERED A CANDLELIGHT SERVICE THAT EVEning in St. George's Chapel in gratitude for her safe deliverance on the river. She sat in the first row between Robin and her cousin Harry, staring at the altar, hardly hearing what the minister said. However much she loved this ornate, gilded, and carved place, which lifted hearts to heaven with its soaring arches and spires, she could not help but stare at the high altar.

The black-and-white tiled floor before it seemed to shift and shudder in flickering light as a thunderstorm rumbled into the valley outside.

For beneath the tile and stone, interred in lead caskets, lay her father and his third queen, Jane Seymour. Somehow, whatever sermonizing tone the current cleric took, in her ears it always turned to her father's outrage at something she had done amiss.

*You shall not speak of your mother in my presence!* he had thundered once and stomped toward Elizabeth, favoring his sore tree trunk of a leg. *Be grateful, girl, you are not declared bastard again! You and your sister had best learn to hold your tongues and tend to your brother's wants, as he shall rule here after me, not a weakling in petticoats. No woman shall sit on this throne without a man to guide her, is that not right, my darling Tudor rose?*

He'd softened then as he turned to beam at his young fifth wife, Catherine Howard. He'd not gone closer to Elizabeth but chucked his Catherine under the chin while she giggled and preened. And then the silly chit had trusted him and, worse, trusted a young, dashing paramour and got her head cut off for following her heart.

Elizabeth jolted back to reality as Robin shifted in his seat beside her, bumping her skirts. She forced her brain back to the sermon from the Old Testament about King David.

"And David saw and coveted a married woman, wife of his trusted soldier Uriah. 'And it came to pass in an eveningtide, that David arose from off his bed and walked upon the roof of the king's house: and from the roof he saw a woman washing herself; and the woman was very beautiful to look upon.' And the monarch sent Uriah," the elderly minister went on, "to be killed in battle so that he might possess another man's wife."

Again Robin shifted sharply beside her. Elizabeth heard whispers, mayhap even titters farther back in the congregation of courtiers. Her quick mind closed on the sermon like a trap: Did this man dare to imply she, as monarch, was acting in like manner? Did her own people believe she would dare to possess Robin and rid herself of his spouse?

The queen stood. "Leave off, man!" she shouted at the cleric, who jumped back so far he almost tumbled off his lofty lectern. "You have preached too long and too far."

She turned to walk out. Her father had done such when the Papists preached against his will. She needed not some pious insult about her and Robin. This preacher would find himself lecturing the northern sheep of her realm next week, indeed he would!

The queen did not glance behind her until she left the long aisle of the chapel. Her ladies followed her out in disarray and Robin, bless him, sat still and rose slowly, as if the message had naught to do with him at all.

THE NEXT MORNING ELIZABETH WALKED OUTSIDE ON THE north terrace with her ladies to survey her favorite lofty view of parks and woodland below. She'd rather be hunting, but she had promised Cecil an hour for business and had also sent for that two-faced liar, Franklin, alias Felicia Dove. First he—she—had claimed to be a lad, then admitted to being a eunuch, but had turned out to be a woman.

" 'S blood!" Elizabeth muttered, and did not deign to explain herself when several of her ladies asked if she were in pain. It vexed her too that Robin was packing to go to London to try to cozen the Spanish ambassador on her behalf—and she was the one who would miss him. And if it weren't for her sister Queen Mary being besotted by her husband, King Philip of Spain, the money to repair this terrace would not have been squandered on a damned Spanish war. Planks and rails, some decaying, covered the earth and stones at the top of the escarpment and made footing a bit slippery, however lovely the blue-green vista below.

"Your Grace," her cousin Harry called to her. Both he and Luke Morgan joined her, with the lutenist between them as if she were some vile state prisoner. "You wished to see Mistress Dove."

Despite the muddy wooden walk and the fact she was finally garbed as a girl, Felicia went down on both knees and stayed there. She was quite a fetching female, slender as was the style.

"Rise and walk with me," the queen ordered, treading the very edge of the terrace, turning away to overlook the stretch of vibrant scene again. "Well," she said when Felicia stood at her side, shaking soil from her gray skirts, "is there some excuse, some explanation?"

"Aye, Your Gracious Majesty. I feared you'd never take a mere lass in, not on a lute. 'Tisn't done, no more than wenches on the stage, and I so longed——"

"Women play the lute and sing in their own homes," Elizabeth interrupted. "I play passably well, but not in public."

"You play *very* well, Your Majesty, and I was thrilled you asked me for a bit of further instruction. You see, I knew the music was God's gift to me and I yearned to play for you, to know you, to just be near you, a woman who is queen in her own right, and that is not done either, as e'en your royal sister was wed."

Elizabeth's temper flared again, but this was not Cecil in some you-must-wed harangue. "Well said, Felicia," she admitted. "It *is* Felicia, with no more surprises, is it not?"

"Oh, yes, Your Grace. If I can no longer play in your gallery with the men, can I not be your privy player and——"

"I have not decided," Elizabeth interrupted, turning to study the girl's eager face. "I will not—cannot—abide those who deal treacherously with me, not a lutenist, not the highest peer in the realm, not the dearest friend. I had friends who lied to me the very month I was crowned, the Haringtons, and they are yet cooling their heels in the country out of my sight."

She saw that revelation startled Felicia. Elizabeth bit her lower lip and glanced away again, remembering how she had sent her dear friend Bella and her Lord John into rural exile. She longed to summon them back. Yes, perhaps it was time. With these unfair rumors about her and Robert flying hither and yon, she needed all the friends she could grapple to her.

"Your Majesty?" Felicia broke into her thoughts, sounding even more shaken now. "I admire you greatly. I am so honored to be at your court, so please do not send me back to oblivion."

"Not to oblivion, girl, but you cannot get off scot-free for such deceptions, and you will remain in Lord Hunsdon's household until I send for you again. He has a soft spot for brilliant talent and, no doubt, a lute or two for you to practice on there. Practice hard—lute playing and truth telling—and mayhap I shall decide to trust you again."

Tears puddled in the girl's eyes, and her face flushed. She gripped her hands together so hard in supplication that those skilled fingers turned white as sausages.

"Will you argue more?" Elizabeth challenged, sensing anger battled with the girl's shame.

"N-no, Your Majesty."

"What has saved you, Felicia, is your clever point that you dared only to do what I have done in my own realm. We'll show them, won't we, those men who say a woman cannot play in public, cannot rule?"

"I MUST REPORT," CECIL INTONED AS THEY SAT AT A TABLE in the withdrawing room where he'd finally gotten the queen off alone to attend to business, "an affair of state that I believe will not please you." When she looked up from the pile of papers, frowning, he added hastily, "Bishop de Quadra has followed us to Windsor."

"He has?" Elizabeth cried, breaking into a smile and clapping her hands, astounding Cecil. "He's here? Then I must stop Robert's plans to go to London."

She jumped up from the table with the top document only half-signed. She threw her quill down, spattering ink.

"Lord Robert was going to London to see de Quadra?" Cecil asked. "On what business? I thought the bishop annoyed you, and why send Dudley?"

As she ran from the room, he cursed and hit his fist on the pile of papers. He gathered his work, refusing to sit here waiting while the queen of England bounded after a married man like some tavern doxy. On his way out, he ran nearly headlong into de Quadra on his way in.

"She's not here," Cecil muttered as de Quadra wheeled about and fell into step beside him down the long gallery.

"In other words, you told her I was coming," the man said with a hint of a grim grin.

Cecil almost chuckled despite his frustration with the queen.

"I hear she's been in a mercurial mood for days," de Quadra continued, as careful as Cecil not to talk when they passed clusters of courtiers in the hall.

"To put it mildly."

"Even banished that brilliant new lutenist she was so enamored of," he said matter-of-factly.

Cecil tried not to act surprised at the depth and breadth of the Spaniard's knowledge of the queen. "Your eyes and ears here keep you apprised of the most minute details, bishop. Or should I ask instead if you have some other, special interest in the lutenist?"

"Now that he has been found a she, you mean?" he parried. "Why, my Lord Cecil, do you suggest I covet the girl? I tell you, I do not take my vow of chastity that lightly."

"I meant, bishop, that my eyes and ears tell me that your eyes and ears are someone close to the queen, so why not a lutenist?"

"But a woman? Like Eve in the garden, as I hear Lord Robert called the queen, women are too fickle and untrustworthy. Best guess again."

They exchanged wary yet bemused looks of admiration. But Cecil's observations of the so-called Dove of the lute had convinced him, at least, that the lass was a survivor and a clever one at that. Chameleons who could change their skin and story and had fire in their fingertips and in their belly always were. After all, that was how Elizabeth had survived to claim her crown.

FELICIA DOVE, USING A BORROWED LUTE SHE'D NEVER SO much as seen before, played for Lord Hunsdon while he ate a little venison stew and drank a great deal of Burgundy wine that evening at his small leased house at Eton. The tiny college town was just upriver from Windsor, where Felicia longed to be.

She felt as caged as she had at home. You might know Lord Hunsdon thought Windsor Palace so drafty and rickety he leased a place. Compared to Richmond Palace, these rooms were small and dark. And that poxy lackey, Luke Morgan, hovered about as if he were her father. He appeared now from some brief errand and sat at table with his lord, glaring at her from time to time over the rim of his flagon. Hoping Lord Hunsdon didn't notice, Felicia glared back.

True, Luke had saved her from drowning—she couldn't swim worth a fig—but she'd paid the price. This was the second time he'd tat-taled to the queen about her for his own advantage. It was bad enough she'd had to agree that her carefully crafted persona, Franklin Dove, was a eunuch. Oh, how she'd like to cut Luke Morgan down to size and condemn him to that very estate right now, the lickspittle.

And worst of all, how was she to keep herself flush with coin if she couldn't send court information to her secret sponsor? Cooped up here, she'd never get her daily written missive to the courier who got them to her employer, whether nearby or elsewhere.

"Play 'Greensleeves' again, Frank—Felicia," Lord Hunsdon put in, his voice slightly slurred. "You play it the mos' melancholy of an'one I've e'er known."

"No wonder, seeing all my dreams are dashed," she dared, and modulated into the minor tones of that sad ballad again.

"But Her Grace sent for you righ' away," he said, stopping for another swig. Luke was savoring his wine and had hardly eaten much for such a big man, she thought. Instead, the blackguard had been watching her, as if he'd devour her for dinner. "And," his lordship went on, "if she forgives tha' fas', she'll have you back in her service in a trice."

"May I ask a question then, my lord?" Felicia said, not stopping her fingers through the tune's sonorous swells.

"Indeed," Lord Hunsdon said with a hiccup and a grandiose gesture.

"Her Grace mentioned having banished someone called the Haringtons, someone who must have been dear to her. I just wondered, in light of my own chastisement, what is their plight and status now?"

"Suffice to say, she trusted 'em, and they misled her," his lordship said, his sibilant words coming out in a strange hiss. "Can't tell you details, sworn to secrecy. But don't fret. She did not imprison 'em, as I believed she would, as I would've if I were the queen—er, king."

"So she didn't 'cast them off discourteously'?" she sang her next question to the tune.

"As a matter a fac'," his lordship said as Luke poured him more wine, "she helped 'em search for their wayward daughter, who's Her Grace's half niece—ill-illegitimate, a course."

"Through which of King Henry's lovers, my lord?" Luke put in, pricking up his too-sharp ears again.

"Mm, a certain Jane Dyngley in the parade of them, 's I recall," his lordship explained, frowning as if trying to remember. "Any rate, their child—Audrey, I think's her name—was fostered out. Great Harry kept the court clean of bastards that way. . . ."

His voice trailed off, and he frowned into his goblet. Felicia knew servants' gossip said Henry Carey, Lord Hunsdon, could be one of the lusty king's bastards, though his mother, Mary Boleyn, had denied it.

"So," his lordship went on as if speaking to his drink now, "this Audrey was Harington's firs' wife, and their daughter, Hester, ran away coupla years ago—no doubt a wench after your own heart, eh, my little revolting lutenist? Well, meaning you revolted to run away from parents too, not that you were revolting, righ', Luke? But Her Grace'll have you back and if she won't, I'll be your patron . . . pay you better than Her Grace, the penny-pincher, 'spite a what you see."

His lordship rose and fumbled to unbutton his breeches, leaning an arm on the mantel over the hearth as if to use it for a chamberpot. She'd seen the practice even at court, when they all thought she was a lad and the ladies weren't around because the queen didn't allow it. But he evidently remembered his lutenist was female and strode hurriedly from the room, listing a bit like Her Grace's barge on boulders in the Thames.

"However much Lord Hunsdon would pay and coddle you," Luke said, reaching out to spear a hunk of bread with his dagger, "I believe you'd choose to serve the queen, even if *you* had to pay *her*."

"You should understand that, as you scramble hard

enough to please her at cost to anyone," she countered, stopping her playing with a dissonant chord.

"That's the pot calling the kettle black. I've watched you watch her, you see, Mistress Dove. You adore her, even more than most of us do." He laughed harshly and popped a hunk of bread into his big mouth. "Poor, petty lutenist, you not only want to be like her, you want—lust—to *be* her."

Her heart began to thud. This man was dangerous. "You don't know the first thing about me—under the skin," she countered, and rose from her seat in the window. Since the lute was not hers and she needed no more accusations, she put it down carefully. Though she'd not been dismissed by his lordship, she made for the door.

Luke leaped up so fast to block her way she panicked and jumped back against the wall. Her small purse, stuffed with coins from Lord Robert Dudley and those that a lad at Richmond had slipped her as another payment from the Spanish ambassador, clunked as if it were one melted mass.

"What was that?" Luke demanded, swaggering closer, nonchalantly sheathing his dagger as he came. "It sounded as if you have a lead bottom, mistress."

"Let me pass. Let me and my affairs be."

He stalked her the rest of the way to the wainscotted wall, both arms out stiff to trap her there. He grinned wolfishly. "Would that your affairs, at least one of them, were mine."

He dared to lower one hand behind her to feel her

bum, but his purpose must have been to find the purse. He cupped it in his palm and bounced it once.

"Been earning extra on your back with your legs spread instead of those clever arms and fingers spread?" he murmured, so close she could smell garlic on his breath. "Or came you by this some other way?"

" 'Tis my inheritance, so keep your filthy hands off of everything. You've already caused chaos in my life!"

"And likely to cause more if you don't do exactly as you're bid and quit that lying—lying with your lips, though I wouldn't mind it if you'd lie with me tonight. Then I'd hold my tongue on all your little secrets so—"

She shoved him back so hard he bounced into a table and sent a chair crashing to the floor. Felicia was out into the hall and up the stairs to her tiny servant's room under the eaves with the bolt shot before she heard the dining room door slam far below. And if that blackguard so much as told on her or touched her again, she'd be sure he'd face royal wrath, and not the queen's.

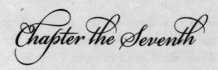

*Youth will needs have dalliance,*
*Of good or ill some pastance;*
*Company me thinketh the best*
*All thoughts and fantasies to digest.*
*For idleness is chief mistress of vices all;*
*Then who can say*
*But pass the day*
*Is best of all?*

— KING HENRY VIII

 "YOUR MAJESTY," NED TOPSIDE SAID, HIS fine voice carrying out over the courtiers and servants assembled in a corner of the great hall of Windsor, "I am honored that you will grace my masque with your presence onstage rather than having the revelries presented to you this time."

"I decided," Elizabeth replied, "that if Lord Robert is to enact the part of Apollo, I would never hear the end of it were I not to take the part of the goddess Diana myself."

"But they were brother and sister and not enamored," she was certain she heard someone behind her murmur, and it sounded like her once-trusted Lord Cecil. Though he and de Quadra would not be in the cast for the drama, they were quite the hangers-on lately. Did the unease she'd felt since she arrived at

Richmond this summer, she wondered, mean that those statesmen were spying on her, even if not in person? When she'd lived in exile, Cecil had stooped to having a cook keep an eye on her, entirely for her own good, he'd said.

"Now, the key parts are these," Ned said, gesturing grandly and striding about to position people. "If you wish to catch a glimpse of the scenery or costumes later, I have sketches done by Her Majesty's clever Gil Sharpe." The queen saw that Ned already had some of the two-tiered set erected and draped with diaphanous cloths. She tugged one long piece free and wrapped it about her shoulders and throat, just to feel more in the part of this fantastical setting.

Looking nervous that the queen was undoing his scenery, her principal player and fool—who was never, indeed, a fool—plunged on, "This is a rendition of the myth of Niobe, who dared to defy a goddess and to place herself above her."

"And that goddess was?" Elizabeth encouraged, fully expecting him to say it was her part as virgin goddess of the hunt, Diana, the part he'd promised her.

"That would be Leto, Diana and Apollo's mother, Your Majesty, a Titan who bore Zeus those twin children."

"But they are not children in the drama, I hope, man," Robin prompted.

"No, my lord, for you see," Ned said, "they are grown to adulthood now and, besides, I've turned it into a political allegory also and you can't have children in something like that."

Elizabeth heard Cecil snort and this time turned to glare at him. Cecil and the Spanish ambassador huddled together near the stairway of the set as if they were boon companions rather than competitors who would turn to enemies should events warrant. But seeing de Quadra gave Elizabeth a thought.

"Ned," she said, her voice low, "we do not insult Spain or King Philip in this play?"

"Oh, no, Your Grace. 'Tis France takes the brunt of it."

"Fine," she clipped out, amused to see him look relieved and pleased for once. "Say on."

"Now everyone, hearken please," Ned said, rapping his knuckles on the wall of the set to recapture their attention. "Her Grace is Diana, and we need four ladies to be her attendant nymphs for the first act. Meg Milligrew will serve as the queen's tiring woman backstage to fetch her bow and quiver, et cetera, and perhaps have a bit part onstage. Lord Robert Dudley as Apollo must needs have at least one follower too—Jenks, are you up for that?"

"I'm more used to guarding Her Grace, but fine," Jenks agreed, and stepped closer to Lord Robert.

"Ah, now," Ned went on, "the mothers' parts. Kat Ashley had best, I believe, portray Apollo and Diana's mother, Leto, who is insulted by Niobe's braggadocio. But who shall play that pompous woman who puts herself above Leto and Diana, so—"

"Katherine Grey is young but her voice is strong and we can deck her in white hair," the queen cut in. "She shall play that role. And what is the allegory then?"

"You and Apollo, Your Grace," Ned explained as Katherine stepped forward, somehow looking both pleased and piqued, "shall represent not only the children of Leto, but fair England herself. Therefore, Lady Ashley stands for Mother England. Katherine Grey is not only Niobe, but France, always criticizing England. But in the play when Diana and Apollo strike down Niobe's—that is, France's—children, she learns never to challenge a goddess again."

"A timely theme," Elizabeth declared with a decisive nod. "Perhaps since rumors and gossip flow from the court of France as if from a gutter, some of you will spread the word what we English do for amusement."

Some grinned, some snickered, yet the queen seethed inside. Mary, Queen of Scots, and France had no right to sully her reputation or Robin's either. Someone had said that Mary claimed not only that the queen of England would wed her Horse Master, but that she would dispatch his poor wife to do so. That was blasphemy and grievously dangerous.

"Now," Ned went on, "each time Diana appears, Felicia Dove will play a bright theme on her lute from behind the facade of the scenery."

"Since," Elizabeth interrupted, "Apollo is the god of music, Felicia may play for his entrances and exits. Trumpets, I think, for Diana. By the way, what is the name of this masque?"

"I had thought," Ned said, drawing himself up to his full height and lifting his chin, "*The Lesson of Niobe*."

"Too obscure," Elizabeth said. "Try *The Triumph of Diana*."

"Oh, of course," Ned agreed, shuffling papers and passing them here and there for a read through of the lines, but looking more confused all the time. He gestured his betters to their positions but tugged people like Meg and Felicia into place.

"Now, Apollo had the art of healing too," Ned went on, "so at the end, perhaps he should resurrect those children of the grieving Niobe whom the twins have slain."

"But that would give Apollo the last say in this drama," Elizabeth protested. "Besides, Robin is no doctor, which reminds me, I meant to send for Dr. Dee. My Lord Robert, send my new barge and bargemen to fetch him at his house in Mortlake, will you not? He used to help present plays years ago with fantastical effects. Yes, send for Dr. Dee posthaste."

"To—to be in the masque, Your Grace?" Ned asked, looking nearly beside himself.

"Perhaps to give the goddess Diana a grand finish," the queen said only, leaving her sudden inspiration a secret. "You all read through your parts, and I will add my voice, and perhaps a few new lines, later. I believe this entertainment will be even grander if we can move it outside to the fountain court."

"B-but," Ned stuttered, his eyes darting at the half-erected set.

"Don't fret," she told him. "You'll have much help to move it outside, and of course, if it rains, we'll have to do it here." Elizabeth turned to leave the room, for she had promised Cecil she would sign the writs she'd ignored and she wanted to get that over, to have the rest of the day free.

She bumped smack into Luke Morgan, who must have been hovering. They momentarily clung to each other to keep from going off balance, then let go but not before Robin jumped at them to pluck Luke's hands from her. Jenks leaped forward too.

"Watch where you stand and not so close to Her Majesty's person, sirrah," Robin clipped out.

"Lord Robert, this is a trusted man of Lord Hunsdon, so unhand him," she ordered. "He has done me good service and may yet do more."

Though it was the slightest of incidents, she saw Robin's jaw clench and his neck vein throb. Was he embarrassed or jealous? she wondered, and a shiver shot through her. Or was he just annoyed she yet kept him in his place? Poor Jenks had just reacted instinctively from years of oft being her sole protector. But what was strangest of all was that the lutenist, far on the fringe of the crowd, had also flung herself forward, as if to protect her queen.

AFTER HER MAJESTY HAD FINALLY SIGNED THE SMALL PILE of papers Cecil set before her, he went back down to the play practice to see if de Quadra was still about. He found that the ambassador and the players had flown, but Felicia Dove sat in a corner, playing some doleful lament while wrapped in the same swathe of material the queen had draped herself in earlier.

He was nearly to her before the girl noticed him and glanced up, stopping her fingers in mid-melody. "I see you are left-handed," he observed as she scrambled to her feet and pulled the cloth from around her slender shoulders. "Do you know the Latin for left-handed?" he went on, stopping a few feet from Felicia to study her closely. When she shook her head warily, he told her, "*Sinister*, which used to imply unlucky or fated, though, of course, it means evil now."

"Say what you intend, my Lord Cecil."

Ah, he thought, the girl had pluck too, but he continued his little charade of an interview with her by shrugging slightly. "If Her Majesty has taken you back, it is your lucky day and you can do naught but good for her with those quick hands and quicker brain."

"I'm not exactly back in Her Grace's good graces," she said, straight-faced at her own witty wordplay.

Yes, cleverness would help too, Cecil mused. "I'm a man of business, Mistress Dove, so I will cut to the quick and be brief," he explained, "not that I wouldn't like to hire you to write me a song for my dear wife or one to soothe the savage beast that rears its head about here from time to time lately."

"I tell people I cannot write, my lord, but in truth I can—a bit, though please tell no one else. So I could write a song for your lady wife, e'en the notes. I've already done one for Lord Robert, though not for his wife. But no, for you, it must needs be a song like this one."

> *The service is unseen*
> *That I full long have served,*
> *Yet my reward hath been*
> *Much less than I deserved*
> *Yet for those graces past*
> *And favor that I found*
> *Whilst my poor life shall last*
> *I find myself still bound.*

"Ah," he said, stunned this mere slip of a girl had read him and perceived the political situation here so well. "Did you pen those lines, mistress?" he asked.

"I believe they were by a courtier the queen banished a while ago."

"Ah," he said again, beginning to be annoyed this girl kept surprising him. "And who was that?"

"I think I heard it was John Harington, but I know him not."

"I did. A loyal man, but one who went astray, though I think Her Majesty's been missing him and his lady wife lately and may have them back soon."

Felicia stopped playing. "That remains to be seen, as does everything with this queen," she whispered, frowning.

"Quite so, especially this summer. Then, mistress, I am hoping you and I can come to an agreement, at least while we are both on the edge of Her Majesty's favor. If you will follow my guidance, I shall become your

patron—of sorts," he added, and slightly rattled the
coins in his dangling purse. "Might we work together
on something that is not a song, not exactly, at least?"

"A deal that is a duet, my lord?" she said, and her
eyes lit. "You know," she added, carrying her lute and
walking with him toward the door that went down
toward the river, "the fact I play left-handed makes it
easier for me to teach others because—for example—
when the queen looks at me to copy my fingering, it's
just like looking in a mirror, almost as if I were her.
And then, she trusts me more."

Before he could garner a reply, the girl began to
strum and sing,

> The night right long and heavy
> The days of my torment
> The sighs continually
> That throughout my heart went
> My color pale and wan
> To her did plainly show
> That I was her true man
> And yet she thought not so.

The queen's principal secretary almost stumbled. For
once, William Cecil was at a loss for words.

"YOU WERE ROUGH ON ME AT THAT PLAY READING TODAY,
my queen," Robin complained almost peevishly as
they strolled the fountain court in the shade while her
retinue promenaded the intersecting paths.

"Robin, I merely want the masque as it should be. By the way, I'm planning to have your friend Dr. Dee fly my Diana out with his ingenious, invisible harness."

He looked shocked but quickly recovered. "But if we're holding it here in the courtyard, what if a big wind comes up?" he protested. "I'll not have you hurt."

"Do you not trust your friend you have oft recommended to me?" she countered, as if they were fencing. "With my approval of such a feat, that silly rumor he is some sort of sorcerer or wizard will be ended and he can be of more use to me. Besides, my lord, it is you who are the sorcerer or wizard."

"You mean of your heart, I pray. My queen, may I not come to your rooms this night? Keep Mary and Kat about if you will, it is just that I long to have you alone . . . nearly alone . . . to show you how much I adore you."

"That is one of the costs of being queen, Robin, not lack of privacy, for I manage that at times, but not being certain whether proclamations, however impassioned, of adoration are to be trusted. A little voice inside me asks if my subjects love me for myself or for the fact I hold might and riches in my hand. *Chi ama crede* is not such an easy thing."

Looking furious that she had turned his own lure upon him, he stopped walking. "You don't mean you question how I truly feel? You cannot mean that, and if so, it is because, as I just said, you will not let me *show* you fully."

"Ah, well," she said, and turned down a cross path to take him unaware and make him hurry to keep up.

"Elizabeth," he said, when he almost never dared her Christian name, "do not doubt that I love you as a man does a woman. Why, if you were a country lass and I some rural swain, I would love you 'til I died."

" 'Til you died . . ." she whispered, closing her eyes dreamily.

When she caught her toe on a brick, she stopped to kick at it as if it were that object's fault for ruining her reverie. Pain shot through her toes. That reminded her she wanted to talk to Robin about Amy's health, but she could not bring herself to so much as mention it now. If anyone found out she had asked, would it not give credence to rumors she awaited Amy's demise? But if Robert Dudley were indeed free to wed, would it change anything? Worse, if Amy were to die, her enemies could say the queen caused it somehow, so she'd best pray for Amy's health, more even than her own.

"About tonight," she whispered, "I do not know."

"We could talk naught but politics," he said, his lips tilting in the hint of smile.

"Talk that now," she commanded. "You have spoken with de Quadra about the Grey girl as my heir, I take it?"

"I did, and he wanted it so badly he trusted me and took the bait whole. He says I am his friend now."

"I knew it, but never trust or believe him fully. Do you think he might already have hatched a plot to help her?"

"I—truly, Your Grace—I think he still has hopes you might consider a Catholic fiancé who could then wed and bed you and in one generation have a Papist back on your throne."

"Then he has a lot to learn," she said, hitting her fists one atop the other as they walked, though her toe still pained her.

"He does indeed, but then, like me, he is merely a man."

She turned to study Robin's expression. Hurt but hopeful too. She did love Robin and want him desperately. But that made her fear him too—or was it herself, her womanly weaknesses, she feared?

"Robin, some evening soon," she whispered, pointing upward at the Round Tower that so dominated Windsor, "I will walk there on the battlements, around and around, and mayhap I will see you there at twilight—before darkness falls."

She turned and swept back toward the royal apartments, while others hurried to keep up. The wind lifted the fountain spray to coat her salmon-hued bodice so it seemed to turn a shiny, bloody crimson.

MEG HAD BEEN RELIEVED TO HEAR THAT EVEN THOUGH Her Majesty's new London barge and rowers had arrived today, she'd already sent them away to fetch Dr. Dee. Not that Meg liked doctors. Though she could recall little of her life before the queen's aunt, Mary Boleyn, took her in and nursed her after a kick in the head by a horse, Meg sensed they had not trusted doctors at her family's apothecary shop in her earlier life. When her mother was dying, the old woman had warned against trusting them too, and Meg had been forced to bar the old leech Her Grace had sent in good faith from hurting her mother more.

As Meg kept cutting more roses, she glanced through the leafy, leggy autumn bushes down the slant of lawn toward the landing. The barge that had been repaired bobbed at its moorings, guarded by two louts arguing about something. Their angry voices carried clear up here. Of course it was just her imagination, but one voice sounded familiar and filled her with foreboding. Mayhap he was the bargeman who had called out the rhythm for the oarsmen from time to time.

"Can't believe the varlets couldn't keep this barge off the rocks," the man in question told the other. "Why, I been shooting the rapids under London Bridge at high tide and hardly e'er lost a one."

The other lout hacked and spit into the river and said something back about the queen, but Meg heard no more. Ben Wilton was a bridge shooter. It—it could be him. But it had been over a year since she'd seen him, and then she'd been far off or had hidden her own face with hair.

She squatted down behind the rosebushes and carefully parted two stems, ignoring the prick and scratch of thorns on her hands.

"Mercy, oh Lord, have mercy," she whispered.

It looked like Ben Wilton, sounded like him too. Somehow he'd been brought here, then left behind when the other new oarsmen went to fetch Dr. Dee. Meg grabbed her basket and, hunched, did a low duck waddle to get farther away from the barge landing. A few times the queen had ordered her to take to the royal bed while Her Grace went somewhere else garbed as an herb girl, but now Meg would have to take to her own bed. Anything to keep clear of running into that man or she was as good as dead with Her Grace and probably, literally, with Ben Wilton too.

But she backed right into a pair of sturdy legs, gasped, turned, and looked up. She was half expecting Ned had been spying on her, but it was Lord Hunsdon's man, that Luke something-or-other. Like the queen had taught her, the best defense was an attack.

"Do you dare to spy on the queen's strewing herb mistress?" she demanded, rising to her full height but keeping her back to the river.

"Looks to me like you're spying on those two men talking down there, and the question is why?" he said with a smirk. "Do you fancy them, then? I don't know their names but I could present you just like a fine lady. They say bargemen have strong arms to hold and please a lady and great thrusting thighs to—"

"Leave off!" she ordered, putting a bit of the metallic clang in her voice as the queen sometimes did. Ned hadn't taught her to mimic Her Grace's carriage and tone for nothing.

"Leave off?" Luke threw back at her, and hooted a laugh, hooking his thumbs in his belt as if he were lord of all he surveyed. "Now what red-blooded man—

including those oarsmen, I warrant—would want to do that when he came upon a blushing wench hot and flushed out here amid these sweet flowers?"

Furious with this lout and with herself for getting caught where he might force her to face Ben Wilton—damn all men—Meg grabbed her rose basket and fled toward the palace. But he caught her easily and swung her around to face him.

"Don't run off. Since you're so close to the queen, you and I can strike a bit of a bargain, all right? I long to serve her closer too, to know what pleases her so—"

"What pleases her is her cousin Harry's lackeys, kin or not, keeping their ham-hock hands off her servants!" Meg cried, and shook herself free to run again. This time he let her go, but she didn't like that he'd seen her spying on the bargemen, especially since he had the habit of tat-telling to the queen.

"YOUR MAJESTY, I'VE JUST RECEIVED MISSIVES FROM AN informant in France about certain occurrences there," Cecil told Elizabeth, stretching his strides to keep up with her as she led courtiers down to the barge landing to greet the eminent Dr. Dee.

"Has war been declared on us again, my lord?"

"No, Your Grace, but—"

"More of that she-wolf's lies about my character?"

"There are subtle hints of religious unrest and cruelties against the Protestant Huguenots that—"

"Save it for later, mayhap for the Sabbath. Besides, Cecil, Dr. Dee might just be one to give us better intelligence about France someday than subtle hints and rumors. Hurry, everyone, as I want this to be a good welcome, and then we get to work on the masque again!" she called to her stampeding entourage behind her.

Cecil swore under his breath and stopped trying to keep up. He was done with this, and if Elizabeth of England wanted him out of her frivolous path to destruction, so be it—except for his card up his sleeve.

He waited to let everyone stream by toward the landing, as if he were a stone in a brook. But he snagged the lutenist's sleeve as she passed.

"Behave yourself," he muttered.

She nodded. He turned up toward the castle to pack his things so he could go to town to hire a barge of his own. But he heard Felicia sing the saucy lyrics to a catchy melody, and he wondered if it was meant for his untuned ears:

> *I shall do anything for you*
> *To stand in your good graces.*
> *Perhaps if you won't favor this,*
> *I'll put on other faces.*

"CECIL WHAT?" ELIZABETH DEMANDED AS MEG HANDED her the goddess Diana's bows and arrows just before her final entrance. Her silk mask was bothering her too. It kept slipping, so she had trouble seeing straight ahead. And as if this bejeweled bodice wasn't already tight enough, she wore Dr. Dee's flying harness under it and had to keep a good watch not to tangle the ropes and wires over her head.

"They say my Lord Cecil packed and left posthaste yesterday, Your Grace," Kat repeated, tying the strings of the queen's mask tighter. "Mayhap his wife was of a sudden taken ill or some such thing—"

"You have the wrong wife for that," Elizabeth interrupted. "Don't you think I've been fearing Robin might be so called away? Besides, Mildred Cecil is as healthy as a horse, and I will settle with my lord secretary later. For now, tell Ned to have someone else of some gravity read the final moral I've newly written for our masque, then." Kat hurried off, out of breath.

Indeed they were all rushed and breathless, Elizabeth thought, feeling a bit nervous herself. Plenty of things had gone wrong at the last moment and with the courtyard packed with courtiers and townsfolk for this masque, the first she'd been in for years. And, it seemed, everyone—except herself, of course—was just trying to get attention.

Meg had pleaded a sour stomach and tried to beg out of acting in this play, but agreed to keep her small part when she saw her costume included a wig and veil in addition to a mask, so Elizabeth could only surmise that the girl was trying to catch Ned's eye again, and she simply would not have that going on. Stephen Jenks was still in a fine snit since Elizabeth had picked Luke Morgan to hoist Diana up to heaven with Dr. Dee's wires. Robin had continued to sulk over Luke's attendance on her too, as if the poor man were some sort of foreign suitor she could wed instead of just a handsome, smitten young man whose attentions pleased her.

Even Felicia was evidently out of sorts, probably because she played not for the queen's entrances and exits but only for Robin's. From time to time, no doubt in protest, Felicia had amazingly hit a sour note from where she sat just behind the painted canvas, far across the stage from where Luke was stationed.

The trumpet fanfare that marked the goddess's final entrance blared. Elizabeth walked onto the alfresco stage as Robin joined her from the other side to Felicia's strummed chords.

"O rare Diana, sister," Robin said, projecting his lines out over the mesmerized crowd through his full-face mask, "never again will the pompous Niobe censure or disparage our dear mother, Leto, for we heavenly beings have taught her the lesson of her life."

"And so must others learn," Elizabeth's voice rang out, "that we, the folk of fair England, cannot be separated nor conquered."

"I go now on another charge to do my duty," Apollo cried, and strode from the stage with his quiver of arrows raised high. Felicia struck more chords, one or two, the queen noted, most annoyed, misfingered again.

"And I must return to my heavenly realm from which I shall dispense justice forever," Elizabeth concluded, and braced herself to be lifted off her feet.

As Ned himself stepped out onto the stage and began to read the closing moral, which she'd meant for

Cecil to say, she waited for the tightening of the harness and the upward ride to the platform above. In their two rehearsals it had worked well, and she had soared above them all, keeping her balance until her feet touched down on high. Now the distinctive trumpets blared again to fill this void of action. At last, she felt the lift.

A set smile on her face under her half mask, she heard the winch Luke used to elevate her. She rose only about ten feet above the pavement of the courtyard and, strangely, hung there suspended. Why was she not swung over? The trumpets played, longer and louder, evidently holding their last note not to leave her dangling like a target on the archery range. When the trumpeters were out of breath, Felicia's lute filled the void. At least, the queen thought in the back of her mind, the girl got to play for the royal exit.

"Curse Luke Morgan," Elizabeth muttered, trying to keep control. The two main wires above her, cantilevered out from the corner tower above the scenery, did not seem snagged. Where those two joined behind the scenery, Luke held a master rope. He needed to counterbalance her weight by walking his scaffold plank to pull her over. Then he must put her down gently, and he knew that well enough. If this was his idea of a jest . . .

She saw Dr. Dee leap to his feet in the front row of the audience where she'd had him sit. He'd been watching with his observation cylinder to see close-up that his wires and ropes worked. But now he took the cylinder and his hands from his face. He looked so alarmed she panicked too, her eyes darting up, all around, though a scream snagged in her throat. Horrified, Ned ceased his speech and ran behind the scenery.

Everyone looked up, gaping at her. No music sounded, neither trumpets nor lute. Her heart began to thud against the constricting harness. Surely the ribs of it and of her body would break. Though the breeze was cool, she began to sweat. Her mask slipped from her forehead and nose so she could not see but she could not right it. No one could reach her from above or below. A trembling began deep inside her. She kicked her feet, trying to swing over. Was this all happening in a moment or eternity?

The wires jerked her hard once, twice to lower her a bit. Dr. Dee began to run toward the stage, while Harry, Jenks, and others gathered under her to break her fall. Another jolt shook her and then the lines went slack.

The men below her broke her fall; yet she went off balance to her hands and knees on the pavement. Her voluminous skirts both slowed her fall and cushioned her, but for a goddess and queen it was damned undignified. Disheveled and dismayed, she could have skewered Luke Morgan.

The final trumpet fanfare pierced her ears, the crowd's shouts, a woman's scream, then a man's voice—Ned's—shouting from behind the scaffolding.

"Luke Morgan tripped and fell, and he's not moving!" Ned cried, bringing back her black memories of Geoffrey's fatal fall. At least she was alive. Shakily, Elizabeth got to her feet, helped by those around her.

# Chapter the Eighth

What should I say        I promised you,
Since Faith is dead,      You promised me,
And Truth away           To be as true,
From you is fled?         As I would be,
Should I be led           But since I see
With doubleness?          Your double heart,
                          Farewell, my part . . .
Nay! Nay! mistress.

— SIR THOMAS WYATT, *the Elder*

 "HE FELL JUST LIKE GEOFFREY!" THE QUEEN heard Meg cry.

'S blood, Elizabeth thought, it was not just like Geoffrey, for Luke Morgan lay flat on his back. Wrapped yet around one hand, the rope that worked Dr. Dee's flying wires had evidently snapped from the master rigging. But from ten feet away, the queen could see Ned had been correct that Luke was not moving. He looked dead.

As Elizabeth neared the fallen man, her snagged harness ropes pulled her back as if she were a child in leading strings. When Jenks saw her struggling, he rushed to take their weight upon himself. With one hand, he drew his stage sword to cut her free, but she stopped him.

"We will not tamper with things yet," she whispered, ripping her mask strings from around her neck.

Looking startled, Jenks nodded. With his strength giving her slack, she strode closer to the prone, unmoving body.

Tears blurred her vision. Two strange falls by those who had served her well, both strong, young men, Elizabeth grieved. What tragedy in the midst of her happy summer.

She bent over as Dr. Dee came running and knelt quickly. His observation cylinder still in his hand, he held the larger glass end of it under Luke's nostrils. He studied the slight misting of the glass.

"Breathing but faintly," he announced, looking up at her. "Keep the others back, if you please, Your Majesty."

"Stand clear, all of you but Dr. Dee. Give them space and air," the queen commanded until she saw her cousin Harry was among the gathering. "All but for Lord Hunsdon," she added, and Harry fell to his knees beside his wife's injured cousin. This close, Elizabeth thought Luke looked merely asleep.

"You had best send for your physicians, Your Majesty," John Dee told her, not looking up this time, "for though I have studied the medicinal arts, they are not my forte. But I warn that this man must be lifted carefully. We must hold his head still, for he's not moved any of his limbs, and I fear some sort of paralysis through a broken neck or back."

"Will he be long unconscious?" Harry asked, his voice breaking. He pressed his hand to Luke's shoulder as if to comfort him. "How can we be certain he has not just knocked himself out?"

Dr. Dee did not answer, but pulled up each eyelid and stared into the man's pupils. "Perhaps no severe head injury, as his irises are not dilated," he muttered. "Your Majesty, a tabletop or door would be best on which to move the man, not just jostling hands."

"Jenks, fetch such as Dr. Dee requires and summon my doctors from the audience," she ordered.

Elizabeth saw Robin was helping to hold the crowd at bay. Their gazes snagged as if she'd called his name. He nodded to her, but she looked back to Dr. Dee as he carefully unwrapped the broken rope from Luke's right hand. His fingers had gone white, though color came slowly back to them now.

The thick, twisted hemp had nearly cut into his skin while his left hand, with which he should have held it too, looked barely bruised. Then, Elizabeth reasoned, he must have fallen from the scaffold with but one hand on the rope, not two as should have been. And that rope had not broken in rehearsal. It looked not frayed but cut clean. Had he let go of the rope with one hand to try to retain or regain his balance? That could have been the two jerks she felt.

As Dr. Dee oversaw Luke's carefully designed exit to the palace where her physicians would tend to him, Elizabeth squinted up at the walkway where Luke had held the master rope.

Nothing she saw could have tripped him unless his unknown stumbling block had tumbled down too and then been quickly removed. The four boards were narrow, but the man had practiced on them. What had gone amiss that he had begun to lift her, then stopped, then fell evidently just as his rope broke—or was cut free?

Only then did Elizabeth recall she was still tied to the scenery. She began to tremble again, not this time at her deliverance or even her fierce concern for Luke's recovery, but from the fact that—as had not happened during the performance—she sensed she was being watched with great hostility.

Frowning, she looked around, only to see familiar faces: Kat's, Katherine Grey's, both women still in their masks; Robin, of course; Harry, who had played a bit part; Felicia, cradling the lute Elizabeth had once given Geoffrey; and the huddle of servants who had been in the masque, Meg, Ned, Jenks.

She looked upward again, this time scanning not only the entire backside of scenery and the castle courtyard walls against which it was nestled, but the tall, dominating Round Tower beyond. Had it now been midnight rather than noontide with the sun streaming down, she could not have felt more frightened.

"Dr. Dee," she called in a wavering voice to the obviously distressed man, "loose me now."

The man's skin looked ashen as he hastened to obey. "Your Majesty, I swear by all I hold dear I cannot fathom what could have gone wrong. Though Luke Morgan seemed surefooted, the man must have simply stumbled and perhaps cut himself free so he would not hang by his hand."

Just, she thought, as Geoffrey must have suddenly been drunk or dizzy and had fallen or thrown himself off, after carefully preserving his lute. Ned and Meg had been certain her musician had met with foul play, and she was certain that life-loving, ambitious Luke Morgan would never have just stumbled. The man had instinctive aplomb and grace, nearly as much as Robin, though with none of the breeding nor training.

"Your Majesty," Dr. Dee's voice droned on, "neither was your getting suspended in mid-flight any part of my plan."

"Not *your* plan, perhaps," she muttered, more to herself than him.

As the hovering Jenks and Dr. Dee unhooked the wires and ropes from her shoulders and the back of her bodice, she felt she could breathe again. Her feet stood steadier on the ground. And for the first time in days, mayhap the entire summer, she knew she had business to which she must attend, however much she simply wanted to throw herself in Robin's arms and be carried off to safety in the palace or that sturdy old Round Tower.

"Everyone stay well back from this scenery," the queen commanded. "Do not so much as touch any of it. Lord Robert, clear out even the players of this masque, but tell them they may be summoned to give witness later. And find my little artist, Gil." Yes, Elizabeth thought, Gil had started out life as a climber—indeed, as a thief who had helped his mother hook goods from other people's lofty windows in London. Climbing and sketching were needed now.

"Doctor," she added in a more muted voice, "please show me again exactly how the ropes were rigged back here and how that man—my counterbalance—could possibly have fallen."

"Fallen," Dr. Dee whispered, "at the precise moment that—"

"That I as well as Luke could have been harmed or killed," she finished for him.

"HARRY, I WOULD SPEAK WITH YOU," ELIZABETH TOLD HER cousin as he entered her withdrawing chamber where she sat alone an hour later.

"So I heard, Your Grace, and came forthwith."

She had sent for her cousin from Luke's bedside on the first floor of the palace. Her physicians had decided it was best the gravely injured man not be carried upstairs.

"First, how fares Luke?" she inquired, clasping her hands tightly in her silken lap.

"Unconscious and unchanged, though he may yet wake. Your doctors say it may not be permanent insensibility," he went on, his voice wavering, "though he stands—lies—in danger of death."

"Sit, Harry," she said, her voice soft. He slumped in the big chair next to hers at the table where she had eaten next to nothing despite Kat's coaxing. She saw Harry had crumpled his hat in his hand and his hose were stained from kneeling on the paving stones. Now, in darkest despair, Harry stared at those smudged knees.

"Have you sent word to Anne that her cousin has been injured?"

"Not yet," he replied, head down. "I was hoping—praying—he would regain sensibility or movement, so I would have some hopeful news to tell her. She trusted me to care for him, you see, and . . ."

Elizabeth heaved such a sigh he stopped talking and looked up. "I know, I know," she said. "He is a man full grown and yet you feel responsible for him. 'S blood, imagine what it is to feel that for an entire kingdom! It is more sometimes than one can bear." He nodded but still did not seemed to be listening, his eyes unfocused, his expression distracted.

"Harry, I have decided we must probe this seeming accident, though it is not yet a murder like the tragedies we have delved. But perhaps it was attempted murder and tied somehow to Geoffrey Hammet's demise—and to intent to harm me."

"A conspiracy?" he whispered. "A plot?"

"I cannot believe Luke simply stumbled, can you?" He shook his head, then looked away. "I regret to cross-question you at this difficult time, but if foul play is afoot we must move swiftly before the trail to—to someone dangerous grows cold. Is there any reason you can give me that Luke could have fallen? When Geoffrey took his fatal tumble at Richmond, evidence suggested he had been drinking heavily, and Meg tells me he had suffered at least one dizzy spell."

"Luke had *not* been drinking, not at midday, not with something like holding your flying wires in his charge. He yearned to please, you know, please you especially, Your Grace. Besides, I was with him most of the morning to know whereof I speak. I admit that at times he did drink, but not much—not as much . . ."

"Not as much as you?"

He sat up straight. "If I drink overmuch, it is always in privy chambers, Your Grace. Did Luke tell you such? I know he had told you other things—about Felicia. Why, you'd think he was your man, ordered to report to you with—"

"No, Luke did not say aught amiss about you, nor is he my man, as you put it. I have not stooped to using domestic spies—yet." She hugged herself as a chill swept her. Though closeted with her trusted cousin, she yet felt the walls had evil ears and eyes. And she was still terribly shaken from her fall.

"Then Felicia Dove said something about my drinking?" Harry asked, startling her back to reality.

"No, cousin. You have a guilty conscience about your drinking, and, I hope, for naught else."

"You don't imply that I would want to harm Luke or, Your Gracious Majesty, ever harm you, no matter what rumors say?" he whispered, leaning toward her avidly, his bloodshot eyes wide.

"Harry, my various cousins or other kin scattered here and there may want my throne—Katherine Grey, indeed, not to mention Mary, Queen of Scots. Then too, my cousin Margaret Douglas and her Scottish husband, the Earl of Lennox, fancy that either she or their son, Lord Darnley, deserves my throne more than I. They hate me and are always intriguing, even if they do know enough to stay in their northern castle

these days. But you—I know you have been true
to me."

"And will be," he declared, rising only to fall upon
his knees nearly on her skirt hems. "I have never
said—as have Katherine Grey, Mary Stuart, or Margaret Douglas—that I had any claim on your throne.
My sire was Will Carey, not your royal father, so, unlike them I have no links by blood to—"

"Get off the floor," she said wearily, putting out a
hand as if to pull him to his feet. "You leap too far
afield. I believe you would never harm or wish me ill.
But this—this mischance today must be examined
since it is the second fall and the first was fatal. And
because this time I was tied to the disaster too—literally. And I thought some were simply set on ruining
my reputation because of my friendship with Robert."

Harry rose stolidly. "You will assemble the Privy
Plot counselors?" he asked, all too obviously avoiding
her mention of Robert Dudley. "But I heard Cecil's
hied himself back to London."

"Is that where he is?" she said, getting to her feet
also. "Then best he stay because I am vexed by his
rantings about the way I have conducted myself this
summer, scoldings as if he were my brutish father!"

Her last words echoed in the room, though she had
not meant to shout and certainly not that. If the walls
could hear, they indeed got an earful that time. She
reached out to pat her cousin's shoulder.

"Return to Luke's bedside, Harry, and send word if
his condition changes. I will visit him myself this

evening after I privily assemble those who are both my helpers and, in some cases, the first people I must question."

"I was the first you questioned," he corrected her. "But I swear that each time I ducked behind the scaffolding to make an exit or await my entrance for my paltry lines, I saw naught amiss. Others darted in and out too."

"Yes, I included. If someone somehow tripped Luke up or cut that rope to harm me, we can narrow it down to far too many, but I must start somewhere. Actually, I do wish Cecil were here, as bitter as he's been, or that I could call in Robin's help. Without Cecil, I shall needs rely on Lord Robert Dudley's advice even more," she declared, talking more to herself than him, "but mayhap not in these privy investigations."

Harry murmured something, bowed, and left the room, though she stood lost in agonizings again. *Chi Ama Crede*, Robert had written for Felicia to sing. *She who loves trusts.* Surely she could trust Robin, trust him with her very life.

"IT HAS BEEN FAR MORE THAN A YEAR," ELIZABETH SAID to call the meeting to order, "since we have met thusly to solve a crime. At least," she added, staring down Kat, Ned, Jenks, Meg, and Gil in turn, "since we all met officially rather than gathering in some fleabitten horse stall."

Jenks and Ned, the queen noted, shifted uneasily. Kat dared not look her in the eye, but Meg shot back a sullen stare. Perhaps the girl was still fuming from their not being summoned to probe Geoffrey's death. Then too, she still looked peaked. As for the queen's little monkey of an artist, Gil Sharpe, the boy instantly produced the sketch she'd ordered when she looked his way.

Elizabeth studied it as Ned asked, "Are we still to be on first-name terms when we work together like this?"

Elizabeth frowned at the intricate sketch of Dr. Dee's rope rigging and winch. "You may call me Bess and the others' first names will do. Will and Harry are elsewhere, of course, and I would like to supplement our crew here with a few others to replace them, but—"

"Lord Robert?" Jenks asked. Ordinarily Elizabeth might have rounded on someone who assumed such, but Jenks was ever loyal to whomever he served, and she admired that.

"Yes, especially since William Cecil—Will—has flown the coop," she muttered. "But for now, we stay with those of us who are adept at this, with Gil our only new addition, for he has helped us before. I have asked him to draw the wire and ropes for the masque, and Dr. Dee has made certain not only that this was the proper arrangement, but that the rigging, even after Luke Morgan fell, had not been tampered with. Someone or something must have tripped or shoved the man off the walkway, for nothing else went awry but a rather cleanly broken—or cut—master rope."

Everyone began buzzing, talking at once. Names flew by, whispered, hissed.

"Quiet!" the queen ordered. "I know full well who could have been back there to place something on the walkway to distract Luke, to trip up or even push him. I have reckoned out that at the very time he fell, Kat and Harry stood behind me onstage and Lord Robert had just exited. But Katherine Grey had made an earlier exit, so was unaccounted for. I shall question her soon, I assure you. But meanwhile, that leaves the three of you and Felicia to give your explanations."

"Are we here," Ned said, leaning back and crossing his arms almost insolently over his chest, "to help you solve this crime or be questioned for it?"

"To help, of course, but sometimes that entails answering questions—as witnesses, not suspects. Now, let me take Will's approach to things, though he is not with us. . . ."

Her voice trailed off. She was furious with Cecil for his protest and unauthorized departure, but she missed him too—at least she missed his rational approach in this upheaval of emotion, his loyalty to her in the past, though that had gone atumble to the winds somehow.

"You do intend to probe for motives?" Ned asked, making her realize she had been silent for a while, "As Will says, *sui bono*?"

"Precisely," she said, recovering her control and turning to look at Jenks first, since Ned seemed suddenly so assertive. "Jenks, you had words with Luke about his being the one given the responsibility of working those ropes instead of yourself."

"Yes, but I'd hardly climb up there and throw him

down for that," Jenks protested, and shook his head so
hard that his thick hair, straight-cut across his wide
forehead, bounced.

*Throw him down?* Elizabeth thought. She had not
pictured that scenario, though few but Jenks could
have bested Luke that way. Would Luke's strength
imply the culprit must be a man? That turn of phrase,
*throw him down*, did not mean, she reasoned, that
Jenks was giving something away. That his strength
and temperament would mean a physical struggle
was the only way her seldom astute Jenks could imagine it.

"At the time he fell I was standing on the other side
of the scenery," Jenks continued, "though I'm not sure
who saw me there. Besides, my argument with Luke
doing your ropes was that I'm the one been keeping
you safe for years. So if I'd knocked him down and
you got hurt . . . I would die before I'd see you hurt,
Your—Bess."

"Thank you, Jenks. I owe you a great deal and have
always trusted you," she said, her voice nearly breaking. It was true. Why was she questioning this man?
He and Kat had been closer than kin for years.

"Ned, just to clear the decks here," she pursued,
turning in the chair to face him, "you had naught
against Luke Morgan, did you?"

"Nary a thing," he declared, looking steadily at her.
"It's Jenks and Lord Robert jumped down his throat
when Luke merely touched you the other day."

Robin? Well, yes, and he had made a slightly earlier
exit behind her, but it had been in the other direction,

away from where Luke waited to hoist and swing her. But surely Robin would not get in Luke's way on that scaffold, especially not if he thought she could be injured. And yet the other evening he'd told her of a dream he'd had where he rescued her when she fell from an apple tree in a garden and all the apples thudded down around them, crimson and shiny and juicy as her lips. But if he'd knocked Luke off his perch to give himself an opportunity to grandiosely save his queen, he'd done a wretched job of it.

Realizing she was blushing, she rose from the table and strode to the withdrawing room window. "Meg," she said, "there is no bad blood between you and Luke Morgan?"

The queen turned back. Perhaps the girl should be put to bed. She did look a bit greenish about the gills.

"Hardly. I didn't even know the man," Meg said, sounding uncharacteristically snappish.

"Luke's good-looking," Ned put in, "and a bit forward, a rank and position climber, I warrant too. He didn't say something or—"

"Something like what?" Meg cried, smacking her hands on the table. "If you mean flirting with the female servant staff, you ought to know, Ned Topside! If Luke Morgan was a climber at court, it's not going to be on the skirts of the strewing herb mistress, that's sure. No, I hardly spoke to the man, and anyone who says different better get Dr. Dee to lend him that glass cylinder of his so he can see better. Forgive me, Your Grace, but I'm going to be sick," she muttered, and lurched for the door.

Frowning, Elizabeth let her go, but as Kat started after her, she added, "Kat, see that she's all right, but then we need to discuss Geoffrey's demise too."

Meg ran back in, right around Kat, her hand over her mouth so they could hardly catch her garbled words. "Lord Harry sends word to come quick, Your Grace. Luke can't talk, but his eyes are open."

THE QUEEN CONSULTED WITH HER PHYSICIANS, COMforted Harry before he went off to send a message to his wife, then emptied the small room to be alone with Luke. For the time being, the patient could not do much but blink and breathe, Dr. Spencer had told her. It would, Elizabeth thought, have to be enough for what she intended.

"Poor man," she said, standing by the side of his makeshift bed so he could see her as she leaned slightly over him. The doctors had put his head in a carved-out block of wood to keep his neck stable, and he could only look straight up. "I am sorely grieved for your condition and pray you will recover. I will do all I can to see you are well cared for. Luke, do you recall anything of your fall from the high walkway? I know you cannot answer, but can you blink once for yes and two for—ah, that's it. Good man," she said, and her eyes filled with tears at his single, deliberate blink. "You see, Luke, I intend to find who harmed you and make them pay."

His appearance frightened her. His once ruddy skin had gone waxen white, and his usually expressive eyes seemed flat and dull. He was too exhausted—or worse—to manage facial expressions, and the doctors had said his capacity for speech was temporarily gone too, and they knew not if it would return. Still, it seemed to her he frowned. Perhaps he blamed her for everything.

"Luke, I hope you can help me with this. Do you think you can?"

One blink. His mind was intact, and he was willing. Yet those eyelids drooped.

"First of all, I know you are exhausted just now, and I will not overtire you but to ask what I can do for you. Lord Hunsdon will return to your side soon, but would you like the doctors to return?"

Two blinks.

"Are you quite warm enough?"

A surprised look—a slight widening of the eyes, then one blink. She knew that the doctors had siphoned some wine down his throat with a poppy potion to make him sleep. She would let him rest an hour or so, carefully guarded, then come back.

She put her hand on his big shoulder, so limp now, all of him, but she had no notion if he could feel her touch or not. The queens and kings of England held traditional curing ceremonies for a disease called scrofula—the curing of the king's evil, some still called it. She wished desperately that, like the Lord Jesus' touch, hers could heal this man.

"Sleep, Luke, sleep," she whispered, and left his side. She was pleased to see Robin waiting down the corridor to escort her upstairs.

"I know this grieves you, my queen," he said as she laid her hand properly on his arm, "so let me comfort you. Meet me in the Round Tower tonight as you had hinted you would."

"As I had said I might," she corrected him. "But tonight, with this great sadness, I can hardly . . ."

"Not for our own pleasure, but to talk everything out," he coaxed, his voice so strong and yet so gentle.

"To talk out something about Luke's fall?" she asked.

"I know naught of that, as I stood far across the stage near Felicia's playing post. Now that Cecil's turned tail and run off, I want to advise you about replacing him."

"I will think on it," she said, but she was only thinking how much she needed Robin's strong arms around her. She almost told him so, but Felicia sat on a bench outside the royal apartments, cradling Geoffrey's lute to her as if it were made of solid gold.

"Felicia," she said, and the lass jumped up and hurried to them. "Lord Hunsdon is sitting with the injured man downstairs, so go down and play them both something soothing—nothing sad and nothing lively."

"Of course, Your Majesty," Felicia said with a quick curtsy to her and then one to Robin, before she evidently realized she need not show him that courtesy in the queen's presence and stopped in mid-bob.

"And though you were playing from too far across the backstage setting to see what went on," the queen told her lutenist, "I still would speak with you later about everyone else's entrances and exits."

"Yes, Your Majesty."

"And, Felicia, I heard those sour notes of protest that I used the trumpets for my masque music instead of your lute. Considering all the changes in your life in the short time you have been at court, best learn to be both obedient and grateful without sour notes."

"Yes, Your Majesty," the girl repeated as if she were some sort of pet parrot. Elizabeth glared at her as she hurried off.

"So," the queen whispered, "she gave you a curtsy too—of sorts, Robin. Does she know something I do not about your being elevated to the peerage or some such?" she inquired as she swept on down the corridor.

"A distant dream but entirely in your hands, as am I," he whispered. His lips twisted in a rueful smile as he strode faster to keep up with her. "As for the lass, she's green but yearns to learn, and at your side, my queen."

"That sounds like the lyrics to another song," she murmured, then stopped and bit her lower lip.

"Your birthday is in but four days," he whispered, "and I long to give you the best gift I can offer—myself."

"There is no time for celebrations or such talk now," she insisted, but she was appalled that she almost tilted into him. She longed to cling to those broad, sturdy shoulders. Instead she forced herself to leave him standing alone outside her door.

# Chapter the Ninth

*I find no peace, and all my war is done,*
*I fear and hope, I burn and freeze like ice,*
*I fly above the wind, yet can I not arise,*
*And naught I have and all the world I seize on;*
*That looseth nor locketh holdeth me in prison,*
*And holdeth me not; yet can I 'scape nowise,*
*Nor letteth me live nor die at my devise*
*And yet of death it giveth none occasion.*

— SIR THOMAS WYATT, *the Elder*

 FELICIA WAS SURPRISED TO SEE NO ONE BUT Luke Morgan in the room where they'd put him. She knew which chamber it was; she'd been keeping an eye on everything and would send the details soon to both Cecil and de Quadra, without letting either of them know she worked for both. Holding her lute by a stranglehold on its neck, she tiptoed in.

The man was sleeping. They had his head in a carved-out block of wood with a leather strap across his broad forehead, evidently to keep him still, for she'd heard he'd broken his neck and they weren't sure what faculties he would recover. She could discern the slight rise and fall of his chest but no other movement.

She'd like to think this was God's retribution on the whoreson bastard for making her life so hard since she'd been at court, but she believed only in fate now. Ever since she had realized she'd been born into an illegitimate line, despite the fact King Henry's blood roared through her veins as royal as Elizabeth's, she'd felt cursed. So she'd get as close as she could to the riches and power that could have—*should* have—been hers if fate had but twisted crooked circumstance the other way.

"Luke, can you hear me?" she whispered nearly in his face, and gave his shoulder a good rock. "Luke Morgan!"

She'd overheard the royal physicians tell the queen he had brain swelling and was partially paralyzed. The physicians had also privily told Her Majesty that they were not even certain if he would live or die, though Felicia would like to have a say in that.

Slowly Luke opened his eyes. His gaze flew wide when he saw her. So he did remember who she was and what had happened between them.

"The queen sent me to sing you a song, and I have a special one," she hissed, her spittle flecking his face. "It's called 'I Find No Peace,' and it's all about being in a hellish earthly prison. Probably an escape to hell itself would be far better," she whispered smugly.

She leaned against his high, narrow bed, began the intricate melody on the strings, and sang in a quiet, controlled voice the lines, ending with,

> *Without eyes I see and without tongue complain;*
> *I desire to perish and yet I ask health;*
> *Likewise displeaseth me both death and life.*

"A fine song, just for you," she said, and went back over the earlier lines about fearing and hoping and not being able to arise. "I suppose your state is like a prison now," she interspersed her own quiet torments between the lyrics. "And since you've been so curious about me and wanted to tell Her Majesty each thing you learned or even imagined—you know, I warrant *you're* a eunuch now—I'm going to confide in you truly, Luke Morgan."

She heard stirrings in the hall, distant footsteps, the buzz of voices. No time to savor the horrified look that had fixed itself on his face. Amazing and delightful, she mused, how a man dazed, drugged by the doctors, and mostly paralyzed could show such fear. But she had no time to revel in this revenge. She had much more of that coming to make her rejoice.

"I know," she went on, still strumming, leaning close into his face, almost breathing in unison with air from his flared nostrils, "what it is to be trapped, you see. To have your parents and betters bid you wed and bed someone you cannot stomach. To realize the only playing you will ever do—lute or otherwise, however gifted you are—will be in your own parlor while you breed brats for some lackbrained country squire who can hardly afford an uncracked chamberpot. Someone just like you, I warrant, who expects to just crook a little finger to get a willing woman in his bed. I wager you can't even crook so much as a finger now, can you, clever man?"

She giggled, then went on. "So you should never have tampered with me, Luke Morgan, never have tried to bring me down with the queen. I have run away before, you see, but don't intend to again, not unless it's to run to something better, something I deserve—or something to put her in her place. Do you know the Spanish ambassador believes Her *un*gracious Majesty's behavior with Lord Robert could even cost her her crown? Now, I'd like to help that happen and then to reveal some surprises."

She changed to yet another melody, but did not break her lyrics she was writing just for him. "What, nothing to say, man? I thought you always had something to say. Can't back me against the wall and ogle me and think I will gladly couple with you at the snap of your fingers? *That* part of you—and I don't mean fingers—doesn't work anymore, I warrant, my Lord Luke!"

He stared aghast in raw fear, or was it smothered fury? No matter, for she had the power now and could swim in it all night. That thought reminded her that this man had jumped into the Thames to save her, but—no, she told herself. That was just another of his ploys to find favor with the queen. He would have jumped in for the royal lapdog.

"You can't keep me from her anymore," Felicia said, segueing into a quicker tune. "She wants me near, her lover pays me to write songs, I spy for great men. I fit perfectly into her clothes, and I could fit perfectly into her skin. Because her blood is mine, you see, her very blood—"

"Felicia, Her Grace said she sent you to play for

Luke," Lord Hunsdon's voice came at the door. "How is he faring?"

"I've been playing various tunes, my lord," she said, straightening and stepping back from the bed a bit, though she kept up the melody. "Shall I stay the night with him then, even if you and the doctors must withdraw?"

"I would count it a great favor and reward you thusly," Lord Hunsdon said. Felicia saw Luke was trying to blink oddly at his lordship, a series of double blinks, then a rest, then two blinks again.

As Lord Hunsdon, who evidently didn't notice, sat on the single chair beneath the window, beyond which the sun was sinking, Felicia stared at Luke, putting herself between the two men for a moment. "I'll do all I can to take care of him, my lord," she assured the older man while she gave the prone, paralyzed one her sweetest smile.

MY DEAREST WIFE AMY, THE LETTER BEGAN, AND IT WAS taking her the longest time to read it. It wasn't just that the sun was setting and shadows were eating up everything out here behind the house at Cumnor. And she was used to reading Robert's hand. But the dead abbots' voices had plagued her today ever since her physician left. She had asked for more potions to dull the pain, but he had said he feared she might overdose herself. And indeed, she admitted, she might.

Since she'd had that unholy thought, the holy men

had been chanting from under their turfy graves, dissonant, nasal. Because their Latin drowned out Robert's words in her head, Amy decided she should read them aloud. She sat on the low stone wall surrounding the graveyard and bent over the letter again.

•

*I cannot visit you now, for Lord Cecil has deserted Her Grace, and this is my best opportunity to advise and counsel her the more. When the court returns to London, I fear she may lose some of the frivolity—*

What did *frivolity* mean here? Amy agonized. Robert had used that word to refer to her love of fun and little gifts, so how could that refer to the queen of England? Didn't she have to stay stately and regal, and wouldn't the gifts anyone gave her have to be very grand?

*—lose some of the frivolity that our sojourn in the sweet countryside had provided this year—*

"The sweet countryside," Amy said aloud, crumpling the letter in her lap. "*Our* sojourn in the sweet countryside." Cumnor wasn't sweet anymore without Robert. It was more and more like a prison. She felt trapped here with that tumor inside her body, maybe reaching for her heart, the heart Robert had already broken.

She smoothed the letter out over her knees again and bent over it, trying to shut out the *Glorias* and *Aves* buzzing in her brain.

*My dearest wife, trust that you are yet and ever queen*
*of my heart. And so, soon I shall send Fletcher with a*
*gift fit for a queen for you.*

"While you stay with her," Amy cried, "with her!"

There! She had drowned out the abbots for once. Yet as she had before, she lay flat on the grass on her back between two gentle grave mounds. She wished the earth would swallow her. Then the voices came louder, sweeter, so she didn't have to be seduced again and again by Robert's promises of gifts, when she wanted only him.

THE QUEEN WAS PLEASED THAT FELICIA STILL PLAYED AND sang, standing close over Luke's bed when she entered. Then Elizabeth noted he was awake and looked agitated. At Felicia's side, she bent over the prone man, then gestured for the lutenist to step to the foot of his bed.

"Does music not please you, Luke?" the queen asked.

He blinked twice. Felicia gasped and stopped playing. "I thought it would soothe him, Your Majesty," she protested, sounding hurt. "Is he—giving you answers in code with his eyes?"

Elizabeth fixed her own gaze on Luke's as he kept glancing deliberately toward Felicia—or mayhap Harry, who sat at the foot of the bed—then blinking twice for "no" over and over. They were such big blinks the queen could almost imagine he was shouting, "No! No!"

"Felicia, step out, and you too, my lord," she commanded.

"I hesitate to leave his side, Your Grace," Harry began, but got up directly when he saw the look on her face. Felicia, pouting, shuffled slowly out, and Elizabeth went to close the door behind them.

"Luke, I am going to list the names of everyone I can think of. You must blink once if it is the name of one who hurt you. Can you do that?"

One decisive blink, then the sudden darting of his eyes toward the door she had just closed. Surely he was not trying to tell her Harry had harmed him, because he had been onstage nearly until the accident and then exited in the other direction. That slip of a girl Felicia? But both of them—and Robert—were far across the wide expanse of scenery and could vouch for each other. And Felicia's playing had never missed a cue during the masque despite the sour notes. . . .

Missed a cue . . . A sudden suspicion struck Elizabeth: Had she herself missed a clue? Young Hester Harington had run away from home, and so had Felicia, according to one of her early stories. The musician had gone white as bleached linen every time the queen had mentioned the Haringtons. Over a year ago, Elizabeth recalled, when John Harington had first described his rebellious daughter, he had said the girl cared deeply for her lute and music. It was a longbow shot but could Felicia—possibly—*be* the lost Hester?

Somehow, the queen vowed, she must find a way to test this possibility without making her musician bolt.

Elizabeth jumped as someone knocked loudly on the door. "Your Grace!" Harry called. "Word's come Kat Ashley's fallen!"

The queen leaped for the door. "Fallen? Is she all right?"

"In pain and calling for you. It's nothing like Luke," he whispered, "but she insists she needs you."

Elizabeth glanced back at Luke, lying immobile. Kat had been a mother to her, comforting her through all her pains both large and small.

"Guard," she called to the yeoman warder standing just down the corridor, "to me."

When he came running, she told him, "Lord Hunsdon may sit at Luke Morgan's bed and my doctors be let in, but no one else. You will stay in his room every moment until I return."

Holding up her skirts, she nearly ran herself.


"KAT, DEAREST, WHAT HAPPENED?" ELIZABETH CROONED as she held the old woman's shoulders while both of her court physicians set her broken arm. She was old now, the queen had to admit, shocked into viewing Kat truly for the first time in years. Seeing her in pain like this made Elizabeth admit to the gray hairs and fragility of the yet ample frame. She knew Kat had become forgetful of late too, but she'd written that off to her being busy and a bit burdened with her double duties.

"I—I simply turned away from overseeing the maid scrubbing out your hip bath, and the floor came up to meet me. Perhaps it was slippery with the boiled soap and scouring powder. My leg—I think it just twisted under me and I came down on my elbow. However will I tend to everything with but one arm, and my left one at that?"

"Worry not for that, for you must rest. But, Kat, many are left-handed, and you shall learn to be too," Elizabeth said to encourage her, but the mention of left-handedness made her think of Felicia again.

*Sui bono?* as Cecil would say. Felicia had certainly profited from Geoffrey's death, as that had vacated the spot of royal master lutenist, but Felicia had not even been at Richmond then. Could it be Felicia was angry that Luke Morgan had exposed both of her disguises? Yet Elizabeth admired the girl and felt fervent sympathy for her pluck in conquering the world of men through masterful lute playing. But as Luke's eyes had darted so in the Dove of the lute's direction, she must question the girl. Mayhap those sour notes at the masque were caused by Felicia having to walk across the scaffolding to get to Luke. If only she could recall if the sound of lute music had moved behind the painted canvas during the play, but her mind had been on too much else. And if only she knew if Felicia resembled the runaway Hester Harington.

Elizabeth held tight to Kat's shoulders as the doctors splinted the painfully set arm. "I pray it won't heal crooked, Your Majesty," Dr. Browne said as Kat swooned. "A woman of this age—one can never tell."

"A woman of any age," Elizabeth whispered to herself, "one can never tell."

EXHAUSTED, THE QUEEN LEFT KAT IN MARY SIDNEY'S capable hands and headed back to Luke's bedside. It was getting late, but she must wake him if he slept and get this over with. The first name she would start with was Felicia Dove, though it was folly to think the girl could keep playing the lute, not to mention topple a sturdy, alert man like Luke Morgan. And something else had been nagging at her that she wanted to ask the girl. Perhaps with Gil Sharpe's help she wouldn't even have to ask that directly.

When she came to the doorway of the sickroom, the queen saw not only Harry kneeling by Luke's bed, but a black-garbed figure bending over him. At first she feared a stranger in disguise, and she'd told the guard—who was now going down on both knees before her—to keep strangers clear.

But then she saw the black-garbed man was a cleric, the Reverend Mr. Martin, who assisted the chapel minister she'd sent to Northumbria for his preaching against her friendship with Robin.

"What—is this?" she whispered, fearing the worst.

"Luke became most agitated," Harry told her, lifting his head. His face was a mask of grief. "A few minutes ago, he began to choke. He gasped—and died. I sent for the minister, sent for you and the doctors . . . even Dr. Dee."

As if merely saying his name had conjured him up,

Dr. Dee filled the door behind the queen. She turned to stare at him.

"I see I'm too late," he intoned. "Your Majesty, it was probably too late for the man the moment he fell."

KAT WAS SNORING LOUDLY IN THE ROYAL BED, BUT ELIZA-beth knew she could not sleep anyway. And Felicia was not at her assigned post just outside the chamber door to play soothing music. Though she had not been anywhere nearby when Luke died, Elizabeth would send for the girl first thing in the morning.

But now, what to do about so many things and people. Not only Felicia, but Cecil. Robin—she longed to meet him atop the Round Tower as they'd discussed. Katherine Grey, still suspect in Luke's fall. Meg, ill of the greensickness had taken to her bed. Assigning Mary Sidney to Kat's duties for a time without unsettling Kat. And she would order that Luke be buried in Eton's graveyard on the morrow, she decided.

Beyond her own servants and courtiers lay her countrymen and beyond that, hostile foreign kings and other countries. Things seemed to be slipping from her control somehow, the queen thought, pacing back and forth between her bedchamber and adjoining privy closet.

Since most of that must wait until tomorrow and she could not sleep, the queen sent one of the door guards to wake and summon Katherine Grey. And, at the last moment, she told the other guard to fetch maids to pour her bathwater from the kitchen kettles.

Katherine came tardily and bleary eyed, her usually smoothly combed, Tudor-hued red hair resembling a bird's nest in her haste. She wore only a robe and flannel mules on her feet.

"Oh, Your Grace," she said in that insipid voice with the bovine look she affected lately, "I thought you wanted help with Kat, and here she's snoring like a pikeman in your bed."

"Then we shall keep our voices down. Ah, here come the maids with my bathwater. You may scrub my back instead of Kat, as I would talk to you," Elizabeth said, gesturing the two kitchen girls in with the four buckets of steaming water.

"In other words, I am to take over some of her duties?" Katherine whispered. "But you know, taking a bath in the night air can be unhealthsome."

Elizabeth ignored that and motioned Katherine into the small tiled room behind her. Though it was not widespread custom to bathe the body often and most certainly not at night, Elizabeth wanted to keep Katherine Grey off balance. She suddenly wished, for the first time all summer, that she were back at cozy old Whitehall in London, where her father had installed in his privy chamber a sunken tub with glazed tiles heated by hot air. Like much of aging Windsor, this room for her bath paled by comparison.

"Luke Morgan died earlier tonight," Elizabeth began as the maids sloshed water in the scrubbed tin tub.

"I heard," Katherine said, stepping behind the tub to rearrange the stack of flannel towels. "Choked on his own saliva, desperate to talk, I heard."

"You hear things quickly, do you not?" Elizabeth inquired as she nodded to the sleepy maids and they scurried out. For one moment she reconsidered the wisdom of facing this ambitious little chit alone in the dead of night, but that must be part of her plan to get this girl to—well, to come clean, the queen thought with a small smirk as she removed her own robe and settled down into the hot water. Her knees were nearly in her face.

"Fetch that sponge and a handful of those rose petals over there," she said. Looking mutinous, Katherine obeyed. The girl handed the queen the sponge, then scattered the petals wildly, with deliberate abandon, so most fluttered beyond the tub.

"Did you note anything amiss during the masque?" Elizabeth asked as Katherine stepped back behind her. Perhaps the girl did not realize that her interrogator could glimpse her face in the mirror on the far wall.

"About his fall, you mean? I didn't know a thing of it until I heard the shout that Luke had fallen."

"You noted no stranger behind the set?" Elizabeth said, sloshing water up over her shoulders, her eyes fixed on the mirror.

"No one," Katherine maintained, straight-faced.

"Then was someone you did recognize lurking backstage—say, your secret friend and confidant, Edward Seymour?"

Katherine gasped. Ah, mayhap she had her now, Elizabeth thought, craning her neck to look up at the girl.

"Not Edward either," Katherine said, recovering

quickly. "Frankly, Your Majesty, I had my hands full, forced by you to play the villain of the piece and trying to parrot all those wretched lines. 'I vow I shall vanquish one and all and drub Leto's reputation in the dust of time.' Such drivel and—"

"It is drivel indeed. Now why did I ever think to give you such a part or lines? And then the ones about your willfully disobeying the goddess Diana—"

"Yes, but at least my character Niobe had children while Diana was forced to be so chaste and virginal that—"

Elizabeth threw the sponge behind her, splatting the girl full in the face. "Kat catches that," the queen said, reaching up to seize a towel from Katherine's arm. "You have a great deal to learn. And one thing is not to lurk behind me, all eyes and ears like a spy. And I hear you raced off to see Edward Seymour the other day, when you know he is forbidden you and you know why, with his seditious family's past and your veins flowing with some part of royal Tudor blood."

"But you yourself have set the standard that one's most intimate friends and paramours can come from treasonous families," Katherine countered cheekily. "Robert Dudley's past shows—"

Half rising from the bath, Elizabeth slapped her face and nearly slipped back in. Katherine, looking down her nose haughtily, lifted her hand to her cheek but did not flinch or flee. "And this is how you treat someone of your blood," the girl dared whisper.

"Only ones that devoutly wish my downfall and are open to treasonous plots against my person."

"Then you'd best send someone to Paris to slap down Mary Stuart, Queen of Scots and France, Your Grace, or to chastise your other cousin, Margaret Douglas, spinning her webs in Yorkshire, for I am innocent of all such compared to them."

"Comparing yourself to them is as foolish and dangerous as your ever trying to compare yourself to me," Elizabeth said, boldly turning her back on the girl again. "I hope, for your own good, that you understand this warning, cousin Katherine. You may go now."

Elizabeth saw in the mirror that the girl opened her mouth to say something else, then evidently thought the better of it. Flipping another flannel towel onto the edge of the bath, where it immediately became half-soaked, Katherine stalked from the room. Slowly, carefully, Elizabeth rose from her bath, which was usually such a fine, protracted exercise in blessed rest. The water had gone very cold.

Though the interview with Katherine had rattled her, the queen turned her mind again to Robin. She stared at herself in the mirror as she dried off, shifting to see her entire body. If she ever ungarbed for him, what would Robin think of her long limbs, flat breasts, and tiny waist? And if he gazed upon her like this, what would he do and how would she respond? The birthday gift of himself he had mentioned—ah, that would be a fine package to unwrap.

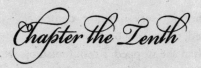

# Chapter the Tenth

*Set me in earth, in heaven, or yet in hell;*
*In hill, in dale, or in the foaming flood;*
*Thrall, or at large—alive whereso I dwell;*
*Sick or in health, in ill fame or in good;*
*Yours I will be, and with that only thought*
*Comfort myself when that my hap in naught.*

— HENRY HOWARD, *Earl of Surrey*

 EARLY THE NEXT MORNING, ELIZABETH stared aghast at her bathtub and the devastated room where she'd interviewed Katherine Grey. Someone had tossed the stack of flannel towels hither and yon. All Meg's rose petals had been flung about. Sodden spots of pink littered the floor and stuck to walls and ceiling. Lavender and fragrant herbs from other baskets peppered every inch of space. The smell sat in the pit of the queen's stomach, sickening sweet, rank, and overpowering.

It looked as if some wild animal had shredded the sponge and cast bits of it everywhere. Though the tin tub had not been tipped, its water had been sloshed out to make a flood on the tiled floors and sop the Turkish carpet. And in the midst of that mess, the velvet-seated close stool that traveled everywhere with her was tipped to add its acrid smell to the chaos.

"Katherine Grey must be demented," the queen whispered, staggering back out.

But then she stopped. Fresh footsteps, which surely would have dried from last night, tracked into the bedroom in which she'd just arisen. Her head down, she followed the wet prints—shod feet, not bare—past the wide bed, where she gasped as she nearly bumped into Mary Sidney. Meg stood dressed but disheveled behind Mary with a tray of what appeared to be herbal remedies. They had evidently just entered from the next room.

"I got Meg up to see if we could tend Kat," Mary whispered with a quick curtsy Meg mimicked, "but since it's you astir and not her, I suppose we'd best let her sleep."

"Were either of you just in my privy bathing chamber?" Elizabeth asked, whispering in deference to Kat, when she wanted to scream.

"Just now?" Mary asked, looking puzzled. Meg shook her head.

" 'S blood, of course you weren't," the queen muttered, yanking a heavy robe over the towel she'd slept wrapped in last night. "It was that dissembling, whey-faced bitch Katherine Grey, and she's getting damned dangerous. Mary, run to her room and see if she's in bed—pull her covers off to see if she's dressed or wet."

"But I saw no one come out into the hall past the guards," Mary protested. "And I stood outside the door a good quarter hour until I heard you in here." But she went back out posthaste as commanded.

Meg came closer as Elizabeth followed the footprints toward the concealed door of the outer wall, rather than the one to the main hall. As in all of King Henry's palaces, a back exit led to hidden stairs. They went down to ground level, where Elizabeth had posted a guard who also frequently checked that the roof door was bolted from inside.

"Meg, fetch me a light," she ordered, seeing the door was not latched from the inside as it should be. Was this how someone had been spying on her? Never in this room had she felt that unease. Half expecting to see Katherine lurking on the other side, the queen put her hand to the latch, lifted it, and yanked the door wide. It creaked slightly but revealed nothing except the stairs up and down from the small stone landing.

Yet even before the girl came with a lantern, a glimmer of morning light reflected in the silhouette of a damp footprint going up, clearly a small foot, not a guard's boot. But someone must know the guard was at the door below. And that someone had been here recently.

"Toward the roof," the queen whispered. "I don't like this. Katherine Grey on the roof?"

"You're certain it was her, Your Grace?" Meg asked, hovering so close she stepped on the edge of Elizabeth's robe. "So if she's on the roof and sneaking into your apartments, you think she could have pushed Geoffrey off at Richmond?"

Pulling her hems free, the queen shook her head, but she knew the girl could be right. Mayhap Katherine Grey was behind all this, for she'd have the motive to terrify the queen at the least and to have her murdered at most. But committing violent deeds on her own did not seem like the sly, snide Katherine.

Nor could Elizabeth believe that of Felicia Dove, though the girl was adept at a medley of sexes and stories as well as songs. Mayhap Felicia was working for Katherine, though Elizabeth couldn't fathom that this Grey girl, unlike her bright sister, Lady Jane, had enough brains to mastermind a plot. Maybe the wily de Quadra had his hand in this. She must again send Robin to him to try to learn more.

But then her two other distant, though close-as-kin enemies, Mary Stuart and Margaret Douglas, were Catholic up to their ears. They could be behind a long-distance conspiracy. Why must it always be that those most dangerous were blood related? Even her archenemy King Philip of Spain, her brother-in-law, had dared propose marriage after her sister died, and he'd like nothing better than to possess her entire country, not her body or heart.

"But," Meg's voice interrupted Elizabeth's agonized thoughts, "this door's always locked from inside."

"Kat's the one who secures it, and who knows if she did last night?" She spun back two steps up. "Come with me, but fetch us a guard first."

When Meg had summoned the guard from his post below, Elizabeth took the light from Meg and let him precede her up the twist of stairs. She could feel the breeze now and see wan daylight from above.

"Door's blown open up here to the roof, Your Majesty," the guard called down. "I checked it several times last night. Best let me look out first if you're set on this."

Yes, she was set on this, on all of it now, Elizabeth fumed as she waited impatiently for his all-clear call or a shout he'd spotted someone. The queen tapped her slippered foot. " 'S blood," she whispered more to herself than to Meg, "it wasn't many years ago my father had the Earl of Devonshire arrested and executed on the charge of merely being an aspirant to the throne that was not his by right. I may have to return to such measures!"

Wide-eyed, her face white as whey, Meg nodded.

"No one here'bouts," the guard called down.

"Let's go back to Kat then," Meg wheedled. "I brought comfrey knitbone tea and a wreath of pennyroyal for her head, since she says she's been dizzy of late and—"

"Fine, but I want to look out up here," Elizabeth interrupted, and shoved the door wider behind the guard.

The view was breathtaking with the roll of land and town to the sparkling ribbon of river and the deep blue-green of forests beyond. Surveying the span of flat roof that stretched to small turrets overlooking the courtyards below, the queen gazed at the top of the massive Round Tower. Standing sentinel on its mound, it was the last sanctuary if the enemy encroached or invaded. And Robert had asked— pleaded—that she should meet him there.

She stood as if entranced until her hair blew in her

eyes and Meg said, "Shouldn't we go back down now, Your Grace?"

Elizabeth spun to look her full in the face. "I meant to tell you that I am glad to see you out of your sickbed, Meg Milligrew."

"I still would rather not get up, but Kat has done so much for me. . . ."

"As have I. Therefore, you will bring sweet strewing herbs and accompany my entourage today but a short way by barge to Eton, to Luke Morgan's funeral and burial."

"By barge?" Meg cried, looking truly anguished. "If it's by barge with all that rocking, I just know I'd lose my insides again, Your Grace, so if I could just beg off, I pray you."

"You're angry Geoffrey had no formal burial," Elizabeth accused, "but remember, Luke is related to Lady Hunsdon, so that elevates him as kin to—"

"Oh, not that, Your Grace, but I really think I'd be like to puke if I set one foot on your barge today, so if I could but be excused this once . . ."

Elizabeth merely nodded and turned away. She had no time for such trivia, however much she cared for the girl. Yes, she must see Robin privily, and the assignation might as well be in the Round Tower tonight. But right now, she must prepare herself to face down Felicia Dove.

WHITEHALL PALACE, THE QUEEN'S MAIN LONDON RESI-dence, stood a vast skeleton stripped of its interior grandeur when she was away. Draperies and tapestries were taken down to be stored, and the few upholstered pieces covered. Plateware and table utensils, whether pewter, gold, or silver, were put under lock and key or taken with her. Her favorite books, pets, and pieces of art made the journey too. Even the royal bed and particular pieces of furniture were carted along on royal progress.

The crowds disappeared: No courtiers clung to the walls awaiting favors, no clerks and secretaries scurried, no flapping-eared servants hovered, no ambassadors came calling. It was blessedly quiet and, usually, William Cecil loved it. But today, he felt he was preparing a corpse for burial, perhaps his own.

Yet he had kept two clerks busy all morning, doing his bidding. He had weeded out old papers from his desk, finished up on business matters hanging fire, and completed correspondence he might never pick up again. He was quite certain he'd depart Her Grace's service now, but would neither leave a mess, nor his privy matters, for the new man. Especially in case Her Majesty had completely taken leave of her senses and intended to name Robert Dudley as her chief adviser.

Cecil finally let his clerks go down to the nearly empty kitchens to see what food they could flush out for a little repast. Alone, he paced the wainscotted anteroom to the royal apartments where he had always worked within reach of the brilliant queen's questions and demands. It seemed dusty, dim, tomblike now, this entire sprawling palace and capital city of her realm.

He startled as he heard a noise, perhaps shuffling footsteps and the creak of a floorboard. It was not the sound of his young clerks coming back.

He peeked out into the corridor and came face-to-face with Bishop de Quadra and one of his men, whose name he could not recall. A pox on it, soon it wouldn't matter one whit if he knew who was attached to whom in international circles, Cecil thought. But to de Quadra, slippery enemy though he was, he thrust out his hand.

"My Lord Cecil, I heard you were here," the Spaniard said, smiling and taking his hand before quickly releasing it.

"Heard from whom, bishop?"

De Quadra smiled and wagged a finger. "Not cleaning up and moving out, I hope," he parried. "If she lets you go, she is doomed indeed."

"Doomed?" Cecil repeated as the two of them went into the anteroom while the bishop's man waited in the corridor. They sat in chairs facing each other before the empty hearth. "I mislike that term or implication. Doomed, how?"

"*Santa Maria*, come on, man," de Quadra challenged, sitting forward and shifting his legs under his black bishop's cassock. "The queen may have been known for some clever fence-sitting at times, but there's naught clever about precipice sitting. And if she throws herself off into Robert Dudley's arms, that will mean damnation, not salvation. Europe, not to mention her own kingdom, is atwitter with scurrilous stories of her lust and looming ruination."

Cecil wanted to tell him he was insane, to order him out, even to strike him, but he knew full well the man was right. When one was royal and the realm rode on a pair of shoulders, however slender, appearances were often reality. Cecil heaved a huge sigh, then said wearily, "I have heard such but pray you overstate your case."

"All of France and beyond will soon know of that elaborate masque that mocked her royal cousin Mary Stuart," de Quadra pursued. "*With* Robert Dudley as her fellow Olympian god."

"I know, I know, but I certainly hope you will have no part in spreading such news. After all, masques and satire are *de rigueur*," Cecil muttered, "and perhaps the queen and courtiers learned their lesson, since there was a fatal accident."

Having tossed out that bait and hook, he watched de Quadra closely to see if he too had someone feeding him fresh information from Windsor. Without batting an eye the man said, "Accidents do happen. As for fatal, the queen should realize she can lose much more with someone pulling her strings—and I do mean Dudley, not that poor man who was hurt. But he died, you say?"

Cecil sensed that de Quadra was not one whit surprised by the revelation of Luke Morgan's death, so he didn't even answer that. It almost made him wonder if the ambassador had more than one spy in Elizabeth's court. King Henry VIII's crafty chief minister, Thomas Cromwell, had always said it was wise to have a second informant watching the key informant, so Cecil had taken that advice, especially because Felicia Dove seemed so flighty, but then musicians and artists often were.

Suddenly Cecil tired of this game he himself had played for so long. Just today Felicia Dove had sent him lines from the doctored-up script Ned Topside had supposedly written, but which certainly bore the queen's stamp too. He wondered again who the bishop had feeding him information so quickly and efficiently, but the Spaniards always did pay well.

"I take it you're not going back to Windsor unless she commands you?" the bishop asked, obviously pleased to change the subject.

"Mayhap not even then. I'd like to simply retire, but if the Tudor temper rears its head, I could be cooling my heels in prison. If so, bishop, I hope you will visit me from time to time to tell me what's going—"

A woman's shrill voice brought them both to their feet. An argument between a man and a woman followed. Cecil hurried out into the corridor with de Quadra clinging like a burr.

An unkempt woman with one child in her arms and one tugging at her skirts was berating the bishop's man. He was gesturing wildly and jabbering at her in Spanish with the occasional English interjection of "No queen. Queen go 'way. Queen gone. You go too."

Despite the fact those words were not meant for Cecil, they fed his worst fears. What if, indeed, Elizabeth's stubborn nature and passion for the sports of love she had inherited from her father, along with her vast power, brought her down?

"What is the issue here?" Cecil demanded in a loud enough voice that both the girl and the Spaniard stopped shouting at each other.

"Your lordship," she cried, peering around the frustrated man until he stepped aside, "Polly Hammet, that's me, widow of the queen's late lutenist, one Geoffrey Hammet. I know the queen's not here, but I want someone to tell her how grateful I am, yes, right grateful."

"For?" Cecil prompted, walking toward the agitated blonde. At least she had been blond once, maybe pretty too, though she looked only weary and worn now. The toddler, a girl, cowered behind her mother's stained skirts at his approach.

"Grateful for the coins she sent, a course, for Geoffrey's services rendered," Polly Hammet spoke up. "A note said so in her own hand—her own hand. The minister, he read it to me. God preserve Her Grace, she saved us from this hard winter coming on, so I been praying she can save herself."

"Save herself?" de Quadra interrupted.

"You know, what all folk been talking 'bout," Polly said, shifting the baby to her other arm. "Either damned if she does or doesn't, the minister said."

"If she does or doesn't what?" de Quadra put in, though Cecil glared at him for his meddling.

"You know," Polly said, dropping her voice conspiratorially. "If she makes Robert Dudley put 'way his poor lady wife or just has someone dispatch her 'fore she weds him."

"I rest my case," de Quadra said.

"WHAT'S THE BOY DOING HERE?" FELICIA ASKED AS SHE faced the queen in her privy chamber. The musician kept rubbing her hands together, the queen noted, perhaps feeling naked without a lute in them for once. She had requested that Felicia leave it by the door. Elizabeth sat in a chair, Gil perched on a table, and Felicia stood facing them both.

"Gil is my artist, and he's very good at faces," Elizabeth said to play her first card. Mary Sidney had reported that Katherine Grey was not in bed, but had arisen and was washing her face and hands. So, Elizabeth had reasoned, that proved neither that she was guilty or innocent of sneaking into and defacing the queen's chamber. Meanwhile, Elizabeth stared harder at Felicia. It was high time to force the lutenist to tell all she knew.

"But why my face?" the girl asked. "I'm just a musician—a servant."

"Then, as a servant, you'd best answer the questions I put to you straightaway."

"But my face—it's mine, Your Gracious Majesty, so why should it be taken without my permission?" she wheedled, arms spread beseechingly.

Time for another card, though not the trump. "I want to send it to friends of mine in exile from court."

*That* rattled the girl even more, the queen noted, gripping the carved arms of her chair. She was about to win this hand. Gil kept drawing madly.

"Who are those friends, if you please, Your Majesty? And if they are in exile, doesn't that mean they've displeased you, so why would you send them a gift—and why that?"

"Felicia, did you *ever* leave your assigned place during the masque?" Elizabeth countered. "You see, I'm trying to fix in my mind's eye where everyone was when Luke fell. Someone must have seen what happened."

"I didn't see but I heard—when he fell. But then so did everyone else, I warrant, and came running. Besides, you know I was playing and that takes all my concentration."

"Really? I've seen you play while walking, while talking, and who knows what else you could manage while your music seduces, like Sirens luring Odysseus's ship upon the rocks. Then too, there were those sour notes. And, come to think of it, during the trumpet fanfares, who knows if you were playing or not?"

"Don't you recall, up on the roof at Richmond I found I was scared of heights, Your Grace? I assure you, I was not going one whit higher than that little landing I was standing on. I believe the scaffold where Luke stood was much higher, and I couldn't have set foot on it even if I wanted to."

"Ah, well, then that is a fine alibi," Elizabeth retorted, her voice dripping sarcasm.

Wringing her hands, Felicia shifted from foot to foot. She was wearing a new green gown that swayed rhythmically back and forth. "Your Gracious Majesty, I pray you do not accuse me of harming Luke. It's true that he annoyed me mightily in playing up to you at my expense, but I live to create beauty, not to mar or ruin it, neither the masque with your fine performance or a handsome man like Luke Morgan. And I would do nothing e'er to bring on your displeasure, for my dream in life is to play for you, to be near you."

So the girl had admitted Luke annoyed her. No prevarication there. And she hung her defense, such as it was, on her dislike of heights, her love of beauty, her passion for playing the lute, and her admiration of her queen. Indeed, some or all of that could be valid. Best, Elizabeth thought, return to the tack that seemed to be shaking her more than mere suspicion of murder.

"Let me see the drawing, Gil," Elizabeth said, and held out her hand. With a flourish, the boy reached over to give it to her. It was a good rendering, even bare bones without shading, cross-hatching, or details so far. Gil had somehow caught the pluck and pride that came through, even when Felicia Dove was in a precarious position.

The queen held the sketch toward Felicia. "Do you think he's captured you?"

"*Captured* me? Oh, I see what you mean. He's good. But he's made me look . . . too defiant when I am once again begging Your Gracious Majesty just to let me do what I was born to do, no matter what others accuse me of, no matter what men or the whole kingdom says about me behind my back."

"Meaning?" Elizabeth asked icily, thrusting the drawing back at Gil, who snatched and bent over it again.

"Like you, I defy rumors and accusations."

Elizabeth knew full well what she meant, but how dare she pull this stunt again, the implication that they were alike that had so softened her royal wrath before. And that had been the second time she caught the girl in a lie, in a change of identity. Who knew if the girl was Felicia Dove or not? Suddenly Elizabeth glimpsed something almost familiar about her.

And then it hit her as it never had before. She jumped up and snatched the sketch from Gil again, sending a jagged streak of charcoal pencil right across the paper.

That was it! Felicia Dove resembled John Harington, whom the queen had sent into exile with his wife for not telling her the truth in a murder investigation. She had not noted the similarities before because Felicia always seemed to be changing. But this girl, who had the stamp of his face softer on her, the broad forehead, the full mouth, reminded her so of John when he too was distraught. Her wild guess that Felicia could be Hester suddenly looked like brilliant strategy.

Elizabeth got hold of herself and cleared her throat. She sat back in her chair. Trump time. "Since you asked, Felicia, and I am deciding to trust you again, I will tell you this sketch is being sent to my friends, John and Isabella Harington. They have a daughter of your age who has a passion for the lute and ran away.

It seems she would not wed the man her father wanted, would not stay in the countryside, though God only knows what has happened to her since. I had imagined once she might come to me. Has she?"

"Despite some chance similarities in her life, what is she to me?" Felicia dared.

"It is more a question of what the Haringtons shall be to you. When I summon them back to court, you may fill some of their loss for them, playing for their pleasure. I will tell them so in a letter I shall send them with this drawing."

She had studied the girl minutely as she spoke, almost as if she had her fixed with Dr. Dee's observation glass. Felicia had hardly moved, even stopping her swaying. Was she listening intently or shocked to immobility?

"I have ne'er heard of your friends," Felicia said, each word calm and clear, "though I am sorry for their loss, Your Majesty. I look forward to meeting and playing for them when they arrive. But now I shall play a song for you," she cried, and lunged for her lute across the room as if that would change the subject. Her movement was so quick, she startled the guard at the door, who moved to block it. "Lord Robert has given me a new song he wrote for you," Felicia added hastily, "but I shall play only its melody now."

"No song now, not even that one," the queen ordered. "You will return immediately to Eton to live in my cousin Hunsdon's house as you did before until—"

"But I thought you believed and trusted me," she

said, holding the lute and striding closer. "Then I can stay here, play for you."

"I will send for you when I think best," the queen commanded, pointing toward the door. When Felicia came closer, the queen summoned the guard with the flick of her wrist.

But as Felicia knelt before her chair and bent her head over her lute, Elizabeth noted something caught in the top of her sleek hair. The queen's slender fingers picked out one small brown piece of matter and then another.

"How, pray tell," she asked, "did you get bits of a sponge in your hair?" She displayed them on her open palm before the girl's face.

Felicia boldly blew the pieces away without missing a note. "It's just tree bark," she said, still playing the plaintive melody. "I was practicing outside, leaning back against a tree, that's all. You know, one of the things I love most dearly about a lute is that when you hold it against you, the notes resonate all through you, become part of you. Perhaps that's how it is to be pressed against one's lover, to feel his very pulse beat, to adore someone so that . . ."

Her words were as smooth as her countenance, her turnings of topic and mood as subtle as twists in her song—and heart. But the queen knew she could not trust her now, not until the Haringtons said she was not Hester. For Hester—as her niece, illegitimate or not—had a strain of Tudor blood in her that could make her nearly as deadly as her Tudor cousins.

"Guard," the queen said, standing, "keep my lutenist close restrained at the Hunsdon House in Eton until I send for her. Lord Harry will be attending a funeral this afternoon, but he will be back after."

Felicia's wails and shrieks were the only truly dreadful sounds Elizabeth had ever heard from her.

# Chapter the Eleventh

*Fortune and you did me advance.*
*Me thought I swam and could not drown,*
*Happiest of all but my mischance*
*Did lift me up to throw me down.*

*And you with all your cruelness*
*Did set your foot upon my neck*
*Me and my welfare to oppress.*

— SIR THOMAS WYATT, *the Elder*

HIDDEN BEHIND A CRENELATION IN THE roofline wall of Windsor, Meg Milligrew watched the royal barge depart with Luke Morgan's coffin and mourners, including Lord Robin and the queen. Wishing she had Dr. Dee's observation glass to be certain the man she feared was Ben Wilton was indeed on that barge bent over his oars, Meg waited until it was out of sight. Then, rubbing her belly, for she had not lied to the queen that she felt queasy, she went down the outside steps of the old guard tower and headed out the King Henry VIII gate into town.

Despite the warmth of the late afternoon, she kept her cloak pulled tight and her battered, broad-brimmed garden hat low. She wanted no one in the thatched, wattle-and-daub house where she'd learned the bargemen were billeted to be able to identify her later. And if by chance Ben Wilton was not at the oars today, she didn't want him recognizing her. Nothing on earth could make her go back to a man she didn't recall and was quite certain she'd fled over three years ago because of his brutality. Sometimes in nightmares she heard his loud voice and felt his hard hands upon her.

Pretending a stone was in her shoe, Meg waited outside the house on the palace-side edge of town. If only she could trust Ned to have come along. He could have played some part and asked questions for her. But she feared he'd tell the queen, just as she had feared Luke Morgan would if he guessed the truth, God rest his soul. Besides, Ned would never grow to care for her if he knew she was already wed, even though that hardly stopped some of her betters at court. Mercy, not even counting Lord Robin's longing for Her Grace, Meg had overheard and seen a thing or two of cheating on one's spouse in the hallowed halls of the queen's palaces.

Meg strained to shut out the normal street noises. Through the front door set ajar, the house sounded quiet but for a muted thumping. Hoping she didn't puke, she edged to the doorway and peered in. It took her eyes a moment to adjust to the dim interior. A bent, white-haired woman in the common room was putting pewter plates onto a bare trestle table.

"Excuse me, good woman," Meg called out once, then louder until the old dame looked up.

"Ey?" she said, making the web of lines around her eyes and mouth deepen even more.

Meg pushed the door open a bit farther. "Is this the place where the queen's bargemen live during the queen's stay here?"

"Ey. Looking for some'un special? Mostly, they's out."

*Mostly?* Though Meg saw or heard no one but the woman, she almost turned and fled. Still she went into the little speech she'd rehearsed.

"It's just I lost my stepbrother years ago in the north of England, name of Benjamin Wilton, and someone told me there's an oarsman here by that name, though of course it might not be him, seeing there's probably lots of Ben Wiltons."

"Ey."

"Ey what?"

"He's here."

"Now?" Meg cried, jumping back.

"For the queen's visit. Out rowing her now for a funeral but don't know whose."

Meg's heart nearly thudded out of her chest, but she stood her ground. Ned had taught her never to make hasty exits, even if you'd made a mistake onstage.

"A Ben Wilton, thin and blond—from the north?" Meg forced herself to go on with this charade, her voice a mere squeak.

"Ben Wilton all right, but no barger's ever thin. This 'un a brawler, not blond, and hails from London. Brags a being a bridge shooter, a lusty, loud 'un too, worse 'n most. Where you live in town? Thought I knew 'em all in town. Ey, where you going?"

Meg turned back and, thinking of Ned's admonition,

said, "I told the man who mentioned it that our Ben
Wilton would never have been an oarsman, not even for
the queen, so pray don't mention a thing to him. My
Ben was a traveling player, and a fine, handsome one
too. Good day to you."

When she turned the first corner, she picked up her
skirts and hustled back to the palace.

THE SUN WAS SETTING OVER THE TWISTING THAMES WHEN
Elizabeth climbed the steps of the Round Tower alone,
exhausted from facing down Felicia, and Luke's funeral. She had asked Jenks to examine the tower, from
foundation to lofty parapet, to be certain it was deserted and safe. Then she'd sent him to fetch his Lord
Robert and keep a watch down below so they weren't
disturbed.

Other than Jenks, who was loyal to both her and
Robin, Elizabeth had told no one where she was. Ordinarily Kat or Mary Sidney would have known, but
Kat was sleeping from the concoction Meg had given
her under Mary's supervision. Now though, the mere
thought of Robin's soon joining her poured strength
into her walk and made her heart beat faster.

The queen had circled the high walkway of the tall
tower only twice when Robin appeared before her,
gasping for breath from his quick climb. Twilight
muted his robust complexion and his gold velvet and
forest-green satin garb to make him seem all shim-
mery silver. She felt caught in a trembling trance between daylight and nightfall.

"You see, my queen, you always leave me breathless."

"And you me," she countered, laughing nervously, "but only for your clever quips and puns and wordplay."

"Alas," he said, mock serious, with one hand on his chest as he bowed to her, "I had hoped for more than that backhanded compliment. I would die to hear you say you are left breathless by my love play."

She shook her head but put her arm through his and walked with him on a slow circuit of all they could survey. Yet they looked only at each other. "We must not speak of dying on this sad day," she said. "But as for love play, I hear you have another song for me."

"Did Felicia say so?" he countered, squeezing her wrist firmly against his ribs. "And I hear you are keeping her close confined at Harry's again."

"Does everyone know, then?"

"Do you still believe that anything you do won't be known, remarked on, and spread even abroad?"

Elizabeth noted, as she had before, that whenever Robin did not want to answer a question directly, he simply made his own query. "You said once, my Robin, if we were but common folk, even a country swain and milkmaid, you would love me forever. But things shall never be so simple. Would that we could be fast friends as we are and not have others scandalized."

" 'S blood, we can stand up to them! I wish you could trust me enough to take my advice. To let me become your next Cecil and your only love."

She tugged her arm free and leaned her elbows on a gap in the wall. Tears prickled behind her eyes but she blinked them back, thinking of poor Luke with his desperate blinking message, of how far he and Geoffrey Hammet fell. Thinking of the burden of being queen, loving and longing as a woman but caught in this dim realm between bright surrender and dark self-control. Her mother had held her power only as long as she held her father at bay, for when she gave in to him, her world collapsed like a—a tower of cards.

"What is it, my beloved?" Robin whispered, leaning close but not touching her now.

"I am thinking of my parents. Great Harry, wed to a wife he could not love when the alluring Anne Boleyn became his passion. To have her, he thrust the Catholic church aside, he executed friends who would not back him, and made this once Papist place into the Pope's hell on earth. The king set aside his first wife, but when he wed Anne—and she bore me—things went so bad between them."

"Stop this melancholy train of thought, or you'll make yourself ill," he protested. "Our estate is naught like theirs, though I could set Amy aside, if you'd but give the word."

She pushed away from the wall and him, pacing faster around and around while he hurried to keep up. "That's just it, Robin, I will not give the word and not only because she is ill."

He snagged her elbow to spin her around into his arms. "Let's not talk of Amy then. Let's just talk of us."

"You know, I actually told myself I agreed to meet you here just to find out if you'd seen aught amiss when Luke Morgan fell and to ask you to go to de Quadra again so we may keep an eye on Katherine Grey from that end too."

"Firstly, I did not see Luke fall, I swear it."

"Then I told myself I would be bold enough to demand if you had hired Felicia Dove to spy on me as well as sing your songs to me."

"I—spy on you? Elizabeth, my love, I watch you with my own hungry gaze and ever shall, but no, I have not asked her or anyone to spy on you," he vowed, emphasizing each word and staring deep into her eyes while his hand on her chin made her look at him.

"I believe that, truly. I've just become so obsessed with finding out who's watching me and who is murdering my men and why."

"Murder? You believe so?"

"More and more. I long to close my eyes and have it all go away, to have our happy, carefree summer back again, to have Cecil here, keeping his mouth shut about a foreign marriage, to have Kat recovered— Meg too—and to have . . ."

Somewhere in her recital, she had closed her eyes. He crushed her in his arms and kissed her. His mouth moved against hers, opening her lips, tearing away her defenses. As always she felt his masterful kisses down deep in her belly. She sagged into his strength as he leaned against the outer wall.

Her head spun so that the top of the tower seemed

to tilt at them. She had to stop this madness before she begged for more. Somehow she managed to step away from him. "Whatever that changeling Felicia has done or not done," she plunged on, clearing her throat and shaking out her skirts, "I want to hear the new song. Since she is not here, you must sing it for me."

He grinned rakishly, making her insides flip-flop again. How quickly he'd recovered from a kiss that had shattered her poise. Dusk embraced them, and she could barely see his face clearly when she stepped away. Mayhap they should have brought a lantern, but then all could look up and see the strange light on the tower. No, they were better in this dark that followed twilight.

"Shall I order you to sing it for me, my lord?" she asked.

"I am only thinking you will no doubt also imprison me for my shoddy lyrics and unworthy voice."

"If I ever imprison you, it shall be here in this tower, and I shall come to bring you bread and beer each day."

"You are already my gaoler, my queen. And anything that comes from your hand, my virgin goddess Diana, is pure ambrosia. But since you command this birthday gift early, I am thinking I must find you another for that grand occasion."

"If you can be so glib in mere conversation, I must hear this song and now."

"All right, though it shall suffer from lack of your Dove's lute. Really, you must free her soon, but here it is then.

*At twilight time I climb the stairs.*
*The sky is silvered everywhere.*
*If my foot slips the fall is long,*
*And yet it pulls me on, this song*
*Of lovers' tryst high in the tower,*
*Of union in this glimmering hour.*

"You wrote it for this place and time," she whispered, awed. "You knew I would agree to meet you here. You are a wizard or sorcerer like your friend Dr. Dee."

"I'd like to tell you your future," he said, stepping forward again to press her hands in his. His breath, like sweet cloves, embraced her before the wind tugged the scent away.

"But since you cannot," she said, fighting again for reason over passion, "at least you must interpret that falling apples dream you told me. I thought it was strange that it came just before I fell during the masque, and I wish you had rescued me then."

"I would give my life to do so. . . ."

She pulled away and began to walk again. "Stop saying these life or death things," she insisted. "I know you were vexed that Luke Morgan put his hands on me, and then to have a fantasy of rescuing me when I fell . . ."

He pulled her to him as he had before. He even backed her up against the curve of the outer tower wall. Elizabeth knew she should order him to unhand her, to step away, but she could not.

"I told you, my love, the dream had naught to do with rescue—for it is you who have rescued me. But must you remain as forbidden to me as Eve's apple? I yearn, I love and burn . . ."

He took her lips again, and she was lost. But for a shred of strength she could well have begged him to press her to the floor stones and ravish her body as he had her heart. When at last he released her, her knees were so weak she pressed against his legs to stand. Pulling back, she leaned against a gap in the wall, staring out over her now black kingdom and the vast reaches of her own soul.

"I shall write yet another verse of my song, which begs you to be brave in climbing the twilight tower," he rasped, his mouth close to her ear. "I shall sing that to yield to passion is like flinging yourself from that tower, not to fall but to fly!"

She felt her bones melt but managed to take another step away. "I will think on that, my dearest Robin. But you must recall, I have already tried to fly—and fell."

Elizabeth felt her way around the tower to the dark stairs. Suddenly she felt the fear of being up so high; a strange dizziness assailed her, like Felicia claimed on the walls of Richmond, like herself dangling on wires above the courtyard paving stones. But the queen must never fear the heights. She put her hand against the solid, steadying stone.

"Robin, stay here for a bit before you follow. And, I swear to you, when I am ready to fly—as you want—you will be the first to know."

.  .  .

THE MOMENT ELIZABETH ARRIVED BACK IN HER PRIVY rooms through the tower door, Mary, Kat, and Meg began talking at once. The queen held up her hands to silence them.

"I was simply out for a walk on the parapets with only Jenks along," she said to fend them off. "What is all this jabbering about peering in windows? Or you mean you saw someone outside—on the roof?"

"No," Mary said primly. "Word has come that your clever lutenist has gone out hers."

Elizabeth cursed and sat down hard on the mounting stool for her bed, her head in her hands before she asked in a shaky voice, "Someone threw Felicia out a window at Lord Hunsdon's? And so this dreadful pattern of murders continues, and I nearly blamed her."

"Oh, no, that's not it," Kat put in, her voice still sounding slow from her medicine. "Someone leaned a ladder up to her window despite your cousin downstairs and the guard you had posted on her door. She climbed out and disappeared, for good, I hope. I'm starting to think it must have been she, not Katherine, trying on your clothes at Richmond. Why, however brilliant at the lute, that girl is like a snake that keeps shedding its skin and emerging all new and slimy once again."

The queen clipped out one of her father's favorite oaths. "Mary," she said, "have a messenger send word to Lord Hunsdon that I will be there at first light, and he's not to touch the girl's room nor anything outside the window. I was just coming to fear Felicia was spying on me for someone—and I fear that someone has sprung her like a woodcock from a trap. And tell them to double the guard on the ground and on the roofs of the palace here, these back stairs too. I must find Felicia—or whatever her name truly is—before she finds me again."

"Oh, something else," Mary said, and went to Elizabeth's cosmetic table to fetch a torn piece of parchment. "I'm afraid Lord Hunsdon's already touched something in Felicia's room. He sent you this. Stuck through with the quill she wrote it with, stabbed right to the drapery at the open window she went through."

Elizabeth took the letter with two fingers as if it would burn her. And Felicia had told everyone she could not write. She obviously was not afraid of heights either. Lies upon lies, the queen thought as she read,

> *The simple Dove in open sky*
> *Whom eager hawk with hasty flight*
> *Pursues to death is forced to fly.*
> *Nor sees she safety where to light*
> *But cuts the air to 'scape away*
> *From present peril as she may.*

"*Pursues to death?*" Elizabeth muttered.

"Lord Hunsdon said it's another song she wrote," Kat explained.

Elizabeth closed her eyes and sank back against the side of her bed. "She didn't write it originally," she whispered. "It was penned by my dear friend John Harington, whom I fear may be her father."

* * *

CLOAKED AND HOODED SO AS NOT TO DRAW A CROWD, WITH Ned, Jenks, Gil, and two guards in attendance, Elizabeth went by working barge to Eton just after dawn the next day. The moment Harry greeted her at the side garden gate, he began his recital of events, obviously guilt-ridden his prisoner had escaped.

"It was yet light, Your Grace, so, of course, who would think such a thing could happen?" Harry rattled on. "I had no notion that, three stories up, she would get out that small window, not with your own guard on her door."

"I shall deal with him later. She must have made some noise."

"But how," Harry went on, "did anyone know she was here to rescue her? I gathered only your inner circle knew, and they wouldn't tell."

"Be that as it may, I just hope, cousin, my guard was not nodding off and you were not downstairs drinking overmuch, from your grief about losing Luke, of course."

"Indeed I was not! So—do you have some idea who could have come for her?"

"For all I know," she said, stepping around to the side of the house to look at the deep prints the ladder had made amidst the white hollyhocks under the escape window, "she could have dropped coins to some knave in the street who fetched a ladder for her. But in truth I have no such hope. I fear she was hired by someone to ingratiate herself with me, for what purpose I am not certain—mayhap simple spying if she meant not to harm me when she could. Nor do I know her mentor's identity, who either came or sent someone to filch her to freedom to do more mischief. But her rescuer appears to be a man. See the large, deep bootprints on each side of the ladder marks?" she added, pointing.

"Indeed, a good-sized man in riding boots," Harry observed, squatting down. "Besides, it would probably take a man to heft a tall ladder."

"A well-off or well-paid man, as his boots were not worn at the heels. Gil," she called to her lithe little artist, "draw me those bootsole prints to size while Jenks and Ned go about in this area to see if anyone saw or heard something amiss or has a ladder that would fit these holes."

As Jenks and Ned hurried off, Gil made hand signals to her that said, "In London, leaving prints, she would be caught and put in prison as an angler, just like me and Bett. Do you think she took goods from that house to sell? If Lord Harry has rich things, there are men who'd pay a pretty penny . . ."

"Never mind all that," Elizabeth scolded. "You are no longer a thief, and I'll not have you chattering about it. You just worry about the pretty penny I'll give you for drawing those marks in the ground. And, Gil," she added, her voice softer, "I sent your drawing of the lutenist to my friends at first light, and it was a fine one."

The boy smiled, nodded, and bent to his work.

Elizabeth let Harry escort her into the house, forgoing the cakes and ale he had waiting for her. Leaving her guards downstairs, she climbed the two flights to the small upper-story room where Felicia had been kept last week and last night. She surveyed the small space under the eaves.

"But," Harry was saying now, nearly on her heels in the slant-ceilinged chamber until she motioned for him to stand back in the doorway, "who would fathom she was so devious? You are thinking, are you not, Your Grace, that she might have had something to do with your lutenist Geoffrey's demise to get in your good graces in the first place?"

"And mayhap with poor Luke's death—not his *final* death, *per se*, but with the apparent accident that led to it. Is this where she stuck the note in the drape?" she asked, fingering the slit there. "It was a lyric by John Harington, you see, and I believe the girl was mocking or defying me with it—for all I know, giving me a clue to her real identity. I had earlier accused her of being John's daughter and Isabella's step-daughter, Hester, who ran away from their country home over a year ago."

Harry gasped. Elizabeth looked back at him. "Oh, yes," she said. "And that would mean she has Tudor blood in her veins from her real mother, John's first wife, one of—of my father's bastards. That would make Hester, mayhap alias Felicia, my niece, kin as close as my cousins Katherine Grey, Margaret Douglas, or Mary Stuart. If her mother had not been illegitimate, her claims could be stronger than theirs, for Hester is directly descended from my father, whereas the other claimants are heirs of his sisters."

"But . . ." Harry stammered, "you can't imply that someone like Felicia—Hester—actually believes you should elevate her somehow or name her as your heir."

"I told you I don't have all the answers yet. But I believe it could have been Felicia as easily as Katherine Grey who had access to my rooms. One of them washed in my bathwater, almost as if baptizing or consecrating herself before she went wild and defaced things. The same person had earlier sneaked in, I believe, and worn my clothes, mayhap laid in my bed. I know not which woman, what else, or exactly why. But I will find out. I swear I will!"

With a vengeance, Elizabeth rummaged in the single, small chest in the room, one carved from a tree trunk. The green gown Felicia had worn but yesterday, a smock, grass-stained slippers, and another gown of brown linsey-woolsey were folded inside. The girl had worn more dresses than these, but she must have left in some haste. The queen yanked them out, shook them to see if anything was secreted here, and threw them on the floor.

"Did you ever take the male garb from her, Harry?" she asked.

"Why, no. I simply told her not to wear it again."

"Then we may be looking for a lad and not a lass, damn her. Ha, another paper," she exulted when she saw a single sheet of parchment on the rough bottom of the chest. She picked it up and turned it over. The paper bore a crude drawing of a pointy-chinned, long-nosed woman in a crown with writhing snakes in place of curls and a dreadful frown. Her neck was long and scrawny and looked either crooked—or broken. Perhaps this was a perverted counterpart to Gil's drawing of Felicia, though it was obvious enough who the subject was here. The words under it were from a song Elizabeth had never heard, but obviously meant to be those of an angry, spurned lover. Did Felicia actually love her or hate her? Her skin crawled as she read,

> *Where are your pleasant words, alas?*
> *Where is your faith, your steadfastness?*
> *There is no more but all doth pass,*
> *And I am left all comfortless.*

> *But since so much it doth you grieve*
> *And also me my wretched life.*
> *Having heard my truth shall not relieve*
> *But death alone my very strife.*

Elizabeth jumped and gasped when a shadow fell between her and the window. Gil's head popped up outside as if he had flown from the ground. The queen ran to the sill and peered over. The boy was standing on the next-to-top rung of a ladder while, below, Jenks held it.

"It fits the marks and has soil in it too!" her man called up, grinning triumphantly.

"Seize the one who owns it," she cried, leaning around Gil to see Jenks better.

"A poor old dame, a thatcher's widow down and across the lane," he called up as Ned joined him. "The ladder was hired last night by a small man with a strange way of talking and a flat cap—she doesn't see well. He seemed to be alone and gave her a whole crown for its brief use."

"A strange way of talking?" she called down, still looking with difficulty around Gil, who was holding out his sketch to her. She took it and hauled him toward the window where he scrambled lithely past. "A lisp, Spanish, French, what?" the queen demanded. "Ned, do some voices for her until she can pinpoint something."

They were drawing a crowd from the street and other windows, so Elizabeth pulled back in. "Not good drawing of you," Gil signed to her with flying hands when he glimpsed Felicia's farewell message. Elizabeth was so frustrated she almost cuffed him. But she heard someone coming fast upstairs. Ned appeared in the doorway, shoving past Harry, who kept wringing his hands.

"I already did voices for her," Ned reported as if their conversation had not been momentarily disrupted. "It's my guess the man was just disguising his voice at first so she couldn't identify it later. She thought she heard him talking different—regular, she put it—to a lad he had with him when he brought the ladder back. She can keep the coin, can't she, Your Grace?"

"What? Yes, all right. Did she see them ride off?"

"Like I said, bad eyes, but she thinks it sounded like just one horse."

The girl dare not run home to the Haringtons, Elizabeth reasoned. Besides, she had sent for them forthwith, so they'd soon be on the road to Windsor. Again she glanced at the mocking, mayhap threatening, drawing and the accusatory verse. The other song that had been stuck to the drapery also mentioned escape and death. Did that imply Felicia meant to commit suicide or—if she had been the cause of Geoffrey's death—meant to make it look as if someone else had killed himself? Or did it mean Felicia would kill someone else and escape again?

*Of my desires I weep and sing,*
*In joy and woe, as in a doubtful ease.*
*For my sweet thoughts*
*Sometimes do pleasure bring,*
*But by and by the cause of my disease*
*Gives me a pang that inwardly doth sting,*
*When that I think what grief it is again*
*To live and lack the thing should rid my pain.*

— HENRY HOWARD, *Earl of Surrey*

 SHE HAD BEEN TEMPTED TO WATCH FROM the old, ruined tower because she loved heights. They made her feel that she could soar, and she often dreamed of flying. She loved looking down on everyone else, the way she would when she was queen.

Hidden in the copse of chestnut trees beyond the old, ruined tower at Cumnor House, Felicia Dove also wished she had filched that observation glass from Dr. Dee. She had to keep her distance to avoid being seen by the wrong people. Her back and thighs ached from the ride here and from keeping watch, hunched over, yesterday. This second day her eyes burned from squinting through the sun, waiting for Amy Dudley to appear.

Without even glancing at her fingering, she'd been playing song after song she intended for Lord Robert's wife. The ones by Surrey and Wyatt were especially depressing and distressing, Felicia thought with a tight grin. And every so often, to remind herself how serious this was, Felicia would hum or strum the melody that she'd meant to present at the queen's birthday celebration on this very day.

"This is my offering to you, Your Most Gracious Majesty, Queen of England, Scotland, and Ireland," Felicia declaimed as if she were at court instead of stuck here. "On this special, blessed event of the commencement of your twenty-seventh year, this momentous seventh of September in the year of our Lord, 1560, I offer this song in the first year of a new decade during which will blossom forth your brilliance and your might."

Felicia spit against a tree, wishing it were the queen. That drivel was almost too much to get out. Yet it was the way her sponsor had wanted it. He was powerful and clever and—but for the queen—the best sponsor she could have right now. Last week Lord Robert had told her he had a sumptuous pearl necklace to give the queen at her birthday gathering, for which he'd nearly beggared himself. This song would have been her royal gift, before everything at court fell apart.

"So now," Felicia gritted out through clenched teeth, "curse you on this day of your birth, Elizabeth Tudor, Queen of England, Scotland, and Ireland. For I will curse you indeed with my deeds and soon celebrate your death day too!"

Felicia startled as she saw the woman emerge from

distant Cumnor House who must be, by the description given to her, Amy Dudley. Soberly clad, she had been out once earlier but with a maid, and that would never do. This time, heading around the back of the house toward the tower, she was blessedly alone.

Gripping the fine, new lute her sponsor had bought her, Felicia emerged from the trees, keeping her prey in sight. For a moment she thought she'd somehow lost her behind a low wall. Had she fallen? Everyone knew that Amy was sore ill with a breast tumor, but Felicia had the strictest orders not to be inquiring of her condition from local folk. Besides, her companion on the fast, furtive ride from Windsor and their endless watch yesterday had told her all that she must know.

As Felicia came closer to the low stone fence, she saw for the first time it set off a graveyard. Amy sat on the turf in the midst of small, sunken headstones, her arms wrapped around her knees, humming in a minor key.

That was a good sign, the lutenist thought as she crept closer. If Amy liked music, it would be all the easier to befriend her and convince her to cooperate.

Forcing a smile to her lips, Felicia leaned on the stone wall, the lute cradled in her arms like a babe, and called out, "Pardon, milady. I'm a strolling player—of the lute, not comedy or tragedy, and would play for you."

Like a doe scenting a hunter, Amy looked up and froze. Her dark eyes were smudges in a pinched, chalk-white face. The lady was ill indeed. Then, as her sponsor had said, in the long run, she would really be helping, not harming, Amy.

"I—I brought no coin out with me," Amy said, getting slowly to her feet. "But I would favor a tune and can get you food from the kitchen for it. If you play something, pray make it lively and loud. I keep hearing old Latin church songs in my head."

Though she had escaped Eton in boy's garb, remembering she was a lass again in the plain gown her rescuer had brought with him, Felicia walked around to the gate and went into the cemetery. She kept her distance from the woman, hoping she would not bolt.

*This,* Felicia marveled, was the lusty, suave Robert Dudley's wife? She looked as if a breath could blow her away, so mayhap all of this would be easier than Felicia feared. Anything to bring the queen down, no matter why her sponsor was paying for this masque without a mask. She began to pluck and sing a bouncy, brazen little tune she hoped would work subtly on Amy's heart.

> *No more shall virgins sigh*
> *And say, "We dare not,"*
> *For men are false*
> *And what they do*
> *They care not.*

Amy's thin face broke into a tight smile.

"Do you like it then, milady?" Felicia asked. "'Tis all the fashion at court, I hear, both song *and* sentiment."

"At court? My husband lives at court and promises he shall send me the finest gift from there, fit for a queen. Have you seen the queen?"

Felicia played on to give herself time to digest all that. She should have realized that Lord Robert would send gifts to his wife since he often gave them to the queen. Either men were skilled at keeping women on a leash with courtesies, gifts, and sentiments, or they weren't, and that man was.

"A gift fit for a queen?" Felicia repeated, fitting those words into her new song. "Then I must tell you, I have played at court and have seen your handsome husband there—"

"Oh," Amy said as her face lit. "Then do you know the lutenist Franklin Dove?" While Felicia gaped at her, the woman picked her way closer through the long grass around the turfy mounds. "My lord hired him once to sing a song for the queen, and I wished— prayed—he would do the same for me and come here to sing it himself. He used to sing to me—we'd sing together." Her voice trailed off and she looked away, frowning and tilting her head as if listening to something.

Felicia fought to keep from cheering at the perfect opening she'd been given. "Yes, I'm Franklin Dove's sister Felicia, whom he himself taught to play the lute," she said, throwing all caution to the winds. She had been told to use an alias and a far different tale, but this was too good to be true. Young Moneybags, whom her sponsor had sent to guide her here, would

have to admit it when she joined him at their forest en-
campment again this evening.

"Indeed *I am*," she said, beginning to play again,
"not only Felicia Dove but the gift fit for a queen Lord
Robert had promised you. I've defied Her Majesty by
playing in disguise with my brother at court, and so I
beg you not to tell the others in the manor house that
I'm here. I will come each day to meet you privily but
will not go into the house."

Amy grasped her hands together. Her eyes, once
flat and dull as gray stones, now shone. "It's the best
gift he could have given me and just like him to have
the lutenist be a woman and not a man, so I would
know to trust you. And if you're out of favor with the
queen, you are especially in favor with Lady Dudley of
Cumnor. You know, Robert used to be so jealous of
me at first. But I thought I'd truly lost him to the
queen."

Felicia kept playing. She didn't want to press her
fine fortune, but she needed to get Amy off by herself,
as soon as possible, down by the stream perhaps or for
a walk along that ravine with all the protruding tree
roots. Still, it would be so much better if this could
happen in a common place and not in one Amy seldom went.

"Play that first song again, Felicia Dove," Amy
commanded quietly with a sweep of her hand, but the
lutenist saw her flinch at some inward pain. She hardened her heart for what she must do.

"Sing with me then, but let's stroll a ways farther

from the house. I believe your beloved Robert would be in trouble with the queen if she knew he sent me, and someone in your household might tell."

"I'll keep your secret, but all right then," Amy said, stretching her strides as she led Felicia out through the cemetery gate. "Let's both sing as loud as we can to drown out other voices."

ELIZABETH COULD HAVE CRIED AS SHE WELCOMED HER OLD friends John and Isabella Harington back to court from twenty months in exile. Their eyes, too, glittered with unshed tears, and it wasn't until Bella rose from her deep curtsy that the queen saw their enforced time in the countryside had given them a great gift, even if they had perchance lost Hester now.

"Bella, dearest," Elizabeth cried. "You are . . . finally, a baby?"

"Is it so obvious already, then?" Bella asked as John beamed. "You know, Your Grace, how desperately I— we—have longed for our own child. But what is the word on my lord's Hester? We don't believe we passed her on the road, not that she'd come home to Kelston, especially after all your messenger told us. We nearly feared you would banish us again for rearing such a child."

"No, no, I would never punish parents for a way-ward child," the queen protested as she hugged Bella and John kissed her on each cheek. "Especially those who served me so well before I was queen, even in the bad times."

"We are grateful to be back for this special day of your birth celebration," Bella added.

"Bless you both for not forgetting," Elizabeth told them, pressing their hands between hers. "Twenty-seven, a lofty age for an unwed queen, some say, but we shall see. You both, of course, will attend the banquet and dancing tonight, though you must see Bella takes to her bed early, my lord."

"Anything you say, Your Grace."

"John, you have always been loyal to those you served, and I have missed you both," the queen declared. "Especially now, I have need of loyal friends."

The Haringtons exchanged unspoken looks that somehow said so much. Elizabeth felt that strange yearning for her own love again. Well, she'd see Robin tonight and pray God he never failed her as these usually loyal people had. Yet the Haringtons had gone to the Tower with Elizabeth when her sister imprisoned her there, and if John had not defied her and lied to her the month she was crowned, they would never have been apart in the first place, sent to their rural home at Kelston near Bath. But all that was over now.

"I deeply regret," Elizabeth told them as they walked together into the royal withdrawing room, "that I had to bring you back to such unsettling news. Once I saw the lutenist was a lass, I should have known she was Hester, but she kept changing her name, her appearance, her sex. . . ." She smacked her hands on her huge skirts. "You did tell her who she is?" she asked them both. "Her heritage—descended from the king, my father, I mean."

"Her mother told her early and often," John admitted. "Knowing Audrey, she probably embellished each detail about the court and her Tudor ties."

"Ties," the queen whispered. "Yes, ties, all right."

"Hester is a brilliant girl," Bella put in, "like her father, skilled in the arts. But even when she was young, she seemed to tread the edge of reality at times."

"Made up fantastical plays and stories, all with music, and wrote them down," John explained, gesturing broadly. "In most of her elaborate musical dramas," he went on, "she became noble or royal—harmless head-in-the-clouds sort of things."

Elizabeth nearly stumbled. Not harmless, perhaps, if one felt thwarted *and* had that treacherous trace of Tudor blood rampaging through one's veins. Elizabeth herself had chafed for years in exile, but she'd had hope for her future; Felicia—Hester—mayhap raged from adoration of and abhorrence for the Tudor queen. *The seething passion held within, I cannot fathom,* Harry had said of Felicia when he first heard her play. The depths of both love and hate she must feel for her aunt, Elizabeth of England, could be staggering.

"Bella couldn't convince or constrain Hester to take up needlework and the womanly arts," John Harington's words rolled on. "But her music—the girl was obsessed with her music."

Elizabeth indicated they should sit and partake of the wine and their favorite dishes she had had prepared for them. "Always good mixed with ill," the queen tried to comfort them, however distressed she felt at what they'd said. "Joy with sadness, hard times with prosperity."

"Your Majesty," John said, clearing his throat, "though I have failed you in the past, I would die to protect your reputation here and anywhere."

Elizabeth stayed her goblet halfway to her mouth. "Why do you stress my reputation now, my lord?"

Bella shifted in her seat. The months away had made this tall, big-boned companion of Elizabeth's youth seem to grow in the queen's mind, and not just because she was showing a belly now. Bella was beautiful, yet athletic and determined as an Amazon. And John looked, as ever, stalwart but a bit willful, with his slightly unruly mustache and beard. That and the single gold hoop in his left ear gave him the air of a brigand, but his eyes were steady and his mouth firm. The queen fought not to see Felicia's face when she gazed upon him now.

"Your Grace," Bella spoke up, turning her goblet around in her hands without drinking, "even in the countryside, your subjects say the wildest things about court doings. I'm sure it is exaggerated, but . . ."

Bella glanced at John as if for support. He nodded.

"Your Majesty," Bella plunged on, "we mean not to be harbingers of bad news when we are so glad to be back with you, but the likes of cowherds and carters say you will marry Robert Dudley one way or the other."

The queen cracked her goblet on the table, slopping crimson claret. She banged her other fist down too, and things rattled a second time. "Then the likes of cowherds and carters—courtiers and foreign queens—are much mistaken! 'S blood and bones, I cannot wed with Robert Dudley because he is already wed, and that is that. And the next person who says different shall spend time in Windsor's old dungeon under the Round Tower! Now drink and eat," she muttered, sliding the sweetmeat dish over the blood-red stain she'd made on the table carpet.

AMY HAD BEEN TOO TIRED EARLIER TO GO FOR MUCH OF A walk with Robert's lutenist. But after dark, when Mrs. Pirto was sleeping sitting upright in her chair, she sneaked out to meet the musician again. It was all so delicious and forbidden, Amy thought with a little shudder. It reminded her of when she and Robert used to meet for trysts when he first courted her.

She didn't like it, though, that Felicia refused to come into the house, so at supper that evening she had cleverly solved the problem. She couldn't wait to tell Felicia, who said she was staying at an Oxford inn but wouldn't say which one. She feared the queen would track her there and be angry she was singing Robert's songs for Amy.

"Oh, there you are," Amy called out as she followed the muted lute music around the far side of the tower. "Good news! Besides this apple tart I brought you, I mean," she said, and extended it to the girl. "You know, I worry about you being out in the dark, not that there's been any trouble with ruffians or such.

Robert should have sent Fletcher or one of his men with you."

"I'm quite all right, and dedicated only to making you feel better in all ways," Felicia said, and sang,

> The smoky sighs, the bitter tears,
> That I in vain have wasted,
> The broken sleep, the woe and fears,
> That long in me have lasted,
> Will be my death, all by thy guilt,
> And not by my deserving,
> Since so inconstantly thou wilt
> Not love, but still be swerving.

"Oh—did Robert write me that—send me that?" Amy asked, her voice shaken. "But it's so sad, and I thought he meant to cheer me."

"He sends it to apologize for any possible grief he has caused you," Felicia said, pleased she'd planted the seed. "He admits guilt for staying away. . . ."

"But it speaks of death and I . . . like not to think on that—though I do sometimes."

"Do you? Then no more of that song. Off with the head of whomever wrote it, though I truly think the more melancholy songs are the best sometimes, the most truthful."

"I—yes, I suppose. But what I wanted to tell you is that I've talked nearly everyone in the house but an old woman, who sleeps away the afternoons, into going to the fair in Abingdon on the morrow, and I shall stay here and you shall sing me songs all day. Then I can feed you and reward you, for I mislike a musician of the queen—especially one who is defying her—staying in an inn. So we shall have a special day to remember."

"Yes, a special day, as you say."

Amy patted her hand even while she was playing a lively ballad and hurried back toward the house.


"YOU LOOK BEAUTIFUL, JUST RADIANT, DESPITE ALL THESE other wretched goings on," Kat told the queen as her ladies bedecked her for her birthday banquet and dancing. Still, even left-handed, Kat kept fussing with the little details of curls and lace ruff and the way her scented pomander hung. The women, without Katherine Grey, whom the queen had banished to her room, oohed and aahed. As Mary Sidney held a mirror for her, the queen straightened the huge strand of pearls Robin had given her an hour ago. They were big as chickpeas and the double strand looped to her waist. She'd partly pinned them to her with a big brooch so they wouldn't bounce right off her shoulders during the dancing.

A knock sounded on the door, and Kat answered it even as the queen's women swept out to complete their own last-minute preparations. When the swish of skirts and chatter quieted, Elizabeth could hear Kat whispering.

"Who is it, Kat?" she called, fully expecting that Robin had come calling a bit early to escort her.

Kat bustled back in. "Two things, Your Grace," she began. "One, Katherine Grey is insisting she be allowed to attend the banquet."

"She will not. What else?"

"You realize she's got everyone saying the queen will permanently imprison her next, just as you did Felicia Dove, only this time in the deepest, darkest dungeon of the realm for her affinity of blood to you."

"How dare she! I am trying to save her from that by teaching her a lesson now, though, God knows, she deserves exactly that or worse!"

"Yes, Your Grace. I just wanted to add that Katherine Grey seems to have known that Felicia was sprung from her prison nearly as soon as it happened."

The queen arched her penciled brows. "Did she? Then, as much as I mislike dealing with her, she needs to be questioned again, but not today, not this special night. She and Felicia and their ilk shall not ruin this night!"

But as Robin escorted her toward the great hall a few minutes later, the queen noted Ned Topside standing at the top of the staircase where he shouldn't be, waving his hand and gesturing toward the musicians' gallery. If the knave was just going to tell her that the lack of Felicia would make the music sound shallow until she was replaced, she already knew that.

"Wait, Robin," the queen said, halting at the top of the stairs, though all those below looked up and a hush held the crowded room. "Ned Topside," she said, keeping her voice down as she turned her back on the others, "this had better be good."

"It's bad, but best you know now," he told her, somber-faced. "A note was delivered by a town boy to your chief lutenist—chief, now that Felicia's flown."

"A note from her?" Elizabeth whispered. When he nodded, she ordered, "Then trace that boy, find out where he got the note. Find *her*!"

"Jenks and I are already working on that, though it may be a dead end."

"I want no dead ends. And the note?"

He pressed it into her hand, all folded up. "At least your lutenist in the gallery could tell it was a song he should *not* sing, not today or ever. And now, Your Gracious Majesty," Ned said, his actor's voice booming, "your musicians and players wish you the bounty of this day and look forward to entertaining you before the dancing!"

In his best bombastic style, Ned swept his arm and graceful body into a low bow. Elizabeth descended the staircase, treading carefully in her long skirts, holding tight to Robin's steady arm. The applause was deafening and the smiles and blinking gems in lantern- and candlelight quite blinding. Surely she could put all the pain of Felicia Dove away for this one evening, Elizabeth tried to tell herself. But the note burned a hole in her hand and she opened it behind the banquet table on the dais to read it.

> *To men that know you not*
> *You may appear to be*
> *Full clear and without spot*
> *But truly unto me*

*Such is your wonted kind*
*By proof so surely known*
*As I will not be blind*
*My eyes shall be my own.*

*And so by sight I shall*
*Suffice myself as well*
*As though I felt the fall*
*Which they did feel that fell.*

The poem or song lyrics were attributed to Sir Edmund Knevet, but the queen knew he'd been gone for several years, dead by his own hand. But none of that mattered. This was utmost defiance thrown in her face, a fierce admission of guilt but also a challenge. More than that, it threatened that she was yet being watched and hinted that there were more falls to come. Whether from a tower or from a throne mattered not at all. However much grief it would cause the Haringtons, Felicia Dove—Hester Harington—must be found and stopped before she lived another day to do more destruction.

"LADY DUDLEY," AMY HEARD ROBERT'S STEWARD, ANTHONY Forster, calling up the staircase as the last of the inhabitants of Cumnor House—but for the Widow Owens, who was staying in her rooms—departed for the fair, "his lordship has sent a gift for you!"

Amy hurried into the hallway and down the top flight of shallow stairs to the landing above the lower flight. "Another gift for me?" she gasped, looking down at him.

"Allow me to bring it to you," he said, and hurried up the stairs. "I didn't want to startle you by just appearing, since we and the old lady are the only ones left in the house."

"But who brought it?"

"His favorite man, Fletcher, my lady, who said he had to head direct back to court. I suppose there is a note with it, but you know how they say good things come in small packages."

"Yes, I've heard that."

As he extended the small leather satchel to her, he added, "It was kind of you, my lady, to insist everyone, even the servants, go for the day. Have a care then," he said, nodding with a half bow. He hurried down the stairs and went out the front door.

Amy stood listening a moment until he rode away, then hurried into her chamber to signal Felicia from the window, waving the fringed shawl Robert had brought her on his last brief visit. It was most unusual for Fletcher not to stay the night, but whatever was this second gift?

She pulled a flat, blue, crushed-velvet box from the satchel and opened it with trembling hands. It was lined with white satin. A short, single string of fat pearls, so fine. And with it a note that said, "As promised . . . a gift fit for a queen. R."

But, Amy thought, if the pearls were that gift, what of the lutenist? She heard her come in the front door downstairs, as Amy had bid, and then a stair creaked. Lute music came closer.

It mattered not, Amy decided, that there was a bounty of gifts from Robert. That was good, not bad.

She hurried down the landing and looked over as Felicia came up strumming and smiling. "Look at the other gift my lord sent me," Amy cried, and reached up to fasten them, despite the ache of pain that spread through her breast and arm again.

"How generous he is!" Felicia declared, and leaned the lute carefully against the banister. "Let me help you."

Eyes shining, Amy turned her back and let the other woman fasten them around her neck. She thought the lutenist hesitated for one moment but she must have simply been fumbling with the clasp. And then the weight of pearls fell against her slender throat and neck, so heavy and so huge.

# Chapter the Thirteenth

"COME THEN, MY LORD CECIL—MINE, NOT the queen's anymore," Mildred called to her husband, gesturing for him to join her at the shuttlecock net their children had just deserted for a game of noisy bowling-on-the-green across the hedge. Sitting in the shade where he looked up from his book, Cecil saw his wife stood in full sunlight, hands on hips, as if daring him not to obey. He'd been reading the same paragraph repeatedly anyway, without retaining one thing, so he got up from the bench.

"I haven't played such in years," he protested. His mental inactivity and lack of purpose, even when he kept busy with the family, was driving him to distraction, and maybe Mildred too. He removed his jerkin to play in his shirt. Trying to appear in a good mood when he was not—for this woman could ferret out secrets better than a master torturer in the Tower—he picked up the wooden battledore and playfully smacked her across the back of her skirts.

She laughed and shoved her sleeves up to her elbows as he took his place across the net. He had to smile. What would he ever do without Mildred? But then, in truth, what would he ever do without Elizabeth? He had not sent her his formal resignation yet, but neither did she summon him to court, so she must be furious with him. She was closer to Robert Dudley than ever, closeted with him at all hours while her kingdom seethed with rumor. If only he could treat the volatile, spoiled queen like a father would and pound some sense into her.

"Not so hard, Will!" Mildred chided when he smacked the little cork-and-feather shuttlecock far over her head. He tried to settle down, concentrating on hitting it back to her, but he soon sailed it wayward again.

"Your mind is elsewhere, and I know where," she declared, plucking it out of the hedge and hitting it back. "Mired in the depths of despair, that's where you are."

"I can't help it," he countered with a whack of the paddle. "More than my shuttlecock game will go to perdition if Dudley helps Her Grace rule this realm. I fear he already rules her heart and there are so few ways of"—he smacked it again—"reversing that."

"But there are ways?" she asked as a coil of hair bounced loose from under her big-brimmed hat. "And if so, you are desperate enough to try them."

"Don't read in overmuch. Though I admit that if

Lord Robert thinks he's in paradise now, I'd much rather see him in that great paradise beyond, one way or the other."

"Will, the servants might hear," she protested, and let the shuttlecock nose into the grass. She came to the net and plucked nervously at it. "The careful, cautious lawyer and counselor I wed seems sometimes dangerously foolhardy lately. My love, if what you just shouted was overheard, someone might construe that you had a plot afoot to dispatch Lord Robert to that very place."

"Ridiculous," he declared, approaching the net, "however tempting. No, he may hang himself if given enough rope. The problem is, he is stringing up Her Grace too, and I cannot bear to let that happen. Yesterday was her birthday, and for the first time since the throne was hers, I was not with her. . . ."

"And de Quadra?" Mildred asked, obviously refusing to allow his own foolish sentiments, so unlike him, to pull him down. "You mentioned he needed watching. Do you think he's doing more than setting up a plan to elevate Katherine Grey if the queen stumbles?"

"The queen has already stumbled, and I fear a great fall."

"Like Humpty Dumpty? *And all the king's horses and all the king's men* . . . But do you think de Quadra would try to harm Dudley or the queen? Mayhap not a direct assassination attempt, but something else, something subtle? There would certainly be no one else to strike at to separate the two of them or to bring her down."

"There is one . . ." Cecil muttered, frowning and hitting the paddle against his thigh in a regular beat that reminded him of one of Felicia's songs.

"Who?" Mildred prompted when his voice drifted off.

As astute as she was, she—and therefore most people—did not see that subtle way out of this damned dilemma, Cecil mused. De Quadra no doubt did, for he knew all the angles. As for Dudley himself, he'd probably not see beyond how it would free him, for the man was the shortsighted type, one who had trouble looking past his own desires and advancements. He might mistake temporary deliverance for ultimate victory.

"My lord, you are woolgathering again," Mildred's sweet voice broke into his agonizings.

"Suffice it to say, God only knows what de Quadra's really thinking or doing," he muttered, turning away so she wouldn't read his face.

"And the same with my beloved William Cecil," he heard her say with a sigh. "God only knows . . ."

Whatever else she said was drowned by the children screeching across the hedge about whose turn came next at bowls.

"*SUCH A GRIEVOUS PITY YOU LIVE HERE WITHOUT YOUR LORD,*" Felicia sang to Amy. "*You, not she, should be loved and adored.*"

Her feet on a padded stool, leaning back in the cushioned chair while Amy slumped in hers across the table, Felicia took another swig of wine and bite of apple before she went back to singing. Amy had ceased crying, ceased protesting that Robert could not have meant all these sad, cruel songs for her. She now just stared into space, though she had stuck her fruit knife into the wooden tabletop in her frustration. It was a pretty, sharp little knife with an inlaid handle, but Felicia really thought she'd best stick to her original plans. Amy seemed not so much afraid now as somehow resigned.

"I told you before, milady, your Lord Robert regrets some of what he's done. Not enough to change his ways or come back again, though he'll no doubt try to ease his conscience with gifts like pearls and notes—and these songs. But I do know how you feel," she said, and sang,

> My thoughts hold mortal strife:
> I do detest my life,
> And with lamenting cries,
> Peace to my soul to bring.

"Did *she* send you, and not my lord?" Amy asked, as if emerging from a fog again. Felicia had thought about drugging her, maybe with her own medicine, but she felt she wouldn't have to now.

"What does it really matter who sent me?" Felicia asked, just picking out the sad tune now. "They both want the same thing—each other—and you alone have the power to stop that."

"Stop that? I?" Amy said, sitting up straighter.

"Haven't you been hinting just the opposite? I am ill and cannot abide the court. Did someone who hates them pay you to take me to court to stop or shame them? But—who sent you then?"

"Someone rich and powerful, but it doesn't really matter. It might as well have been Robert—maybe it was Robert. Only your ability to fight back matters. No, I have not come to take you back to court. There is a better way, a supreme gesture of defiance you can make. Why, if something happened to you, something suspicious, everyone would blame them, and could the queen then ever follow her heart's desire at the expense of her honor? It would forever ruin them and his plans to rule with her as counselor or consort. And, of course, solve your problems too."

"So you cannot come from him," Amy reasoned aloud, getting to her feet. "He did not mean those cruel songs for me. Are you here to abduct me and blame them for it?" she cried. She didn't flee as Felicia suddenly feared, but put both hands on the table to steady herself.

Felicia knew the woman had drunk far too much wine after she'd said the doctor had told her not to when she took her medicine. Mayhap Amy really knew what was coming, what had to be done, and would cooperate. It must be done cleanly, cleverly, with no scuffle, and time was flying. Someone could get ill at the fair and return early. The old widow down the hall could awaken or emerge from her chamber.

Felicia stood and washed her pewter mug in the

water from the ewer. She shoved her chair back under the table and wiped her plate before putting it and the mug back on the sideboard from which she'd seen Amy take it.

"Whatever are you doing?" Amy cried. "Are you leaving?"

"I must and so must you, but you know that," Felicia said, trying to keep her hands and voice steady. "You do realize you can strike at them here and now, don't you, that you needn't go to court or be abducted? You can save them from their sin if you want to look at it that way—or you can save yourself from coming pain and lingering, lonely death from your illness."

Amy gaped at her, then nodded. The girl might be as dull as the queen was sharp, but Felicia thought Amy understood what she meant at last. But had that look meant mere knowledge, or acceptance and agreement too?

"Let me close with the most recent song Robert wrote for his love, the queen—at least a few lines," Felicia said, not making a move to take up the lute again as she sang,

> If my foot slips the fall is long
> And yet it pulls me on, this song
> Of lovers' tryst high in the tower,
> Of union in this glimmering hour.

"But really, Amy, I know he wrote that song for you," Felicia went on, her voice soft and calm. "It's called 'At Twilight Time, I Climb the Stairs.' "

"I have thought of throwing myself off the tower out back. It's all ruined. The steps are dangerous. And I've heard their song there."

Felicia frowned but didn't ask whose song. "Would you like to ruin *them*, but just can't find the strength anymore, Amy?" she asked.

"I have loved him long and love him still," she whispered, then choked back a sob. "Any woman would—love Robert."

"Then do it to save him from her. If the queen of England weds him, either with you put away or gone for good, will it not ruin her as it has you?"

"I don't know, don't know anything anymore," Amy said, pressing her hands to her face. Her voice came muffled. "Your songs and mind are too twisted for me. I am so weary. Should I walk to the tower out back?" she whispered, dropping her hands as her eyes darted around the room. She cocked her head and seemed to be listening again, to someone or something else.

A pox on the people of this house if they came back early and ruined everything, Felicia thought. No more stalling. This must be done now.

"I must leave," she told Amy. "Will you not walk me to the downstairs door?"

"Yes, we must be going," Amy agreed, her countenance suddenly so white she seemed a wraith or ghost.

Felicia began to shake. Amy, like poor Hester Harington, had simply had her life ruined by those she loved. But it was the queen's fall—the queen's coming death—that this was all about now.

They went together down the first flight of stairs to the landing. There, at the top of the lower staircase, unfortunately, Amy turned back and looked Felicia full in the face. "But you've left your lute behind," she said.

"I'll go right back to get it. Oh, look," she added quickly, desperate to have the wretched woman glance away, "they must be coming home already."

"Back from the fair and singing. Is that what I hear?" Amy murmured, tipping her head. She stooped slightly as if trying to glimpse the front door. Felicia glanced up at the banister running along the hallway above to be sure the old woman had not emerged from her chamber. She strained her ears to be sure she heard no sound. Then she slid one leg in front of Amy's ankles and shoved her shoulders hard. The slender woman did an almost perfect cartwheel forward, striking her head on one of the stairs, then tumbling the rest of the way down. She landed almost daintily, as if she'd floated. She lay blessedly still, sprawled at the bottom, face to the floor, one arm flung out.

Felicia ran back into the room, seized her lute, and looked around. It seemed that only one woman had been here, eaten here, but she did take Amy's fruit knife and stick it up her sleeve.

She ran down the stairs and knelt beside the woman. Her head lay at a strange—a wrong—angle. Felicia pictured again the drawing she had done to mock the queen with a crooked, scrawny neck. Amy had not made a sound and seemed not to breathe. Was it so easy to embrace death? Felicia wanted great violence and tumult when the queen and kinswoman who had betrayed her died.

She sucked in a sob as she listened and looked longer for movement, for she'd been told to be sure the deed was done right. Nothing, no motion, no sound. She smoothed Amy's skirts down over her legs and straightened her cap, which had pulled awry.

Felicia Dove stepped outside and carefully closed the front door behind her. Such thick clouds had sprung up in midday that it almost seemed like twilight. She walked around the cemetery and tower to the thicket where Fletcher held his horse. She fixed her eyes on it, not him, staring at his mount's unique, nearly striped mane.

"Deed done?" Fletcher asked.

She only nodded before he pulled her up behind him.

"Then let's rub out the camp and be on our way. Don't want to talk about it but to him, eh?" he prodded.

She still could not speak of it. And she certainly wasn't warning this man who must be next so that she could get to the one who had the farthest to fall.

THE BLUE VELVET, ERMINE-LINED ROBES WORN FOR THE annual Order of the Garter ceremony at Windsor felt heavy on the queen's slender shoulders. They made her feel she bore a great burden and would stumble at any moment.

"No doubt these robes were made for men," she complained to Robin, noting how fine he looked in his.

"I'll tell you one thing about King Edward III, who began this nearly six centuries ago. He thought he had to have these designed for men in full battle armor."

"So was the throne made for men, my queen, but you carry everything off perfectly," he assured her as they led the procession of new garter knights from St. George's Chapel across the middle ward to the royal apartments.

Elizabeth nodded and waved to courtiers and townsfolk alike lining the castle walkways to catch a glimpse of their queen. But, if truth were told, she admitted to herself, sometimes she didn't feel she was carrying anything off perfectly. No one had located Hester Harington, and without Cecil, paperwork was likely to bury her. Kat and Meg were ailing and that wore on her. The continued wild rumors about herself and Robin were a burden too, and she could no longer laugh them off or ignore them. How she would like to simply escape from all this, even if for a moment.

"We have a good two hours before the banquet begins, I believe, Sir Garter Knight and Lord Lieutenant of Windsor Castle," she addressed Robin. "Come cheer me then, and we'll give the others some time to themselves."

He seemed to glow as he escorted her into her withdrawing room and closed the door behind them, even on Kat Ashley. "Allow me, my queen," he said, and unhooked and lifted the heavy robe from her, placing its ermine side up on the big pile of bolsters before the broad oriel window where her ladies often sat. The sun slanted in to nearly blind them as he added his own pristine-hued robe to hers.

"A fur-lined nest for us to rest," he said, and gently pulled her down to sit beside him.

"For a moment I thought you would break into song," she said, leaning luxuriously back on her elbows despite the crush of her golden gown. She heaved a huge sigh and flopped all the way back, half closing her heavy-lidded eyes in the splash of sun.

"You haven't hired another lutenist," he observed matter-of-factly.

"I don't have the heart until that girl is found and stopped."

He leaned closer on one elbow, hovering over her, shading her so she could see him without squinting. "Despite what she's done—or may have done," he whispered, "you have a soft spot for her."

"Do I? Not if she's deadly dangerous."

"But I am here to protect you, so let's not think of anything unpleasant," he whispered, his gaze slowly sliding down then up her tight bodice.

At that mere look, the familiar flutters low in her belly began. She had intended to tell Robin he must go to London to seek intelligence about de Quadra's plans for Katherine Grey. While there, he could deliver her ultimatum to Cecil to return at once and do his duty or be shamefully dismissed. But suddenly she could not ruin this precious moment with either of those pressing issues.

"Elizabeth, let's only think of us," he pleaded as if he'd read her mind.

"Of us? Is there really an us, Robin?"

"If it were up to me, that would be all there is. Us together riding, us at table—for breakfast, supper—and the council table. And us in bed at night, all night."

"Then would you be my master?"

"Never of your spirit and mind, but only your body and heart." He looked and sounded so impassioned. His hand caressed her waist, and he kissed her hotly until the whole room spun. "Let them all go to hell who would stop us," he breathed against her throat as he trailed wet kisses there, lower and lower down her flesh above her square-cut bodice. "Let them heed the Garter motto, *'Honi soit qui mal y pense.'* "

*Evil to him who evil thinks.* The translation danced through Elizabeth's thoughts, though they were getting slower. Something so tight inside her began to uncoil, to yearn to surrender to this man alone.

Somehow Robin dared to ruffle up her petticoat hems, but she did not protest. He squeezed her ankle and heavily, slowly, slid his free hand higher. She thought to trap his intruding touch but she only sighed.

"As a Knight of the Garter, may I not claim at least one of your garters?" he murmured, nibbling her lower lip. "It was a lady's garter that began the order—it should have been disorder of the garter—hundreds of years ago. I would sue for the right to touch and take this one."

She felt him untie the silken ribbon above her knee, then the one above that. When her stocking loosed, he skimmed it down past her knee to bare her thigh. She could feel his calloused thumb against her flesh, stroking her, stroking. Picturing his hands on her, she moaned and reached to embrace his neck and pull him down hard to her.

"Sit up and let me unlace your bodice," he whispered hotly, but she held on tight. Her pulse began to pound, screaming at her to pull him even closer, to surrender at last and become his alone.

"Who in hellfire is that?" Robin muttered, going stone still just above her.

Elizabeth's senses surfaced from a deep, swirling pool. Someone was pounding on the door, shouting too.

"We must answer," she said, and tried to push him off. He didn't budge at first, then sat up to let her rearrange her petticoats.

"Send them away," he hissed.

"It's Harry, much distraught. Open the door."

Yes, it was her cousin's voice, she realized as she tried to stand, only to have her stocking cascade to her ankle. Her heart fell to her feet too. Harry sounded desperate, but then mayhap they had found Hester. If anything had happened to Kat again . . .

Elizabeth stood her ground before the window as Robin straightened himself and walked across the room to open the door.

"What news, Harry?" she asked, her voice far too shrill.

"For Lord Robert—a messenger named Bowes from Cumnor, sent by his lordship's steward, Forster," he said, and stepped aside to let a mud-spattered man step into the queen's privy rooms.

"Your lady wife, Lord Robert," Bowes, a ruddy man, choked out from where he stood. "She's dead of a fall down the manor house stairs."

"Amy?" Robert said, as if he had many wives. He staggered two steps back and leaned against the table near the door. "But how—just fell? And dead?"

Elizabeth took the blow of all that meant. People would say . . . they would believe the worst. . . . They would accuse not only Robin but her too of Amy's death.

Bowes was rattling off a disjointed story of Amy mysteriously sending everyone to a town fair, of being nearly alone in the house, of taking a tumble down stairs she'd walked a hundred times. Her neck was broken but her skirts and cap were not even slightly mussed.

Robin recovered enough to ask Bowes to wait outside with Harry. Elizabeth stood facing him across the table and the width of sunny room that might as well now be the span of the western ocean.

"They will s-say vile things of me—unt-true things," the usually glib man stammered, his big frame trembling. "I have m-many enemies and—"

The queen held up her hand. "You must leave me now."

"Leave you? Do not desert me, my love! I admit I wanted it to happen—at least for her to be gone so that—"

"Wanted *what* to happen?" Elizabeth cracked out,

stepping forward and seizing the back of a chair to keep herself upright. "What did happen to her? Mere happenstance? I reckon suicide a possibility, but they will say we and not her disease drove her to it. Or worst of all, folks will claim foul murder and where will we—I—be then?"

Her words raced, her mind too, but she said again, "Robin, you must leave me."

"I—where will I go?"

"To your house at Kew, nearby but under restraint."

"Under restraint? They will say I am under arrest! If you send me away, they will say you think I am guilty."

" 'S blood and bones, I will say that they know anyone suspected of a crime must be removed from the presence of the sovereign. And—they will say what they will, but we must weather it out."

"But I was not there! I could not have done it."

"You? *You*? What of me now? I see I am not like my father to do as he wishes with lovers and face down all the world. Besides, rumors will fly that we hired someone to do the deed." She panicked even more when she realized Robin would run to her and, if he touched her, she might be lost again.

"Harry!" she shouted.

Her cousin burst in the door as if he'd had his ear to the keyhole. "Your Grace."

She looked only at him, not into Robin's wild eyes again. "Escort my Lord Dudley to his house at Kew and stay with him while he writes to his wife's family.

Not only condolences but a demand for a full coroner's inquest—that a jury must be called to look into this dreadful occurrence completely and truthfully."

"Yes," Robin said. He raised his voice as if the commands were his to give when she was telling him what he must do. "One of her half brothers is a magistrate and another, John Appleyard, has been High Sheriff of Norfolk and Suffolk. Her brother Arthur Robsart could also attend."

"Go now, Robin," the queen said, relieved he seemed to be thinking as well as reacting now. Her face felt as hard and cold as marble, but marble that would crack and shatter. Behind Harry and the messenger Bowes, courtiers crowded into the outer room.

"Do not desert me to the wolves, my queen," he begged, merely mouthing his words now the way Gil sometimes did. With a quick turn, holding his shoulders back and his head erect, he followed Harry out through the crowd.

Elizabeth locked her knees and continued to stand as Kat and her ladies hurried in. Everyone began to talk at once around her, and she heard nothing. Had her good sense deserted her that she had loved Robin so blindly? They would all whisper he had hired his wife murdered, perhaps that the queen of England had led him to it or herself sent someone to dispatch Amy.

"Lovey," Kat's voice finally pierced her darting thoughts, "won't you come sit, at least, or lie down? What can we do for you?"

"Send for Cecil," she said, her voice cold and

clipped. "A dreadful deed may have been done to a lady of my realm, and I must see to it as I do to all court and country business."

She turned slowly, regally, and walked toward her bedchamber as fierce tears burned her eyes. The enormity of this loss loomed before her like a dark hole she could fall down and down. A fall. Amy Dudley had *fallen* under mysterious circumstances, as had Geoffrey and Luke. And Hester Harington was missing.

She made it into her room before she finally tripped on her loosed stocking.

# Chapter the Fourteenth

*O cruel prison how could betide, alas,*
*As proud Windsor where I in lust and love . . .*
*Where each sweet place returns a taste full sour,*
*The large green courts where we were wont to love,*
*With eyes cast up into the Tower . . .*

— HENRY HOWARD, *Earl of Surrey*

"GET UP, GIRL," ELIZABETH ORDERED, AND pulled the bedclothes off Meg Milligrew the next morning. "Ill or not, your queen has need of you."

Who was ill or not? Meg's muddled mind wondered as she struggled to throw off sleep and clear her head. Oh, that's right—she'd been claiming she was puking. The mere thought of Ben Wilton being on the grounds and in town made her sick to her stomach. But the queen had sent his barge to fetch Cecil, so she'd snatched a few good hours of sleep last night.

The queen! Here in this room.

"What is needful, Your Grace?" Meg jolted upright in her rumpled bed.

"I will take no time for my doctors bleeding me, purging me, and lecturing me on my diet because they believe it will improve my choler. I have things to do. Arise and now."

Someone near the door held a lantern that hurt

Meg's eyes. She came finally awake to see the queen had come in black mourning garb to the little room near the kitchen block Meg shared with two scullery maids. Kat Ashley peered in the door with Lord Robin's sister Mary Sidney, and Bella Harington. With the dreadful news yesterday, it was just like them not to let Her Grace out of their sight. When Elizabeth Tudor was in pain, anything could happen.

Wrapping her sheet around her shift, Meg scrambled out of bed. The queen stood between her and her clothes, but she knew that tone of voice brooked no delay.

"What can I do, Your Grace?" she asked, not bothering to look for her shoes under the bed. "I would have come posthaste if you'd but summoned me."

"I need curing herbs that heal the mind and heart as well as the body. I have England's work to do and need them now."

Meg knew it must be early morning yet, as the maids had not been roused. Her wide gaze snagged Kat's as the queen stalked from the chamber, leaving her friends who shared the other bed gawking. Nearly running, Meg padded down the long hall toward the pocket of a chamber she used as her herbal room here at Windsor. Fortunately, since the corridor was pitch black but for occasional sconces set along the hall, the queen's guards carried lanterns as well as pikes.

Her Majesty got there just before Meg did. However did her royal mistress know exactly where this was in the maze of rooms down here? It sobered Meg to realize how the queen, sooner or later, seemed to know everything.

Meg shoved the door in and sneezed, either from her bare feet on stone floors or the fine, sweet dust that always hung in the air from her mortar and pestle. "Get a light in here!" the queen ordered. Someone thrust a lantern into the tiny room, and Lady Harington raised it high. It threw strange, shortened shadows on the walls and cluttered shelves.

Meg cleared her throat. "Which herbs do you require, Your Grace?"

"You said once that sweet marjoram helps those given to oversighing."

"Oh, yes, especially those who are lovelorn and th—" Meg cut herself off and began to scrabble through her wooden boxes for the marjoram.

"What else would serve?" the queen demanded, leaning over her shoulder.

"For oversighing?"

"For what ails me!"

"Let me just recite their virtues and you decide, Your Grace." Meg's heart ached for her queen, but she was glad that Ned was now predicting she would call a Privy Plot Council meeting. More than just Amy Dudley's death needed looking into. Meg had Geoffrey's stained death shirt hidden in this very room, and the cause of Luke's fall needed to be found. She had overheard, however, courtiers wagering that Her Majesty would get Cecil busy and call a governmental Privy Council meeting with her advisers to see to the realm's business—without Lord Robin, of course. So maybe the queen still would not have time to look into Geoffrey's demise.

"I have basil, which is good for the heart and takes away sorrowfulness," Meg announced, racking her still sodden brain.

"Yes, some of that."

Meg pulled out a parchment packet, then a second. "Boiled chervil root gives courage."

"Do you think that I need courage, girl?"

"No, Your Grace," Meg murmured, slapping that box closed. "Rosemary comforts the brain and heart and cures nightmares."

"Yes. Bring that. *If* I ever sleep again."

"Lavender for the nerves, but then that's already in your garments. Oh, I have vervain for contentment, one of the herbs I strew on your floors."

"Yes, all right, but if you already have it all over my floors, it is not worth a damned fig."

"I'll put more on fresh. And a pennyroyal garland helps giddiness."

"Hardly that," the queen said with a sniff. "I have already been cured of such."

"Lastly, meadowsweet to make the heart merry."

"Merry? I shall never be merry again, never. Hurry with them, as I have much to do," she commanded, and swept from the room like a whirlwind.

As Kat followed the queen and her coterie out the door, she glanced back at Meg and shook her head. They both knew that perpetual activity was one way

Elizabeth Tudor tried to stave off grief and heart-break, but they both knew she would eventually spiral down and crash.

SECLUDED AGAIN IN HER PRIVY CHAMBERS WITH A FEW intimates and Meg, who was strewing fresh vervain and meadowsweet on the floor, Elizabeth Tudor flung orders this way and that as she rampaged through piles of papers on her desk, signing some, thrusting others at Bella or Mary. They had suggested she send for one of her own clerks or secretaries, but she wanted only her closest friends around her now.

"Cecil will have to explain that . . . Cecil can see to that," she said as she waded through parchments to clear a place on the abalone-inlaid tabletop. "Now," she said, seizing a fresh sheet and dipping her quill pen again, "I must plan a fine, public funeral for poor Amy Dudley."

Elizabeth noted well that silence descended on the room. She looked up and stared each woman down, including Meg in the far corner, until all nodded or murmured acquiescence. Elizabeth had not slept last night but had paced the floor, railing at what had happened. Now her legs hurt. Her thighs, one of which Robin had stroked so seductively but yesterday, trembled. Her eyes burned with tears, shed and unshed, and she had the most violent headache topped off by a continual urge to sneeze from the herbs hanging heavy on her person and in the room.

"At Oxford, I think, would be fitting," she told

them, swiping at her nose with a lavender-scented handkerchief, then exploding in a racking sneeze. She blew her nose loudly, then went on. "St. Mary's Church of Our Lady at the university will do. Lady Dudley shall have swags of black cloth, painted escutcheons, and a fine choir and chief mourner I shall hire for a good fee. Then a large feast after."

"But, Your Grace," Mary put in, holding a pile of papers to her breasts, "you told me last night to write Robert at Kew to command that Amy's body be buried in Cumnor Church after it was viewed and searched by the coroner. Have you changed your mind?"

"And if I have?" Elizabeth challenged, then softened her voice. "No, this large funeral is for after her early interment, after we have the questions of her death settled publicly and truthfully. And write to your brother that, as all the court, he is to be fitted for mourning clothes, even at Kew."

"You will not write him yourself?" Mary asked, flinching slightly as if she were expecting another explosion.

"It grieves me sore, dear Mary, but I will not write nor see your brother until his name is cleared—pray God, soon—and he may return to us all. Of course, I believe him innocent, but it must be proved to others beyond a doubt." Even as she declared Robin's lack of complicity or guilt, doubts gnawed at her. She saw tears flood Mary's wide eyes as she nodded.

"Write the funeral orders, Bella, and I will sign," Elizabeth said, jumping up and thrusting her pen into her friend's hand before she tugged her into the chair she had just vacated. The queen strode to the oriel window where but yesterday she and Robin had lain together—and nearly lain together indeed. That is what would have happened. That is what she, fool that she was, had wanted to happen before the dreadful news had saved her. Why could a queen not carry on as a king and to hell with what people thought? Must a woman's reputation be so much more pristine and precious than a man's?

"The royal barge," Elizabeth cried excitedly, pushing her nose nearly to the leaded glass window before shoving it farther ajar. "The barge is back."

The queen noted Meg spilled the rest of the herbs she had been carefully strewing, but she seized her cloak and hurried past the girl. Elizabeth was out the door and down the corridor so quickly that her guards, companions, and courtiers scrambled to clear her path and then keep up with her. She fought not to run, to keep her eyes clear of tears, striding out of the palace through the gate named for her father. She walked down the grassy knoll among roses and herb beds, along the edge of town to the royal landing before she slowed her steps. Never had she walked this before, but she did not want to wait for her litter, and Robert was not here to pick a good mount for her.

The September afternoon sun glittered off the Thames as she glanced in the direction of Kew. She blinked back tears, but when she saw Cecil standing at the front of the barge, she was suddenly sure his eyes watered too.

"I am glad to see you, my Lord Secretary of the

State," she called to him in a scratchy voice before he
made his way across the gangplank. He had two of his
clerks in tow, both carrying fat satchels. "I have need
of you as things have been piling up this summer since
you brought us back that fine Scots treaty," she added
as he approached. She had expected him to be re-
proachful or angry but she read naught but concern on
his strong, stern face.

Cecil bowed then kissed the hand she offered. "But
now that the seasons are shifting again, we shall take
care of all your burdens," he said, his voice controlled
and comforting. Always when William Cecil spoke he
said volumes beneath the surface of his words. It was
something they shared, and she realized how desperately she had missed that and him.

They began to walk up toward the palace with a
vast entourage trailing while her guards made a buffer
through the swelling crowd. "And, Your Grace," Cecil
added quietly, "I am here to help in public and in privy
councils."

BY LATE AFTERNOON, WORKING STRAIGHT THROUGH WITH
Cecil's clerks madly copying and ferreting out documents he kept calling for, the queen and her chief secretary had cleared her pile of papers or set things aside
for the Council meeting tomorrow. It was nearly dusk,
seven of the clock, when Elizabeth was finally alone
with her old friend.

"Though I can hardly go rushing to Cumnor to investigate Amy's death," she said as they yet sat side by

side at her big desk, "I mean to call a Privy Plot Council meeting late tonight to do something about it."

"Forgive me, Your Grace, but I think you need your rest. You've obviously been burning the candle at both ends even before this tragedy occurred."

"I cannot rest now. I must know what happened to her so that others far and wide may know and leave off their carping and slanders. Besides, two men in my service have also met with strange deaths through falls."

"Yes, but, as with those, Lady Dudley might have simply fallen. She was ill, mayhap morose or distracted."

She turned sharply in her chair to face him. "Can you assure me there was no foul play in her death, my lord?"

His usually steady gaze wavered before he looked back at her. "Of course not," he said.

"Then I mean to send Ned Topside and Jenks covertly to Cumnor, not to get near the formal investigation but to learn whether Hester Harington, alias Franklin and Felicia Dove, could have possibly been in the vicinity. I suspect her of culpability and mayhap complicity in Luke's death, perhaps even Geoffrey's, so why not Amy's, though that is a long shot? Well, what is it you know you are not saying?" she demanded when she saw the usually stolid Cecil blanch white as marzipan.

When he did not have an immediate answer, she went on. "My Lord Cecil, do not tell me to tread carefully here, as I shall do that. But the lutenist has been snagged in many a lie, changed her identity, and then fled before I could question her more."

"But what motive? If deep-seated anger at her parents, would she not attack them somehow? Because she wanted to be at court, and then became insanely jealous of others you favored? But a motive for three apparently disrelated murders? *Sui bono*, Your Grace, what can be her reasons, not only for harming the men but Amy, if you are striving to link all this together?"

She gaped at him one moment. Why was he arguing so hard, as if this girl were his client in court and not the queen herself? "Cecil, she might have pushed Geoffrey to be able to take his place. As for Luke, he was on to her guise and warned me twice about her, so who knows what else she thought he knew? And," her words came out halting now, "her parents tell me that Hester used to love me—her kinswoman on the throne she feels could have been hers—but now I think she hates me because she thinks I've betrayed her."

"Yes, all right. I can see that much," he admitted, shifting slightly away from her in his armed chair.

"I believe," the queen plunged on, "she's stalked me the way a hunter does his prey. I've felt for weeks someone was watching me, over and above the fact I assume de Quadra and his ilk have spies at court, but it wasn't like that. Hester would, I fear, actually like to *be me*, and with her Tudor blood, however diluted in her veins— My lord, are you quite well? You look too pale, so the barge trip here and then my working you so hard . . ."

As she reached to touch his arm, he shook his head and gathered the last of his papers. "I'm fine. But you said Hester might be guilty of complicity earlier. Do you think there is some sort of plot here?"

"I don't know. Harry says she had a fat purse, and I know she must have been in the employ, even briefly, of others besides—besides Robert Dudley."

She got up and went to the window, leaning her hands on the sills to support her shaking legs. She tried to go on but her voice snagged. Robin. He could have hired Felicia-Hester to go to Cumnor. But he would have had to defy his queen to spring the girl first, mayhap so she would not be further questioned and reveal who had hired her and for what. But if Robin had sent Hester to harm Amy and someone saw her there, what would be easily traced and proved is that Felicia-Hester had been in the employ of the queen of England. Her stomach knotted at the dreadful possibilities that could come from that twisted knowledge.

"Your Grace," Cecil's voice interrupted her thoughts, "I will do all I can to help delve into this. Shall I summon the others, your cousin Harry too, for our Privy Plot meeting?"

"Yes, after dark when I shall supposedly retire, let us say at nine of the clock. And about my needing rest, my lord," she said, turning to face him, "I swear if I let down one moment I will turn into a screaming banshee and everyone will know that I am a mere weak woman."

He rose and came toward her. "A woman indeed, Your Grace, but never mere and never weak, not you."

"Oh, Cecil," she blurted, "Mildred is blessed to have you and I shall never, never have someone to love."

"But you—"

"The other thing you must do, of course," she plunged on, sniffing back tears, "is make marital overtures again to Archduke Charles, Catholic or not." She drew her handkerchief from her sleeve and blew her nose. "Send some sort of grand gifts to keep the Holy Roman Hapsburgs calm and happy right now, my lord. I may want no part of him, but I must put up a bold front. Well, are you speechless at last that I am broaching a marriage, a foreign marriage, or that I can think politically about it and not just personally?"

"Of course not," he insisted.

She thought he lied gallantly, trying to buck her up again, her dear Cecil whom she—God forgive her— had treated abominably but never would again.

"You are a queen who has learned to face necessity," he said.

"Necessity," she repeated, and added a long list of her father's favorite curse words. "And shall that be my bedfellow all these years to come?" She glanced out the window, toward the roofline where Hester or someone had come to spy on her. "Send for our fellow conspirators, my lord," she ordered, "including young Gil. And send the barge to fetch Dr. Dee too, though he won't make it here in time for the meeting. He must bring his signal mirrors, observation glass, and flying harness back again forthwith."

.    .    .

IT HAD BEEN NEARLY TWO YEARS SINCE ELIZABETH HAD
sat with her entire Privy Plot Council. Ned, Jenks, and
Meg looked excited, probably that Geoffrey's death
would now fully be addressed. Kat still seemed
drained and tired; Harry and Cecil resigned. Gil sat
drawing Elizabeth's face until she rapped the table
with her knuckles and gave him a cut-off signal, so he
sat up and paid attention.

"Now, before we turn to the main subject, the latest
death and Hester Harington's possible crimes, I just
want to say that I have never needed all of you more
than now," Elizabeth began their meeting. Her voice
caught. She had been talking so much today, fearing
her own silences within, that her voice was turning rough and made her sound ever on the edge of
tears.

"Anything we can do to help, Bess," Harry said, using her sobriquet for such sessions and investigations.
"Of course, I'm especially interested in Luke's strange
demise, but if Felicia's flight from right under my nose
is somehow tied to Amy Dudley's death . . ."

His voice trailed off and he fidgeted in his chair. It
flickered through Elizabeth's brain that Harry had
once wanted to be the brilliant lutenist's sponsor and
mentor. But he never would have dared to think he
could help his queen find happiness by dispatching
Amy through Felicia. Surely he would have seen the
ramifications of that. But did he sympathize with the
girl perhaps knowing she was the result of one of King
Henry's brazen liaisons? Those rumors Harry himself
was King Henry's bastard never seemed to die.

"I brought Geoffrey's shirt I been keeping," Meg piped up in the awkward pause, pulling out the garment from her lap under the table. "Ned, Jenks, and I think it proves that he was pushed, at least that someone else was on the roof with him."

"How so?" Elizabeth asked, strangely relieved to put off talking about Amy's death.

The girl flapped the garment open on the table and everyone craned or leaned forward. "This red stain is from the malmsey that you thought was a sign of his drinking. Don't you think it looks like someone threw it on him? See this burst of stain, not like he dribbled his own drink, 'cause this is right over his heart, not down under his throat. And since he left the musicians' gallery in a clean shirt with only his own flask of sack like always, because we looked into that, someone else threw this on him for spite or—"

"Or lame proof he was drunk and fell of his own accord," Jenks added, frowning. "And we learned a bottle of your personal malmsey was pilfered from the wine cellar that very night, from the ones marked with your name."

"Not her whole name but just E R," Meg prompted him.

"I am indeed impressed with all you have done," Elizabeth admitted. Jenks sat up even straighter on the bench he shared with the other two. Ned beamed, but Meg's eyes filled with tears again.

"You know, Bess," Kat said, resting her broken, splinted arm on the edge of the table, "I thought some of your food and drink was filched more than once.

Besides, that would fit the pattern of Katherine Grey mayhap wearing your clothes and using your bathwater. . . ."

Everyone stared at the old woman, who blinked back owlishly at them. Though stricken with amazement that Kat had somehow not realized they were all thinking the culprit they would investigate was Hester-Felicia, Elizabeth reached for Kat's good wrist and clasped it. "We are going to focus first on Hester Harington. But I do believe, Kat," the queen said, "that Katherine is a problem and may be in league with the Spanish ambassador."

"I believe so too," Cecil agreed. "I warrant he has had one or two spying for him here at court, and it is possible Felicia Dove, alias Hester, was one of these."

"Ah," Elizabeth observed, "then you have been keeping an eye on him—and on the court—even from afar."

"I have," Cecil declared a bit testily.

"At any rate, Kat," Elizabeth went on, "I cannot fathom Katherine doing de Quadra's dirty work for him, if it entailed either spying or murder. She's too spoiled and haughty to stoop to either, even if she'd like to see the deed done or to replace me as queen. But we are going to try to link Hester Harington to all three crimes. Do you see, Kat?"

"Of course I do. That's what I meant," she insisted.

Elizabeth expected people to speak up, but no one so much as moved. They too seemed disturbed that Kat had drifted far afield. It was the first time Kat had been more than just forgetful or slightly befuddled. If

Elizabeth lost her support on top of Robert's, she would never make it through this.

"Bess, I believe you had an assignment for Ned and Jenks," Cecil urged.

"A key one of the utmost importance and secrecy," she said, grateful for his lead. "I want the two of you to ride to Cumnor tomorrow, pretend to be players just passing through to Oxford."

"To covertly keep an eye on the inquest and investigation there?" Ned asked, looking even more somber and important.

"You are to steer completely clear of that," she ordered, pointing a finger in each of their faces, "or you will implicate me in something of which I am innocent, except perhaps of bad judgment."

Silence slammed into the room. No one breathed. Did they think she did not partly blame herself? She cleared her throat and said, "You are to work closely together to circumspectly discover whether or not a traveling lutenist—male, female, or eunuch—was in the vicinity of Cumnor House recently. Gil will draw from memory two more sketches of Hester Harington, which you may show around with the story of a runaway sister or some such. Meanwhile, the rest of us will sit tight but try to discover more about Geoffrey's and Luke's . . . murders."

Everyone reacted differently to that pronouncement from their queen. Meg and Ned looked triumphant and Jenks solemn. Kat nodded, while Cecil and Harry frowned, and Gil began to sketch Hester-Felicia's face from memory.

They hashed over much else before the queen sent them all to bed, Ned and Jenks with coin for their journey and permission to pick sturdy mounts from the stables since Lord Robert was not here to choose for them. She told Meg to take Kat to Mary Sidney to sleep in her ladies' rooms tonight because she could not bear to see her as distracted as she was. Cecil was the last to head for the door.

"My lord, I want you to visit Robert Dudley at Kew after our council meeting tomorrow. I do not want you to leave me now, but you are the only one to do it."

"To comfort him?" he asked, astounded. "I?"

"I know you don't get on with him, but I trust you to tell me true. My master lawyer, you must accuse Robert Dudley—the fortune-hunting gypsy, others call him—and tell me if you believe he could be . . . could be guilty, and I then have loved—do love—a murderer, who has done me in too when he had someone kill his wife. He's hired Felicia to sing his songs, and I must know if he's paid her to do—his other bidding," she choked out before she felt the last remnants of control desert her.

Elizabeth sank sobbing to her knees. William Cecil knelt with her, holding her as a father might while she soaked his shirt and shook against him like a thin reed in the harsh wind.

# Chapter the Fifteenth

The dread of future foes
Exile my present joy
And with me warn to shun
Such snares as threaten my annoy.

For falsehood now doth flow
And subjects' faith doth ebb.
Which should not be if reason ruled
Or wisdom wove the web.

But clouds of joys untried
Doth cloak aspiring minds,
Which turn to rage of late report

By changed course of minds.
The tops of hope suppose,
The root of rue shall be
And fruitless of their grafted guile
As shortly you shall see.

The dazzled eyes with pride,
With great ambition blind
Shall be unsealed by worthy men,
Who foresight falsehood find.

— QUEEN ELIZABETH

 THE NEXT MORNING, THE QUEEN MET PRIV-
ily with Ned and Jenks, garbed for their
ride to Cumnor, and with Dr. John Dee,
who had recently arrived.

"Has Dr. Dee made it clear to you how you can use
the signaling mirrors he is lending us?" the queen
asked again. "And if you break that precious observation glass, I shall break your skulls."

"We will not harm a thing nor get caught," Jenks
vowed, "and be back to report to you as soon as we
can—if Ned can keep up a fast pace."

"If you can keep up with posing as a traveling player,"
Ned put in, affecting an educated London voice.

"And *that*," the queen said, seizing both their wrists

in a hard grip, "is what I mean by you must get on with each other for this trip. No lording it over him, Ned. And, Jenks, no gibes about your outracing or outfighting him."

When they went down the back way as she had bid, the queen turned to Dr. Dee again. "I cannot thank you enough for your help and the use of your brilliant devices, doctor. I would reward you with a sinecure or coinage, but I do not want it noised abroad that you are in the service of the queen. I regret to tell you there are spies about my court who would proclaim that to their hostile foreign masters."

His eyebrows hiked higher. "It will ever be honor enough for me to be covertly in your employ, Your Majesty."

"But I have something else yet to ask of you."

"You mean you will dare to use the flying rig again?" he asked, glancing at the big bag of ropes and harness he'd hauled in with him. "Since you didn't send it with your men, I surmised so."

"I would speak of that, but come with me now, and I shall show you the drift of my gratitude from one bibliophile to another."

"Bibliophile?" he said, sounding puzzled for once, though she realized full well he knew what that word meant.

She led him from her privy chamber down the short hall to the small, wainscotted room that served as her library when she lived here. His swift intake of breath when he glimpsed the rows of volumes was reward enough for her.

"I bring only a small portion of the royal library with me on progress from London but have numbers of books at all my palaces," she explained, waiting for him to follow her into the room. "But I want you to select three books for yourself from these, one for each of your clever devices you have entrusted to me so that I might climb from the pit my enemies think I have fallen into—or mayhap we shall call it a book apiece for the three deaths we must solve."

"Oh, Majesty, choose from all these? I said it is my joy and honor to serve you," he said, staring at the books instead of her.

"And serve me you shall. But this will be our coinage, good doctor. You shall build a fine library over the years and tell no one its source, and if either of us needs to borrow aught from the other—books or ideas, intelligence, as you say—we shall."

She left him staring at those crowded shelves with the same intent expression on his face she had seen on Robin's when he'd gazed upon her with her skirts up and stocking down.

THE FIRST THING CECIL NOTED IN ROBERT DUDLEY'S SMALL manor house at Kew was that no lamps nor tapers were lit and the draperies were pulled closed. He nearly stumbled in the front hall when Dudley's steward closed the door behind them. One would think it were night outside instead of broad afternoon.

"Ah, some light in here at least," Cecil observed to the queen's prisoner in this velvet cage as the steward led him to the short walking gallery. Hand out-stretched, Dudley hurried to greet him. Though there was a row of windows here, the sun did not enter in late afternoon, and the gallery too seemed muted and grim.

This manor the queen had given Dudley—it had once been the dairy house of a fine estate—had no more than twenty chambers and was tucked away under a slant of hill. Still the land gave him tenants, rents, and men to draw on in his climb back to respectability. But that, Cecil thought, might be all water over the mill dam if Her Majesty learned that Dudley had betrayed her. That was what he was here to discern, yet the man looked actually glad to see him.

"How fares Her Grace? What is her feeling toward me now?" Dudley began to pepper him with questions as soon as they shook hands. He sounded desperate, but was that a mark against him? As ever, his focus centered on his own status and only the queen's welfare as it served his own.

"Her Majesty is endeavoring to stay purposefully busy about the realm's business and prays that all will be settled by the coroner's jury of inquiry," Cecil told him as they fell into stride together down the length of the old flagstone floor.

"She is stronger than I," Dudley murmured, folding his arms across his chest.

"Stronger than most of us, if the truth were known—and it must be known, Lord Robert."

"Through the inquest, you mean?"

"Yes, but I am sent to ask you straight if you had any foreknowledge that your wife would come to harm."

"That she would try to harm herself, you mean? And did I encourage her suicide?" he asked, acting either intentionally or obstinately dense. "No, Cecil, and believe me, I could have. With the tumor in her breast, she was, of course, in pain and deeply melancholy at times."

"But you were hardly pained nor melancholy to hear of her death, I take it," Cecil threw at him. "You would see that as clearing your way to the queen, I have no doubt."

Dudley stopped walking. His chin lifted. "No, my Lord Cecil, I was not saddened by her death, except the loss of life of one so young and that she suffered greatly alone these last years when I was absent to earn my family's way back in the world. I will not—cannot—pretend to grieve for her loss in my own life. Amy and I burned our flame out long ago and had little in common after that, but she was my wife. I sent condolences but not false feelings to her family and do not express them now. But as to your original question," he said, his voice rising again, "I would not doubt the shallow, spoiled woman could kill herself just to spite me!"

Cecil stared straight into Dudley's steady gaze. A frown—perhaps a perpetual one now—furrowed his high brow and his eyes blazed. But in them, the seat of the soul, lurked not deceit but flamed raw self-serving arrogance. The blatant honesty was a mark for his in-nocence, Cecil decided, however much it condemned him as a dreadful husband.

Cecil cleared his throat, uncertain he could find his voice for once. "You realize the evidence, such as we know of it now, looks suspicious for foul play," he told Dudley as they began to walk again. They changed directions often as the corridor had nothing of the length of the queen's galleries or even the one he and Mildred walked in inclement weather at Stamford or in their small country seat at Wimbledon. Suddenly Cecil pitied as well as detested this man: He'd never had a wife capable of comforting him and had been through hell for his family's fierce ambition. And Cecil, of all men, understood ambition.

"As for suspicious evidence, I heard," Dudley was saying, ticking things off on his long fingers, "that her neck was broken and her head at an odd angle, yet her cap was not awry. Two, her body bore no discernible bruises. Three, that Amy had insisted everyone but Mrs. Owens, the doctor's old widow who gets about only with a walking stick, leave for the fair. Bowes also said they questioned Amy's lady's maid, Mrs. Pirto, and she said Lady Dudley had a strange mind. Hell's gates, I could have told them that!"

"That she had a strange mind or all the other details?"

A muscle kept working in Dudley's jaw, Cecil observed. "No one but my brother-in-law in a letter—he sits on the coroner's jury—has told me aught of her demise, I swear it," Dudley insisted, his voice rising in pitch to sound nearly hysterical again. "I have lost my wife, my position at court, my reputation, my hopes, my men . . . my queen. I went to the Tower once and nearly faced the headsman, Cecil, and cannot bear to again."

"But if you are innocent—"

"*If!* Does Elizabeth not believe me—believe *in* me? Then I am doomed indeed!"

"Keep calm, my lord. *Since* you are innocent, once things are settled, you will be returned to court, I believe."

Dudley clasped Cecil's hand and looked intently into his eyes again. "If I can but believe that—that she will take me back . . ."

Cecil gently pulled away from him. "But if she does, it may be only as Master of the Horse, Lord Lieutenant of the Castle, and not as her favorite. I believe you are clear-sighted enough to see all the ramifications of that reasoning. I leave you to contemplate them, as I must be heading back now."

"You know, I entertained her here once when she was at Richmond," Dudley said, almost as if talking to himself. "All glittering and happy, she came riding in for dinner with her ladies and praised all I had done for her, our friendship. Her voice rang out here and her very presence lit this quiet tomb of a place like a torch."

Dudley's voice drifted off as he stared dazedly around the gallery, no doubt seeing, hearing the ghosts here. Cecil shivered.

"I can only pray your name—and hers too—will be

soon cleared, my lord," Cecil said. Strangely, he found he meant it. Though he had often wished to run Robert Dudley through with the sharpest sword, this living death, suspended in dark exile, reminded him too much of his own recent plight. And made him almost, but not quite, regret the lengths to which he'd gone and would yet go to keep Dudley from ever being king.

"Cecil, I am deeply grateful you came to see me, even if she commanded it, and that you have listened to my side. Tell Her Grace I am innocent of all but adoring her. If I come back . . ." he said, and his voice drifted off again as he turned away to stare down the length of flagstone floor.

"If you come back, we must find a way to work together for the common good—her good," Cecil said. Though he didn't want to, he clapped the man on the shoulder before he headed for the door.

"Are the guards treating you well enough?" he asked, turning back. "You said you've lost your men, but they may be returned to you. Do you have a word for them, then?"

"I command they see to the royal stables in my stead, but there is one close groom I may indeed have lost. He disappeared even before any of this happened. I trusted him but fear he might have pilfered the pearls I sent by him to Amy and disappeared with the profit. I long favored and trusted him, one Edmund Fletcher. So if he turns up, tell him I demand an accounting of where he's been or I may send him permanently packing."

"I'll pass the word along," Cecil said, intrigued at how Dudley could do unto others what he did not want done unto him. That hardened his heart for the whole of what he had been sent to do—to confront, not comfort. Hoping it seemed an apparent after-thought, Cecil waited a moment, reopened the door to the gallery, and stuck his head back in.

"I forgot to tell you, Lord Robert, the queen is beginning to believe whomever that lutenist Felicia Dove worked for may have spied on her and urged Felicia to cause Geoffrey Hammet's and Luke Morgan's strange falls too when they got in the way. Put it in writing to me if you can think of any possible ties the lutenist could have had to any courtier who might have wanted your wife dispatched. After all, Felicia was sprung from her confinement two days before your wife's death, so who knows she wasn't sent to Cumnor too."

He went out quickly and, this time, slammed the door as loudly as his heart slammed again his ribs.

IN LATE AFTERNOON STEPHEN JENKS AND NED TOPSIDE rode through the remnants of the country fair in the small town of Abingdon before wheeling back and reining in. Only the booths of a few itinerant vendors who had not yet moved on remained on the central town green. They could see where the crowd's feet had trod the grass between the aisles of makeshift tables of wares and the burned-out circles where meat had been cooked and sold on the day Lady Dudley died nearby.

Splendid, Ned groused to himself. Her Grace had sent them to look for one girl and an unknown man in the area where a popular country fair had drawn people from all over. Talk about a needle in a haystack.

"Yer a wee bit late for the festivities," a big bear of a man called to them, emerging from a low-slung tent and shading his eyes from the setting sun.

One more person they might as well question, Ned thought. He and Jenks had stopped to question numerous people on the road, showing them the drawing of Hester Harington, saying their sister had run off, mayhap with a man on a single horse. Absolutely no one had claimed to have seen her, though many remarked on the fine portrait and touched Gil's charcoal sketch with their dirty, calloused fingertips until they'd smeared it. At least they had a second one. They were completely out of sorts, late, tired, and so hungry that even the smell of rank meat made their mouths water.

This man did not blend in with the rest. He had massive shoulders, a bull neck, no waist at all, and spoke in a broad Scots accent. "Abingdon Fair coupla days over, lads, 'cept for those of us stayed to sell off wares," he told them in a friendly enough voice, though, of course, not every Scot had to be crude and rude, Ned thought magnanimously.

"What a pity," he said, with a hand to his chest and a doleful look at Jenks, who just nodded. "And we'd heard it was at next week's end, not last. We're players, you see, my good man."

"We coulda used a bonny bit a that," he told them, handing a pig's trotter up to each of them from a rusted iron grill over a cook fire that had long gone out. Beads of lard had congealed on the edges of the pig's feet. However hungry, Ned just held and gestured with his while Jenks gobbled his down and heaved the bone into a common refuse pile crowded with loud crows vying with the local dogs for scraps.

"In other words," Ned went on, doing most of the talking as he and Jenks had agreed, "no excitement at the fair."

"Oho, dinna say that," the Scot told them, rocking back on his heels. His thick hair was so slick to his head, Ned wondered if that's what he did with the trotter grease. "Dinna ye hear," he said with a smirk, "the queen's fancy Lord Robert Dudley's wife got kilt nigh here, coupla miles over at Cumnor House? Folks been buzzing and some gone over to look at the place, 'cept they're not letting anyone in to see the stairs where the lass got thrown doon."

"Got thrown down?" Ned repeated. "Someone saw her get 'kilt' then?"

"Nay, lad, but everybody kens someone was hired to do it for Lord Robert or even the clever queen. Elizabeth been besotted by a man and may carry his bastard, but Mary, Queen a Scots, now there's a fine figure of a woman!"

"Now see here!" Jenks exploded, and spurred his horse before Ned nudged his own mount forward to cut him off. "You and others who don't know—" Jenks shouted.

"Dinna ken what?" the Scot challenged, glaring up and around the back of Ned's horse at Jenks. " 'Sides roasting the best trotters, I warrant I can take on one more braw lad in the wrestling ring for a healthy wager!"

"He meant," Ned put in, glaring at Jenks, "you and the others don't know how sorry we are to have missed the fair and all that excitement. So where is this Cumnor House anyway, and are folks sure the poor lady was really 'kilt'?"

"I hear the staircase wasna steep or long enough for a fatal fall, 'lest someone broke her neck first," the Scot told Ned, ignoring Jenks now and lowering his voice conspiratorially. This lout, Ned thought, ought to be on the stage with all his dramatic aplomb. "And there's a coroner's jury convened to hear the case and all, but 'tis said her waiting maid, one Mrs. Pirto, overheard the poor lass at her prayers."

"Overheard her praying aloud and loudly too, I warrant," Ned prompted. He was studying not only what the man said but how he said it. Not often he'd heard the Scots brogue to learn to ape it.

The man nodded. " 'Deliver me from desperation,' the poor, sad, thin thing was saying on her knees with her hands clasped and tears apouring doon her pale cheeks. Goes to show she ken someone was out to harm her," he added, shifting stances and his tone again. "And any jackass would ken who. Now, how aboot doing some bloody war scenes for me, in 'change for them trotters?" he asked as Ned put a booted foot out to kick Jenks and keep him from charging the lout again.

"We'll just have to do that, perhaps tomorrow,"

Ned said, jerking his head toward Cumnor with a glare at Jenks. They were starting to draw a curious crowd from the scattered cottages and tents. He realized they'd best be done with this man and show the sketch around. "We may even work up some scenes and call the new work 'The Sad Case of the Lady Dudley.' But you see, we've lost two others of our players, a man and a girl, through a misunderstanding. The girl, brown hair and eyes, sometimes goes about garbed as a lad, for our work, of course. And often carts her lute with her, or if she's sold it again, she still likes to sing."

"Och, lad, ye ken, I did see such a pair, day we was setting up," the Scot said, scratching his slick head. "A man and a lad on one horse and the lad holding a lute, real careful like."

"Bull's-eye," Jenks muttered, while Ned just wished he'd keep his trap shut and not stir this brawler up again. He could see Jenks had been reaching for Gil's sketch in his saddle pack, but he obviously let it be since the man had only seen her at a distance. "That's them all right," Jenks said excitedly. "Name of . . . Meg and Ned, and we've got to find them and tell them no hard feelings for the fight we had."

"The man, not the one holding the lute," Ned said, leaning down excitedly, hoping Jenks left off his chatter. "Can you describe him?"

"Hmm, a thin lad, ye ken. Good rider. Wore dark common garb, both a them. Their horse looked winded and was a fine one too, well-curried, a chestnut mare with four white feet and a white forehead

and strange, dappled mane. The two of 'em eloping
together or stole something, did they?"

"That lute," Jenks blurted in the same moment
Ned, deciding it was time for bribery and no more blatant lies, fished out a coin to give the man.

"No need," the man protested, puncturing Ned's
theory that all Scots were tightfisted. "Ye not even eat
your trotter yet," he said to Ned, looking almost hurt.

"This money's for the rest of your pile of them over
there," Ned explained, then while the man walked
away to gather the other pigs' feet in a swatch of
greasy cloth, he whispered to Jenks. "No need to tarry
with these others just to get the same information and
tip them off we've been around asking, especially since
it sounds like Felicia and the man were just skirting
the fair. I'd bet the rest of those larded trotters and a
throne that was her and the link to whomever sent her
here. It couldn't be just coincidence she fled here from
Eton, and I doubt if she came to play the lute at this
louse-ridden country fair."

"No, 'cause he'd have remembered that," Jenks
said, making Ned roll his eyes. "But I can tell you the
man was probably Edmund Fletcher, Lord Robert's
man."

"How in heaven's name do you know that?" Ned
whispered, wide-eyed.

"Not just 'cause he's a bony rake of a man. That's
his horse, Firkin, and it disappeared the day Felicia-
Hester did, right along with Fletcher too."

"Fletcher, Firkin, Felicia, Hester! It sounds like one
of her damned songs," Ned muttered through gritted

teeth. With all his hard work and brilliance, it annoyed him to no end it might be Jenks's knowing horseflesh that could link Lord Robert to his wife's murder.

THE SUN WAS SETTING AND THE QUEEN WAS CLOISTERED with her ladies. She had kept herself inside all day, working, seeing only Cecil and her intimates, including Meg, who was one of the few who knew how devastated the queen actually was—not so much over the death of Amy Dudley but the death of her tenuous trust of Lord Robin.

Since the queen was staying inside, Meg decided it was now or never. From her lookout site among her roses, she had seen Ben Wilton working alone on the barge landing. And with no one suspecting a thing, she had contrived to get in and out of the royal wardrobe rooms.

In her tiny distillation chamber, Meg managed to dress herself but for a partially unlaced bodice back. After sneaking out the side servant's door, she ducked outside Windsor's walls, garbed in the queen's clothes: huge sleeves, brocade bodice, and a bush of satin skirts over a farthingale that hung on her hips like a massive birdcage. Best of all for the disguise, she wore a dark blue velvet cape with a huge hood she could try to hide inside. While the court was at supper in the great hall, she had to make both her entrance and her exit on the wooden boards of the barge landing—the stage for her very own masque.

"Oh, Ned," she whispered, hustling through a break in the hedges to hide herself from the castle guards, "wish you were here and would help."

She must pull off a good enough rendition of the queen to convince Ben, but it would not have to be the performance of her life in that respect. It wouldn't be like trying to convince someone who really knew the queen. Meg had always feared imitating her before a person who knew Her Majesty well, but now she must playact before someone who had known *her* well. Meg shuddered in outright fear. This little performance meant her peace of mind and maybe her entire future.

Holding her skirts off the damp grass—for the queen was slightly taller—Meg kept behind the hedges and made her way down to her rose and herb beds above the river. Yes, facing the water, Ben was still alone on the wooden landing, his turn to guard the barges, no doubt. The castle guards proper had stationed themselves farther along the bank. Holding herself erect, she sidled down the slope and strode toward the landing.

"Sirrah," she clipped out as she tried to mimic the queen's commanding voice with what Ned called her metallic tone.

"Ah—you?" he cried, squinting into the setting sun to see her better. She wondered which *you* he meant until he blessedly fell to his knees.

"You may rise," she intoned, then wanted to kick herself that she hadn't let him stay down.

"But you—alone—out here, Majesty?" he stam-

mered, trying to shade his eyes with the cap he had
swept off.

"As you must know, I have received a blow of late
and need some time alone—to walk out to think. And
I thought when I saw you here—you are the Ben
Wilton they said was the bridge shooter from London,
I believe . . ."

"Oh, yes, Majesty, that's me. Took many a boat
through at high tide, saved many a soul."

"So I hear, and that is why I am sending you back to
that duty, Ben Wilton."

"But there are other shooters back in London," he
said. "I just got hired on royal duty here last week."
Meg moved carefully away, keeping her back toward
the sun and not letting him get too close. Their shadows flung themselves long and lean across the landing
to the barges. Meg was tempted to pull her hood farther forward but she didn't want to overdo it on this
warm day.

"Yet I am sending you back to oversee them all—
with this warrant and these coins," she added, thrusting forward the document she'd carefully written with
the queen's signature—thank Ned again for teaching
her to read and write, and the queen for paying her a
stipend. Though she treasured anything Her Grace
ever gave her, she would part with her entire fortune
to have this man go away.

"But, you mean back to London—afore you go?"
Ben demanded, sounding either angry or suspicious
now.

"I have a care for my people," she said, her voice

catching as she aped exactly words and tone she'd heard Her Grace use. "And I send my best barger back to have a care for my people in my capital city."

To her dismay he shuffled slightly closer, head cocked. Mercy, she'd overstepped. He would realize it was her, however long she'd been gone from him, however much he probably thought that she was dead if that old friend of her mother's had not told she came back. When he went down again on one knee to put out his hand for the parchment and the purse of coins, she realized she shaded him now and he was looking up at her with some emotion she could not name.

She wanted to flee. He must be on to her. Ned had not taught her well enough, or her courage to command herself like the queen had failed her. Elizabeth Tudor had been foolish to keep her close so that she could have a double to stand in for her if there was a need in solving a crime or running a realm. She was doomed for sure, she feared, as Ben Wilton frowned up at her and she stepped aside to get the sun in his eyes again.

"Majesty," he said, his burly shoulders shaking, his brash voice as tremulous as hers had been, "I shall ever obey. And I shall never forget this day you commanded Ben Wilton to do your bidding."

Meg knew an exit line without Ned's prompting. Her knees nearly knocking, she turned and strode as quickly as she could in queenly fashion back toward the distant castle. But she kept her head high and her shoulders squared the way Elizabeth of England always did in public, no matter what her burden.

# Chapter the Sixteenth

*Blame not my heart for flying up too high*
*Since thou art cause that his flight began.*
*For earthly vapors drawn up by the sun*
*Comets become and night suns in the sky. . . .*

*I say again, blame not my high desire*
*Since of us both the cause thereof depends.*
*In thee doth shine, in me doth burn a fire*
*Fire draweth up other and itself ascends.*

— JOHN HARINGTON

 "WHAT DID HE SAY?" THE QUEEN ASKED THE moment Cecil entered her privy chamber upon returning from visiting Robert Dudley at Kew. "Do you deem him innocent?"

Cecil sighed and sat in the chair on the other side of the low-burning hearth as she indicated. He heard pounding on the roof above, but neither the queen nor Kat reacted to it, so he tried to ignore it. Had she been keeping so busy she had ordered her long-desired repairs on the old palace already? She should know full well the treasury was too gaunt for such work. Surely she hadn't put some of the castle guards to work, for he'd noted the watch had been greatly cut from when he'd left at dawn today.

Security in the state apartments was not much

better. Kat Ashley was the only lady in attendance, and she kept staring out the window into the gathering dusk. The queen herself poured him wine and handed it to him. Didn't she realize she could be at risk with lessened security? Mayhap he'd have to see to it secretly himself, as he'd been forced to handle other things lately, but he'd best keep his mind on the business at hand.

"Your Grace, I will tell you flat," he said before he took a sip as she hovered over him, "that Lord Robert is guilty of overmuch ambition and arrogance, but I truly don't believe he is stupid enough to have his wife murdered, not since he knew that she was dying. He wanted his marriage over and admits that. And, of course, the man is greatly self-serving and that can be dreadfully dangerous in one close to the monarch."

She backed up several steps and sank into her chair, her hands gripping the carved, clawed arms of it. "I know, I *do* know. But it was not long ago the same things were said of me, when my sister was yet on the throne. And I killed no one to advance myself, though I am sure my enemies would have delighted to prove I did."

Kat drew their attention as she began to sputter about something, then stamped to the door, opened it with her good arm, and went out. Mayhap, Cecil thought, she was going to order that infernal pounding stopped. Elizabeth just shook her head as her worried gaze pinned Cecil to his chair again.

"And there are other things that Robin—Robert— and I have in common," she went on. "We each lost a parent to the headsman's axe, each was sent to the Tower and feared for our own lives. In terrible times, he stood by me, believed in me, comforted me—yes, even loved me from afar. He helped me to pull through."

"It's true then that he sent you flowers when you were in the Tower after the Wyatt Rebellion?" he asked.

"Oh, yes." Her taut mouth bent into a hint of smile, and she closed her eyes as she spoke, tipping her head against the high-backed chair. Cecil leaned forward to hear her better through the racket from above. "One time he sent a small nosegay of early spring posies he bribed one of the guards' sons to bring me," she said, her cheeks taking on a deep blush that reminded him again of Dudley's power. "And the boy was to say that someday he would send me gems the same color as those primrose and forget-me-nots. They lasted for days stuck in a pewter mug of my wash water, and then I pressed them in my Bible. I have them yet. . . ."

She opened her eyes and sat up straighter. "Later he sold the only meager piece of land he had and loaned me a pittance that was a fortune to me when Queen Mary would have gladly seen me go about in rags in exile. He stood by me always when others turned their backs, my lord. Sometimes he's nearly like a brother, my other self—"

"Then, if he is completely cleared and returns, treat him as a brother, Your Grace, the way you do Harry. Favored, but not the favorite."

They spoke of all else Robert had said when with

no warning, the door to the room banged open. As they both shot upright, Cecil jumped in front of the queen, his hand going for the sword he realized he didn't have. But it was Kat, out of breath.

"Oh, lovey," she said to the queen, coming toward them, "I've solved the mystery of who has been wearing your clothes and impersonating you."

"Katherine Grey, or is Hester Harington back?" the queen cried, rushing to Kat.

"I know you kept her partly because she looked like you and Ned trained her to speak like you, but now—without permission—she's . . . she's trying to become you! I saw Meg Milligrew traipsing back to the castle in your clothes and then saw her take them back to the royal wardrobe. Your blue velvet cloak and jade-green skirt and sleeves with heavy ruching and the salmon sleeves, you know the ones. Oh, lovey, surely it wasn't Meg Milligrew harmed those other men for serving you, for I thought Geoffrey was her friend."

"Where is she now?" Elizabeth demanded.

"Gone to her room and taken to her bed again. I followed her there and peeked in."

"Sit down and rest, my Kat, but first send a guard to bring Meg to me. My Lord Cecil, I have tired you out, I fear," she said, turning back to him as Kat obeyed, "so you may go if you wish."

"I will stay, if that's permissible, Your Grace. I want to hear the upshot of this too. I've been racking my brain to find who, close to you and unassuming, could be spying in your court for the illustrious new Spanish ambassador."

"De Quadra? 'S blood, we knew from the first not to trust him. It can't be Meg, can't be," Elizabeth whispered, but he saw her backbone stiffen, and he backed off across the room to a safer seat.

"IT IS THE WONDER OF THE AGE THAT THIS OBSERVATION glass brings things up so close and clear," Ned whispered as he and Jenks took turns with Dr. Dee's device from their night hiding place up in the old tower overlooking Cumnor House.

"They ought to call it a spyglass," Jenks said as he moved it to gaze from window to window.

Ned, itching to take the device back, now had a fairly good idea of the layout of the downstairs of the house. They had crept around the grounds and, keeping their distance, peered though windows with the observation glass. They'd even glimpsed the fatal staircase, short and shallow as it was from a landing that evidently divided it into two flights, a "pair of stairs" most folks called them.

It was a warm enough night that no one had closed draperies, so they'd glimpsed lighted activity within and had also identified where the various people lived in the chambers across the backside of the manor house. It seemed that Amy Dudley's rooms were on the eastern side—a nervous-looking woman who was probably her maid, Mrs. Pirto, paced in a large chamber there, and an old woman, who was probably Mrs. Owens, King Henry VIII's doctor's widow, appeared to have the western set of windows.

Anthony Forster and his family evidently lived in
the building's only wing, so he and Jenks could perhaps eavesdrop on them if they wanted to risk it. Too
bad the queen had told them to steer clear because, of
course, by affecting varied personas and voices, Ned
was certain he could pry a great deal of valuable information out of the players in this tragedy.

"This is as close as we're getting," Jenks whispered,
as if he'd read Ned's mind, "or Bess will have our
heads. One wrong move where someone links us to
her, and people's tongues will start wagging again. I
won't have them saying she has something to do with
it, though I can see them pointing a finger at Lord
Robert."

"Since kings and queens get the praise, it's only
right they sometimes take the blame," Ned muttered.
"It will be our Bess's challenge over the years to see it's
much more praise than blame. Here, give that back a
minute!"

The light had gone out in old lady Owens's rooms,
but Ned was certain she stood now at the window, a
pale ghostly form in white. That is, if Amy's spirit
wasn't haunting the place already like any self-
respecting ghost in an English castle or manor should.
Surely a lamp from the house had not caught the glint
of this glass to warn old lady Owens—no, her eyes
couldn't be that sharp. And Mrs. Pirto was still pacing,
so she didn't suspect a thing either. Ned wondered if
Dr. Dee fully grasped that he could elevate the art of
spying with this leather and glass tube and those little
signal mirrors. They each carried one of them in a

pouch slung over their shoulders because they didn't dare to leave them back in their camp in the woods.

"Too bad we can't stay tomorrow to watch the go-ings-on from this perch," Jenks said.

"We could get trapped up here, though it doesn't look like this tower's ever used. Let's go. Tomorrow at first light, we'll watch from the woods, then search the forest for a possible camp. After all, there is a slight chance Felicia and Fletcher—"

"And Firkin—"

"—might still be about. There's no other good place where they could have hidden close by, we've seen that. Here, I'll carry the glass, and let's watch those crumbling steps."

They edged slowly down, creeping from stair to stair, sometimes sitting, feeling their way, helping each other in the blackness. Too bad, Ned thought, Amy Dudley hadn't been this careful in the house, because she could have saved them all a lot of bother.

WHEN ONE OF THE QUEEN'S GUARDS ROUSED MEG FROM her bed, she prayed that Her Grace only had the need for more curing herbs. But when she saw the look on the royal face, she knew it wasn't that. She imme-diately felt more nauseated than facing Ben had made her.

"You've been seen outside wearing my clothing, Meg," the queen clipped out, "evidently impersonat-ing me without my command or permission." Her Majesty sat in her high-backed chair, while Cecil and

Kat stood by the dark windows. Cecil's presence made Meg doubly apprehensive. "Don't just stand there gaping," the queen said. "Why, girl?"

"I—I haven't felt well, Your Grace."

"I am aware of that. So are you implying your stomach complaints have affected your brain, to make you take my clothes and go outside in them? Or are you claiming forgetfulness, as you did when you came into my aunt's employ to meet me the first time?"

"No, but what does the Lady Mary Boleyn have to do with this? It's just that today, Your Grace, I had to see someone, someone who would listen to me more if I looked fine."

"And that person was . . . ?"

Covering her face with both hands, Meg burst into tears. She was doomed. The queen would brook no excuse, no lie, nor was there one that Kat or Cecil could not ferret out and expose. She saw no other path but to throw herself on the queen's mercy and tell her about Ben. Her Majesty might be angry every time one of her ladies went behind her back to see a man, but— queen's double or not—Meg knew she was only the herb girl. Besides, she tried to buck herself up, Her Majesty hadn't wanted to be married either and had said more than once she didn't trust men.

Meg fell to her knees, her head down. "It's Sarah Scutea keeps getting me in deep distress, Your Grace, not Meg Milligrew."

"Lift your head, as I cannot hear you when you talk to my feet, not with that work on the roof this late. But you told me you had renounced your previous name and life."

Meg gaped up at her. "I wanted to, Your Grace," she said, raising her voice. Yet she didn't dare to look the queen in the eyes. Remembering Ned said a good way to avoid stage fright was to look slightly past a person or over the heads of the audience, she tried that.

"Before my—her—mother died in London and while you let me nurse her, I found out I—Sarah Scutea—was wed to a rough, hard man, one Ben Wilton, a bargeman and a bridge shooter."

The queen leaned closer, gripping the arms of her chair so hard her long fingers went white. "Wed? You are wed? And you've known this nearly two years? You've been hiding a husband from me for nearly two years?" Her shrill voice rose to a shriek.

"But I couldn't remember him—couldn't love him. I—I told you I'm not Sarah."

"But you've known all this time. So the person you went out dressed as your queen to see was . . ."

"He's here with your latest crew of bargemen, Your Grace, brought in from London when the others put you on the rocks. He's a brutal man, I heard, and I cannot bear to—"

"Then you should have come to me months ago," the queen cried, flinging wild gestures. "I will no longer be accused by anyone at any level of keeping husbands and wives apart! This Ben no doubt would have you, if he had been at least told his wife was back from the dead."

Meg saw Kat had come closer, slack jawed in shock, though Cecil wisely kept his distance. "But—please, Your Grace, I've sent him away happy and none the wiser with some coins and a letter. And he doesn't know I'm back and alive, since he thought I was you."

"What letter, if you do not want him to know of you?"

Meg gazed up in sick awe at her queen. She had risen and loomed over her, a face carved from white marble with flashing eyes.

"I—in your name—I asked him to return to London to do his job there and praised him too."

"But what letter? I must tell you, when I summoned you here tonight, I feared that you might have betrayed me—politically as well as personally—and be spying for some foreign power. After all, Sarah Scutea is the daughter of Spanish-bred loyalists of my sister's Catholic cause. Have you played me for a fool all these years when I trusted you too? And now I learn you are sending letters by some bargeman into London. De Quadra is still in London, I believe, my Lord Cecil?" she demanded, turning toward him so fast her skirts swooshed across Meg's tear-streaked face.

This was pure nightmare, Meg thought, worse than the one with Ben. Her beloved queen was now talking of spies, and that meant prison or worse. She had forged the queen's name, though not for some evil cause. But fears of torment or prison were only slightly worse than being forced to return to Ben Wilton as his wife, she was sure of that.

"I wrote him a short note on a piece of your parchment, Your Grace," she continued her confession, the volume of her voice amazingly picking up as she went. "I signed your name—"

"You know better than forgery, girl," Kat interjected.

"Actually," Cecil cut in, "considering it's the queen's name, it's treason."

"I cannot abide such deceit," the queen went on, ignoring them both. "Even if you have not betrayed me to an enemy, you have made yourself my enemy by not trusting me with the truth. 'S bones, I'd have thought people learned their lesson when I sent the Haringtons away. I am going to have you confined until my Lord Cecil questions this Ben Wilton and then . . ."

The queen's voice faded as a dark shroud wrapped tighter and tighter around Meg's thoughts. The noise from the roof, the pounding of her heart . . . Then everything just stopped as Meg hit the floor.

IN THE SHORT STRETCH OF TIME BETWEEN DAWN AND daylight on the morrow, Ned and Jenks had scoured the woods within a half-mile of Cumnor House, reasoning that if Felicia-Hester and Edmund Fletcher had stayed in the area, they would not have risked residing with anyone or even staying at an inn. They had found the remnants of several camps and the skeletons of two fairly fresh campfires in the woods, but nothing that pointed to their prey.

While Jenks, who had better skills in tracking anyway, continued to survey the area, Ned tied his horse

to a tree near Cumnor House. Wishing he had
brought the observation glass, which was back in
Jenks's saddlepack, he at least had one of the signal
mirrors with him. If one or the other of them located
something important, they had found they could play
sunlight from these off the side of the tower that faced
away from the house. Every so often, Ned glanced up
at the lofty ruins but saw no flash of light from Jenks
yet. He took his mirror from its pack so that he would
have it at hand if he needed it.

He crept closer to the manor house. The place lured
him, as if it were a massive stage where a great drama
had just been played out. Even the old, sunken graveyard and the half-toppled tower would make fine
scenery. He imagined he could see each actor, especially the tragic heroine on her knees, hands clasped,
giving her "deliver me from desperation" speech the
Scotsman had mentioned. And of course the scene
with the horrified denizens of Cumnor returning on a
lovely Sabbath, laughing from the fair at Abingdon,
only to shriek in dread at the sight of the corpse, before
they expounded great speeches on the frailty of life.
Someday mayhap he'd do that very play, though not
for the queen and Lord Robert, that was certain.

Ned startled from his grand musings as a character—the doctor's old widow—entered from around
the house, leaning on a carved stick. His pulse
pounded. She was alone and slowly, unsteadily coming
this way as if it were fate he too should enter the scene
to speak circumspectly with her. The queen had said
not to meddle, but who knows what valuable proofs

this old beldam might have to throw light upon the plot?

Ned strolled her way, hoping he appeared nonchalant. He got so close without any reaction on her part that he realized she, like the old woman who had provided the ladder in Eton for Felicia's escape, did not see well. Hell's gates, then she'd not be one whit of help either.

"Who's there?" she called, her voice scratchy. "Halt, for I can hear you."

"Just a peddler passing through, milady," he said, using a warm, friendly Kentish accent.

"A peddler and not another gawker?"

"A gawker at what?"

"*What* kind of peddler, young man?"

He walked slowly closer. "Of, ah, mirrors, milady. See?" he said, and held the glass close to her face to test her eyes.

"A peddler who doesn't know what happened here," she said, tut-tutting. She put a parchment-skinned hand to the mirror and brought it closer to her face while Ned still held it. "Then you are new here and just passing through?"

"That's right, milady."

"Bah, nothing's right anymore. Have you not heard of Lord Robert Dudley's lady wife being dead of a fall?"

"Yes, but—you mean, it was near here?" he asked, pleased by the rising tenor of his voice.

"This very house, just down the hall from me—two doors," she said with a decisive nod. "The coroner and his jury asked me if I saw anything, but I didn't. Nor did I hear her scream, as they asked that too."

Ned figured, since this was going nowhere, he'd best make a smooth exit. "I must be on my way, milady. Got to make a living, you know," he said, and stepped back.

"I couldn't tell them a thing about hearing poor Amy stumble down the stairs either—two sets of eight each I take very slowly and always count—or when she hit at the bottom. You wouldn't think eight stairs enough to take a fatal fall, would you? My hearing's good, but I must have dozed off then."

"Ah, yes," he said, still edging toward the wood. If Jenks saw he was talking to one of the household, he might tell the queen he'd disobeyed her orders and then there'd be hell to pay.

"You know, they didn't ask about the music, though," she said almost to herself, shaking her capped, white head. "But then, I kept dozing off and it might have just been in my head—from my days at the king's court, you know, always fine lutenists about in the old days."

Ned froze in his tracks. "You heard music?" Ned asked, turning back. "Lute music?"

"Probably not. But lutes were always my favorite, so sweet and soft."

Ned wasn't sure what parting he made with her, for he ran for the fringe of forest and frantically signaled to Jenks before he realized he was only matching another darting dot of light on the tower. Whatever

Jenks had found within those woods, Ned was sure he could top him now.

MEG MILLIGREW KNEW HER LIFE WAS OVER WHEN SHE woke in the morning. Bella Harington had brought to the room where she was being held her clothes wrapped in a blanket, a purse with coins, and a wooden chest into which someone had stuffed samples of most of her herbs.

"I grieve for you," Bella had whispered, and squeezed her arm. "I know what it is to be sent away from her for—for deceits. Above all, Her Majesty must have those she can trust and who trust her in her care."

Meg wanted to beg to see Her Grace again, but she was too numb to talk and the big lump on her forehead throbbed from where she'd fainted to the floor. She thought of poor Catherine Howard's ghost at Hampton Court, which—even when the queen's court was in residence there—ran down the hall at night to try to get past King Henry's guards so she could beg for her life. But the guards hadn't let her pass. Screaming her false innocence, like her ghost still did, the queen had been arrested, tried, and beheaded. At least Meg Milligrew was just being condemned to marriage with Ben Wilton back in London, she tried to tell herself.

This all seemed so unreal now, the days she had spent with Elizabeth Tudor when she was princess

and now queen. What a heady brew was the awe and
thrill and challenge and joy of being her herbalist,
even her friend. Dear Kat had mothered Meg just as
she had the queen. Meg would miss Jenks and—Ned.
Ned was not even here to bid her farewell, and when
he heard that she'd been wed all these years, would he
even pity her a little bit? So stuck on himself, would he
ever know how her heart had flown when he so much
as looked at her? Like being near the queen, when
Meg breathed his air, she soared.

She sat slumped on the cot in the dim room, as if
waiting for the executioner. But Bella had explained
that Cecil had spoken with Ben Wilton and had
cleared her of any possible treason. Meg shrugged.
What did it matter now if Ben beat or abused her?
What did it matter when the dream of one's dreary
life—a dream that had come true for a time—was
gone?

She stood to face Ben when he came in.

"They said—the queen's woman said," he began,
twisting his hat in his big hands as he studied her sus-
piciously, "that you got kicked in the head. And you
din't know who you was for a long time and still don't
recall much, Sarah."

Meg nodded. She could just hear Ned correcting
Ben Wilton's grammar. And *Sarah*. She was no longer
Sarah Scutea nor Sarah Wilton, not in her crazy head
or in her hurt heart. Her true self was Meg Milligrew.

"They said," he went on when she didn't speak,
"the coins you gave me and some more you'd have are
for us to start life again in London and I'm to treat you

good." He held up a small, fat purse, then let it drop from his belt again. "You go 'long with me and I'll try," he added, but she saw a vein throb in his forehead as if he was holding back. "Look, Sarah, the money's enough for me to lease back your folks' old 'pothecary shop on the Strand just down from Whitehall Palace so's you can run it. Who knows the queen won't shop there, give you a royal warrant and all."

Meg shook her head as she gathered her things. "That's all over," she finally choked out.

"Her woman said Her Majesty's relying on me to take good care a you. And that this paper"——he produced the parchment where she'd forged the queen's name—"really was from her, delivered by you."

Meg couldn't stem the tears then, at Her Grace's gift even in her anger. How desperately Meg desired to be here to help her through the loss of Lord Robin and all the troubles it had caused.

"Wait 'til everyone hears who you served," Ben's voice droned on as they left the castle. "They'll come flocking to the 'pothecary, put some real coins in our purse, eh? Now, see here, Sarah," he said, spinning her around to face him just outside the walls, "I'm gonna try to take care a you, but you gotta do like I say. Come on now, woman."

She moved quickly so he wouldn't touch her again. She feared he'd take care of her, all right, one way or the other. Not looking back, she followed Ben Wilton down to the public landing where they caught a hired barge downriver to London.

But at the last minute, before the turn in the

Thames, she glanced back to see the top of the sturdy
Round Tower before it disappeared with all she had
left behind and would never have again.

"SO WHAT IS IT?" NED DEMANDED WHEN HE RENDEZ-
voused with Jenks, who was gesturing at him madly
not twenty yards into the woods. Ned couldn't decide
whether to tell him what he'd learned from the old
woman or just save it for the queen, but he didn't even
have an extra moment to decide.

"A body," Jenks told him, breathless, dragging him
by one arm deeper toward a small, wooded ravine.

"What? Whose?"

"See for yourself."

Ned smelled the corpse before he saw it. It had evidently been stuffed in a hollow log with leaves shoved
in after it, for Jenks had not been too careful in its res-
urrection.

"Fletcher?" he asked, nearly gagging. The corpse
was naked but for a pair of linen underbreeches.
"What happened—that is, what did she do to him?"
he asked, his voice nasal as he held his nose.

"Not her usual style," Jenks observed stolidly.
"Looks like she's stuck some small dagger in his ribs
from behind, then cut his throat."

"And took his clothes so no one could trace him?"

"If that was her purpose, she wasn't too careful.
One of them dropped a note about payment they're
due that's signed by some man with a Spanish-
sounding name. We've got to ride," Jenks said, kicking

leaves back over the corpse. "All we need is someone finding us with him."

"Ride where? You mean to confront de Quadra? You think that's where the girl's gone?"

Jenks pulled the paper in question from his jerkin and began to unfold it carefully. Within were long hanks of brown hair.

"She stripped him of his hair too?" Ned asked.

"No. His was always short and thin. She cut her own," Jenks explained as if Ned were the slow one. "I warrant in his clothes, hair cut like him, and on his horse, Hester Harington could make it past the guards to get back in Windsor. We've got to get back there and warn her. Like I said, let's ride, and if you can't keep up, that's just too damned bad."

*The fowler hides as close as he may*
*The net where caught the silly bird should be*
*Lest he the threatening prison should but see*
*And so for fear be forced to fly away.*

*My lady sews while she doth assay*
*In curled knots fast to entangle me*
*Puts on her veil to the end I should not flee*
*The golden net wherein I am a prey.*

*What needs such art my thoughts then to entrap*
*When of themselves they fly into your lap?*

— JOHN HARINGTON

 ELIZABETH OF ENGLAND STOOD BY HERSELF on the vast, flat stone roof of Windsor Castle above the royal apartments, waiting for Hester Harington to find her. For the second evening, she had ordered the guards thinned and had sent her ladies away. The door to the roof from her privy stairs stood open, but she did not yet have that old feeling she was being watched by someone who wished her harm.

Though the queen could command thousands, she had never felt more alone. That was as it must be tonight and mayhap always. It was partly penance for becoming besotted with Robin when she must never trust a man. It was atonement for ignoring the business of her realm and her precious reputation, which she must now resurrect and protect at all costs.

"Like wearing a hair shirt now and hereafter," she whispered as she scratched at Dr. Dee's flying harness under her tight bodice. Her father's fanatical first wife, Catherine of Aragon, had worn a hair shirt when she could no longer please him because Anne Boleyn had danced into his life. Now Elizabeth, their heir, must rid herself of Hester to regain the kingdom and the power and the glory. She must be the bait in her own trap.

Her legs and back ached from standing, her shoulders from the taut, thin, wirelike ropes of the harness attached to the turret above. Just as the sickle of moon sliced through the scudding clouds, Elizabeth saw a shadow emerge from the door. She could discern the pale silhouette of a slender man, mayhap Hester's embodiment of Franklin Dove. From here the hair seemed much shorter, but then he—she—wore a cap pulled low.

"I never thought to find you here," the soft voice, Hester's indeed, said. The queen saw her look up, behind, and all around the dim area before she wedged something into the door to keep it closed. "I have ascertained you have no guards waiting below or hidden here to pounce on me in some sort of trap."

"Where would I hide a guard on this vast stretch of roof?" Elizabeth countered, gesturing slowly. "I felt we must have a privy discussion and knew you would want to come here, even if just to peer in windows at the sorrow you have wrought. Dare I guess you have been visiting my chambers again, niece Hester? I hope the royal food and drink, bathwater, and clothes suited you these last weeks I took you in."

"Took me in—deceived me, that's sure. You were falsely kind, then callous, then cruel. Nothing you have done since has suited me!" she cried, stepping forward with a bit of swagger.

"Why did you not come to me when you first ran away from home?" Elizabeth pursued, standing her ground. "Why did you not tell me the truth of your checkered Tudor heritage?"

"Do you think I do not know you told my parents to exile me to the countryside, make me marry a man unworthy of me so I could breed his brats and dilute my heirs' royal blood? You must have always feared my heritage!"

"Hester, I gave you no thought for years, as I had other problems, other people to worry about, and—"

"That's it, try to belittle me again, the granddaughter of a king and your own niece and heir," she cried, hitting her breastbone with her fist. "Try to say my mother came from an illegitimate affair. The true Catholic believers of this country and this world say *you* came from an *affaire de coeur* the king had with Anne Boleyn when only he believed he had divorced his true wife!" she ranted. "Wait until I tell your French and Spanish enemies who I really am when you are gone, Aunt Elizabeth!"

"But I am going nowhere, Hester," she insisted, fighting to keep calm when she longed to leap forward and smack the girl to her knees. The queen knew well enough zealous Papists would gladly swarm to promote even the likes of Hester Harington as queen over Protestant Anne Boleyn's daughter.

"Had you *known* who I was," Hester was saying quietly, as if she had never slipped into a tirade, "you would never have taken me in—never have taken me *unknown* without my brilliant music. You would never have raised me high, as you have our kin Lady Katherine Grey or Baron Hunsdon."

" 'Raised me high,' Hester? Is that why you've thrown others down from heights? Was it simply that they were in your way, or was it some sort of warning to me that you stood above them in your regard?"

"Here is my last warning for you," Hester whispered, then sang in an eerie voice the children's rhyme, *"Her fall is nigh who climbs so high.* You see, dear aunt, your master lutenist Geoffrey came upon me gazing in your windows at Richmond, but I knocked him unconscious with a brick with which I had thought to break your window. I seized his lute and played as he had before, even after I pushed him. It did not enter his mind that a mere girl who seemed drunk and was offering him a drink—"

"You stole, then splashed my wine on him," the queen accused, gripping her hands hard together. "For many weeks, Hester, you have watched me and stalked me as prey you would entrap. Then Luke Morgan got in your way, but what of Amy Dudley?"

"Amy Dudley?" Hester asked, crossing her arms over her chest and rocking slightly back on her heels as if she were enjoying this. "You mean your lover Lord

Robert's wife, whom you arranged to have pushed down the stairs by some lackey you hired? I just might confess to your counselors, like Lord Cecil—to your entire court and beyond—that you sent me to do it. You only detained me in Eton first so it would look as if I escaped and then harmed Amy at the behest of someone else."

Elizabeth stared at the girl, aghast. For once the depth and breadth of her twisted hatred stunned the queen to silence.

"You think I had something to do with her fall?" Hester went on, taking the inquisitor's part now. "No, I accuse you of causing her death, and you must be cast down from your arrogance for that as well as other crimes and sins."

"Stop playing me for the simpleton, as you have in the past," the queen commanded, her muscles tightening against what she sensed was coming. But she must press on to find out who else was involved. "You and whoever sent you to Amy could only hope her death would be my downfall. That someone was either de Quadra or—ah," Elizabeth said, as Hester sucked in a sharp breath at his name, "that figures, since you mentioned the Spanish Papists. De Quadra it is, then?"

"I am just astounded how you blame everyone but yourself, aunt. Besides, many have hired me to do their bidding, including yourself and your precious Lord Robert. *He* deserves to be brought down too, for the way he treated Amy. But for an accident of birth and cruelty of chance—and your hatred of me because you are in league with my parents—I could be queen."

Her voice became sharper, her expression, even seen through thickening twilight, more contorted.

"I adored you from afar," Hester plunged on in her disjointed tirade. "I worshiped you when I saw you in the crowds, or riding with Robert Dudley, or on your barge, or through many a window. But now it is all over."

"You know I admire your brilliance and talent. Will you not tell me how you managed to kill Amy? You fooled me many times before, but I know your handprints were on her death. However did you carry it off so cleverly?"

Hester swept off her hat and threw it aside. She had severely hacked her hair with a knife or sword. "She sent them all away, her entire household, just to be with me," she boasted. "After all, I told her I was sent from Robert—and it killed me to kill her instead of you."

Hester lunged with both hands raised. The queen shoved her back. She had expected and prepared for this: the double ropes would hold and Cecil and Dr. Dee would rush to her aid from the small roof atop the narrow turret where they waited. But she must know if Robert had sent Hester to Cumnor.

"Hester, who sent you there?" she cried, shoving her back yet again. But the demented woman flashed a knife at her, above her in a huge arcing swipe. It glinted in thin moonlight as it caught one of the harness ropes. The queen feared she had fatally miscalculated. Who could fathom that a murderess who pushed people to their deaths would have a knife?

Though thrown off balance, Elizabeth hardly budged as the shoulder ties yanked. The girl was slashing, sawing at them.

"Now!" the queen cried to Dee and Cecil, and heard an answering shout. She longed for Jenks, for he could have just leaped to her aid, not climbed down a damned, shaky wooden ladder.

Ducking Hester's high swings with the weapon, the queen fumbled for the small stone cudgel she had at her belt, but it was pressed between them. Her shoulder ropes went slack and fell free. Hester heaved her back. They struggled for eternity, the queen pressed to the very edge, the knifepoint nearly in her chest while, with all her might, she counterbalanced Hester's thrust of it. Though the queen kept her feet fairly anchored, Hester pressed her head and shoulders into the wall's deep niche, just like the one Geoffrey had gone through at Richmond.

Elizabeth wrenched the knife away, cutting her palm. They grappled for the weapon at waist level. Despite the slice of pain and her bloodied, slippery hand, she tried to stab at Hester's midriff. The girl's purse broke free, and coins cascaded and clattered at their feet even as the knife skittered away.

"That was her knife—Amy's," Hester gritted out. "She wanted to die, fell so easily—but you . . ."

Elizabeth could have held her ground, except Hester seemed willing to go over with her. Everywhere the queen hit or grabbed at the girl with her right hand, she left a slippery mark of blood. Suddenly Cecil's face appeared, John Dee's too, but Hester clawed and kicked at them. Cecil tried to reach for Hester, Dee for the queen, as both women teetered on the edge of night.

In one last, mad moment, writhing, struggling, their weight took them over. Hester grabbed for Elizabeth, but the queen pulled free. With the queen's blood smeared across her face, the girl shouted a curse and simply vanished.

Flailing upside down, Elizabeth saw only blackness. No, her skirts shrouded her head as her ankle ropes jerked taut and held. Under her skirts, the hidden ropes she and Dr. Dee had tied down from her harness to new stone fastenings on the floor as double anchors had saved her. But where in hell were Dee and Cecil while she dangled upside down?

The men hauled her, ignominiously, back up.

"Thank God, thank God," Cecil kept muttering as he wrapped her cut hand in a handkerchief.

"What took you so long after I shouted?" Elizabeth cried, sucking in a breath of clean, fresh air.

"We came immediately," Cecil insisted, "but it just seemed like a year—to me too."

But, she thought, as Dee cut her free of the foothold ropes, she had outsmarted and outlasted Hester, just as she would anyone else, sane or insane, who wanted her throne.

"There would never have been that much slack to allow you to budge if she hadn't cut the ropes above," Dr. Dee was saying fretfully. "I'll have to restring those better next time."

The queen would have laughed if she were not

afraid of plunging into hysteria. "There will not be a next time for me, good doctor, not trying to fly," Elizabeth assured them, still gasping for breath and fighting dizziness. Cecil was so white it looked as if he were the one who had nearly been lost.

"At least all this, Dr. Dee," Cecil said, his hand steadying her arm, "shows Her Majesty has now learned to keep her feet firmly on the ground."

"Ha!" she countered. "I may have had my feet tied down, but to a high roof under the heavens."

Gingerly, as if they all had fought that slip of demon girl, they leaned over the edge of the parapet to look below. It appeared the dark-clad body of a thin man was splayed on the courtyard stones.

"It ends as it began," Elizabeth whispered. "Dr. Dee, I must get out of this harness, as I shall never wear anyone's again."

Let clever Cecil wonder what that meant, she thought as she saw him hastily stoop to gather some folded papers Hester must have lost amidst her coins.

Still shaken, the queen walked unsteadily down her privy stairs to her rooms, with Dr. Dee and Cecil close behind, carrying a lantern they had lit. She walked into her bedchamber the same moment someone began pounding on the door.

"Your Majesty, it's Jenks!"

"Enter!"

Jenks and Ned, mud-spattered with a cluster of guards behind them, nearly fell into the room in their haste.

"Hester's on her way back in man's guise and she's

got a knife!" Jenks cried, scanning the room wide-eyed.

"And we think," Ned added, breathless, "de Quadra is behind Lady Dudley's death."

"What would I ever do without all of you?" the queen said, turning to take Cecil's arm. "My lord, stay with me, and the rest of you get Hester's body out of the courtyard," she told her astounded men. "Bring her inside and lay her out carefully. I shall tell her parents the dreadful news."

"I will go down with your men and then tell them myself," Cecil insisted.

"No, it is my place."

Cecil stood straighter, as if at attention. "The pinnacle of all England," he said, "is your place and ever shall be."

BELLA SHOOK WITH SOBS BUT JOHN HARINGTON STOOD dry-eyed at Hester's makeshift bier. They would set out toward home at dawn. The queen slipped back into the lantern-lit chamber—the same one Luke Morgan had died in—from which Hester's coffin would be carried to a wagon for the journey back to the Harington home. Her death and burial would be private for many reasons.

"Your Grace, our gratitude is unending," John said when he saw she had stepped back in. "For not making what she did—tried to do—public. For giving us the gift of our son's being born without a cloud over his head and his name."

Elizabeth stepped forward to take Bella's and John's hands, then pressed their palms together. They were blessed to have each other and must never be parted. Though she did not want to gaze on Hester's face again, she frowned down at her peaceful profile.

"In this sad turn of events, it is best to let the truth sleep with the dead," she said, realizing she spoke of Amy Dudley as well. Suddenly she understood and felt kin to both women who had been kept in country exile when they longed for so much more. "John," she added, "find some decent lutenist to play something beautiful before you bury her. Godspeed. Jenks will care for you, and you must come back to me soon so the child can be born at court with my doctors in attendance."

She slipped out into the dim corridor. Flanked by two guards, the queen climbed the broad, lighted stairs toward the royal apartments. She was halfway up when Ned came running after her.

"Your Grace!" he whispered, gesturing her to the side. "There is something you must have."

Frowning, she turned back to him under a hanging lantern as he extended a folded, wrinkled parchment to her. "Not a petition to me about Meg Milligrew," she said. "I will not change my mind on that."

"No," he whispered, though he looked deeply distressed as well as exhausted. "It's a note I found on the body—Hester's—earlier and nearly forgot I'd slid it in my shirt."

She opened it where she stood, unable to wait to see the last insulting song the demented girl must have kept on herself to be found if her cause were lost. Or would it be another letter for Hester linking her to her patron, like the one Jenks had brought back from Cumnor, this time mayhap from the wily de Quadra himself?

Her trembling hands smoothed the small piece of paper on the thick oak banister. She squinted to read it, then gasped.

It was a mere four lines of a flippant little song she had heard Hester sing more than once:

> I shall do anything for you
> To stand in your good graces.
> Perhaps if you won't favor this,
> I'll put on other faces.

But it was not the ditty itself that stunned her. The lines were addressed *To My Master, the Queen's High Man, Lord Cecil*.

A MESSENGER WITH THE VERDICT FROM CUMNOR ARRIVED the next week when the court was preparing to return to London. The coroner's jury had ruled the cause of Amy Robsart Dudley's demise was *Fatal Mischance*, adding, *No one person is deemed directly to blame*.

Yet Elizabeth stared at her face in her looking glass for a good hour after secluding herself, as she said, to pray, and then used her black window like a mirror again that night. Was she to blame, even if indirectly? Or Robert? His man, Edmund Fletcher, had been with Hester, but he could have been in someone else's employ, since Robert had told Cecil that he knew not where the man had gone. At any rate, the queen had summoned Robert Dudley back to court on the morrow.

De Quadra? A mere paper one of his aides had signed saying money was owed the lutenist meant naught, at least not enough to confront the man or banish him from England. The wily King Philip of Spain would just send another Spanish snake, mayhap worse than this one. Cecil and de Quadra seemed to get on, and that would be helpful to keep the peace, wouldn't it?

But Cecil . . . What were the true implications of the note Ned had given her? She had not asked him—was afraid to ask him and thereby mayhap lose her closest adviser and the bulwark of her strength. But Cecil was hardly the type to pay for songs or have time to mentor musical talent. She recalled how quickly he had bent to retrieve the papers that had fallen with Hester's coins. And she could only guess at the depths to which his absence from court had plunged him and to what lengths he might go to be certain he and not Robert was the one to whom she turned in the running of the realm. She recalled how hard Cecil had argued that Hester would have no motive to harm Amy, but was he protesting too much? And on the rooftop, had he reached for Hester to seize her or to shove her over so she would not implicate him?

"Cecil, can I not trust you either?" she cracked out,

jumping up so hard her chair fell backward on the floor. "Then I swear I shall trust but myself!"

Stomping over to her jewelry box, she smacked the lid open against the wall. She folded the Cecil note with the one implicating de Quadra, then rummaged through the deep, crowded chest to the very bottom. She snatched out a flat box. She'd keep both these papers for ammunition if it was needed.

" 'S bones and blood!" she muttered as she jammed the papers flat under the velvet lining of the box of pearls Robin had given her. "I alone am queen, and that is that."

# The Afterword

*Vengeance shall fall on thy disdain,*
*That makest but game on earnest pain:*
*Think not alone under the sun*
*Unquit to cause thy lover's complaints,*
*Although my lute and I have done.*

— SIR THOMAS WYATT, *the Elder*

DECEMBER 18, 1560
WHITEHALL PALACE, LONDON

"MY ANSWER TO HER INQUIRY IS STILL no," Elizabeth told Cecil.

She noted well her courtiers ceased their chatter and pricked up their ears as if they were all in de Quadra's hire to spy on anything she said, even in her presence chamber. Indeed, she herself had grown wiser about using informants lately: She had not only sent Dr. Dee to France for several months, but had dispatched a handsome messenger to her cousin Margaret Douglas in Yorkshire with a fine Christmas gift—and the command he come back with intelligence about what was going on up there in the wilds.

"But, Your Majesty," Cecil protested gently, taking the petition she shoved back at him across the table, "Queen Mary Stuart writes of the burdens of barren widowhood in her young age and how far she has fallen. . . ."

His voice trailed off, and he exchanged a hooded look with the queen before plunging on. "Therefore, the Queen of Scots and France—"

"Former queen of France now her young husband is dead of an ear infection," she interrupted. "We all know her mother-in-law, Catherine de Medici, is regent of France for her second young son, so let Mary of Scots go home and try to rule her nation on her own, as I do—until, of course, my Lord Cecil, we make a fine foreign marriage for me."

"Then let me bring to your attention, Your Grace, that the *former* queen of France did at least finally ratify the Treaty of Edinburgh."

"Which you worked hard for, my lord. But the woman dared to slander me and to quarter England's insignia on her coat-of-arms and to say she should rule here in place of me. I will not have her passing through my kingdom, foul North Seas weather or not. If she means to go home to Scotland, she may land in Scotland."

She noted Cecil sighed heavily before he placed the petition up his sleeve. He would not look so melancholy for long, she thought, not when she sprang her surprise on him today. And the one she had for Robin.

As if her thoughts had summoned him, Robin stepped forward from her coterie, handsome and glittering in his black and gold, the colors he had worn since he had been back at court. She supposed the gold was to imply he could yet be royalty, the black that he remained in mourning. Mayhap he was the latter since she had made him her friend but not her favorite these last months.

Elizabeth inhaled deeply to steady herself for this. The halls, even this presence chamber, smelled of fir and holly boughs the servants had been hanging for the coming holidays. Her own scent of rosewater and lavender—she wondered again how Meg Milligrew was faring, for she missed her hand on the herbs— made her nostrils flare.

"My friends, as you know," she said to quiet them again, "I have summoned you today for the bestow- ment of an earldom on Lord Robert Dudley. But first, now that my comptroller, Sir Thomas Parry, has de- parted this life to leave the office of Master of the Court of Wards open, I must tell you I am bestowing that great office on William Cecil, in addition to his duties as my chief secretary."

It pleased her to see she had taken Cecil by surprise. And Robert, who no doubt thought that lucrative post should be his. In addition, of course, to his elevation to the peerage he'd dared to push for as a outward sign that she believed he was innocent of Amy's death.

"Ah, here is the other matter," the queen said, hold- ing up the patent for the peerage that would create him Earl of Leicester and place him permanently in the House of Lords, as he thought was his due.

Robert Dudley glowed with confidence. He could not help it, she thought. It was his way, and that would make him a dominating king and difficult husband.

But she could not help loving him, though she had grieved for and buried all those girlish dreams now.

She reached for Amy Dudley's knife, which she now used to break seals on correspondence. Whether or not Robin recognized it did not matter, for it was the queen's keepsake, a reminder of many things.

"No," she said, frowning and cocking her head, as she gazed at the document so dramatically that she knew Ned Topside would approve. "I fear not just now, for certain pains still smart and cause agony to us all. Mayhap at a later time."

She stuck the knife in the ornately lettered patent and sliced it cleanly in two.

Some gasped audibly; others stood speechless. Cecil got a coughing fit. A telltale vein throbbed in Robin's neck, and he simply looked the angriest she had ever seen him.

"Are you mad?" he cried, balling up his fists, one on the ornate hilt of his dress sword. "You shame me and my name!"

She stood and, tossing the knife and the torn paper to the table, leveled a straight arm and index finger at him. "I have raised you to where you now stand, my lord, and may someday raise you higher. But I tell you—all of you—there is no master and but one mistress here!"

No one breathed. Cecil knelt first, then the others randomly until only she and Robin were left standing. Their eyes met and held, his fury fading to fear, hers unblinking and steady.

Then Robert Dudley went down on both knees before the queen of England as she swept from the room.
By the time her ladies caught up with her, she walked
alone through the frozen privy garden in the shadow
of the palace towers.

## *The Author's Note*

THE QUESTION OF WHO KILLED AMY ROBSART DUDLEY IS one of the most intriguing historical mysteries of all time. Although the evidence was closely examined and the case formally tried at the time, no definitive conclusion was reached. Robert Dudley was implicated and reviled on and off over the years of his life and even after. In recent times it has even been conjectured that Amy's death was not a murder, suicide, or accident of falling down the stairs: From the distance of centuries, one modern-day sleuth has claimed her broken neck was caused by a spontaneous fracture, a side effect of her advanced breast cancer.

I believe, however, that someone powerful hired a "hit man"—or woman—to dispatch Amy, either hoping to free Elizabeth to wed Dudley or to shame her publicly and discredit him permanently. The candidates for such a "sponsor" are highlighted in this novel. The undisputed fact that Amy herself insisted that nearly everyone in the household go to the Abingdon fair suggests that she had a compelling reason beyond mere whim to be alone that day.

Among the many suspicious circumstances and theories (including my fictional version), one thing, however, seems clear. As writer George Adlard put it after studying the Dudley case for years, "The mystery connected with the death of Amye [multiple spellings were common in Elizabeth's England] Robsart will probably never be cleared up."

The poems and song lyrics included in this story are those that could have been popular at this early stage of Elizabeth's reign. The ones attributed to Sir Thomas Wyatt I found especially pertinent, since he was twice arrested and imprisoned in connection with charges of adultery with Queen Anne Boleyn and in both cases received a pardon and returned to King Henry VIII's favor. It is fitting that a man with such apparent appeal be quoted in a story about the charismatic Dudley's hold on Queen Anne's daughter, Elizabeth.

Katherine Grey is yet to cause the queen much travail; the very month this story ends the girl committed an act of high treason that Elizabeth does not discover until later, with dreadful results. Mary, Queen of Scots, will remain the thorn in the queen's side for years. The people who caused Elizabeth the most concern in her reign were those "blood-kin" who had various claims, however convoluted, to her throne.

Lord Robert Dudley's story hardly ends here, nor does Cecil's, Kat's, Dr. Dee's, or even Meg Milligrew's. Look for the continuation of their tales in *The Queene's Cure.*

I will close with a few lines from a 1559 song that highlights the young queen's increasingly tense and dangerous personal and political dilemma about marriage. It is fascinating that so early in her reign, this songwriter read the queen's dawning realization of her destiny so well:

> *Here is my hand,*
> *My dear lover England.*
> *I am thine both*
> *With mind and with heart.*

> — WILLIAM BIRCH
> from *A Song Between the*
> *Queen's Majesty and England*

## ABOUT THE AUTHOR

*K*AREN *H*ARPER is the author of two previous Elizabeth I mysteries: *The Tidal Poole* and *The Poyson Garden*, as well as a number of contemporary suspense and historical novels. Her new Elizabeth I mystery, *The Queene's Cure*, will be published in April 2002. She lives in Columbus, Ohio, and Naples, Florida.

Turn the page for an exclusive preview of

# *The Queene's Cure*

The new book in Karen Harper's thrilling
Elizabeth I Mystery series

**Available in April 2002**
**wherever hardcover books are sold**

# Chapter the First

*Other distinctions and difference I leave to the learned Physicians*
*of our London College, who are very well able to search this matter, as*
*a thing far above my reach . . . none fitter than the learned Physicians*
*of the College of London.*

—JOHN GERARD
*The Herball*

SEPTEMBER 25, 1562

 QUEEN ELIZABETH WAS MOUNTED AND WAITING. She shaded her eyes and waved up at the parapet of Whitehall Palace where Kat Ashley was taking her first constitutional walk in the ten days since Dr. Burcote had cured her fever.

Kat smiled wanly and waved back. The old woman's recovery would have ordinarily been enough to make the royal spirits soar, but Elizabeth Tudor was en route to visit the Royal College of Physicians in the City. She was even less pleased with them than she had been ten days ago when she had needed them and they were gone. For since then, they had begged off a royal visit—twice.

"A lovely day for an outing," Mary Sidney nearly sang the words as her brother, Robert Dudley, whom they both affectionately called Robin, helped her mount directly behind the queen. Ever the optimist, Mary was quite as pretty as she was pleasant, though that lighthearted humor ill-suited the queen today.

Her Majesty heard a rumbling noise and glanced behind.

Boonen, her coachman, was bringing up her round-topped, wooden and leather coach, pulled by the eight matched white mules. Though a ride in it over ruts or cobbles could shake the teeth out of one's head, Elizabeth's use of the three she had ordered had set a new trend.

This one, her oldest, was upholstered inside with black velvet embossed with gold and outside was richly gilded. Like all of them, it was adorned with ostrich plumes. The effect of the equipage was exactly the awe she wanted, though folk had finally stopped calling it "the monster." She had not wanted to ride in it on the way today, but perhaps it would do for her return if the weather changed or the visit was as trying as she expected. She could, of course, have summoned the College fellows here, but she had wanted to beard the lions in their own den and see exactly what prey they had been hunting lately.

After all, that pride of lions was lorded over by two men who did not wish her well. Peter Pascal, their past president, gossip said, had never forgiven a personal tragedy for which he blamed the Tudors. When the Catholic Church was cast from England, her royal father had ordered Pascal's beloved mentor, Sir Thomas More, imprisoned and beheaded. Some said Great Henry could have saved More, but was angry with his former friend for censuring the king's conscience.

Elizabeth felt that Sir Thomas and others were legally judged guilty only for their refusal to take the Oath of Supremacy. This act granted Henry and his heirs—especially, at that time, the newborn Protestant Princess Elizabeth for whose mother the Catholic Church was dissolved—the right to head both the kingdom and the new Church of England.

But all that was before the torrent crashed over the mill dam: Anne Boleyn beheaded, Elizabeth declared bastard, and four other stepmothers paraded through her young life. Elizabeth could grasp bitterness over someone beloved being beheaded, but she was not to be blamed for what her father had done or for being Protestant either. She was willing to let men, even Papists like Pascal, follow their consciences as long as they didn't rock the royal ship of state.

But of even more immediate concern was the eminent physician John Caius, the current president of the college. Also an ardent Papist, he had never forgiven Elizabeth for dismissing him from his lucrative, prestigious post as court physician when she came to the throne four years ago. But it was precisely the fact that he had served their Catholic majesties, Queen Mary and the Spanish King Philip, so assiduously that made her mistrust the man.

Actually, she didn't approve of Pascal's and Caius's actions any more than they did hers. Though both were learned men, she felt they had their feet mired in the past. Surely new methods and remedies were needed to fight disease today, not old physick. Yes, those two heading the Royal College of Physicians needed a close watch as she urged them to lead England's struggle against common workaday disease and the tragedy of random, sweeping pestilence.

"Isn't it just a splendid day, Your Grace?" Mary's sweet voice repeated as if Elizabeth had not heard her the first time. Her hand on the pommel, the queen shifted slightly in her sidesaddle to see her friend better.

"The weather, my dear Mary, might as well have storm clouds after the learned doctors delayed this meeting twice," Elizabeth groused. "Delayed meeting with *me*."

"I understand, Your Majesty," Robin put in, looking up at her, "that they had an official convocation in Cambridge, then must needs go on to Oxford. And the second time they petitioned for a stay, their messenger said it was to be certain their premises were pristine for your perusal."

"As if they had something to tidy up or hide," she added ominously.

He flashed a smile as he took her reins from a groom, patted her white stallion's flank, and tried another tack. "It is true that they overvalue their power and always have, Your Grace."

"Indeed," she replied crisply, tugging the reins from his big, brown hands, "for I have known others to do such and pay the price." With a narrow look at him, she spurred her horse before he could mount his.

Others fell quickly into their appointed places in the royal retinue. Usually the queen traveled by river barge but she was a splendid horsewoman. She always felt more in control when mounted than encased in a coach. Yet armed guards with swords circumspectly sheathed rode ahead of and behind her.

Only two ladies-in-waiting accompanied her today, Mary Sidney and Anne Carey, the latter wed to her dear cousin Harry Carey, Baron Hunsdon. Two men rode her flanks, Robin, her Master of the Horse, who scrambled to catch up and, because she always felt safer when he was at her side, a man of no rank but in her lofty regard, her long-time protector, Stephen Jenks. If any of the horses balked, a mere look or touch from Jenks would calm them. With the carriage rattling over cobbles behind their mounts, they clattered out of the King Street Gate into the busy flow of London foot, cart, and horse traffic.

The queen gave but a quick glance back at the white towers and glittering, bannered pinnacles of the palace that symbolized the Tudor monarchy. Kat still stood on the parapet of sprawling, rose-bricked Whitehall, the queen's official London seat. Its twenty-four acres stretched between two main east-west thoroughfares of her capital, the broad River Thames and this passageway cutting through Whitehall's grounds. The latter was called King's Street, or more simply "the street." Though the city was awash with people, it was good to be away from the overly ambitious, watchful two-thousand hopefuls who always jostled each other for place and position around her. In bright sun and crisp breeze, she waved to the common folk.

"Give way! Uncap there, knaves! Give access to the queen's majesty!" her first two guards began to shout in repetition. When her people heard the cry or glimpsed the queen herself, they parted like the sea. Men hoisted boys on their shoulders to see better; maids waved scarves or hats; old women peered from second- or third-story windows. The faces of her people turned and tilted toward their queen like flowers to the sun. It was always that way, and her love flowed back to them.

"God save Yer Grace! Long live our good queen, Bess Tudor!" and a hundred other jumbled cries assailed her ears. Ordinarily, that was enough to buoy her up; today it only slightly sweetened her sour humor.

But the shops and taverns did have their doors ajar. She caught glimpses of the wares within. Sometimes she wondered what it would be like to stroll the streets and peek in with no one noticing, to be simply English and not the English queen. Once, when she had Meg Milligrew in her household, she had planned to do just that, for the girl resembled her and, on a whim, she had thought to change places with her for a brief hour. But that was tomfoolery and best put away like so much else. Nothing mattered but being a good queen and a strong one. And commoner to courtier, ignorant carter to learned physician, the folk of her realm had best realize she meant to rule and not just reign.

As the queen's party turned into the long, broad street called the Strand, Elizabeth averted her eyes from the apothecary shop that Sarah Wilton, alias Meg Milligrew, her former Strewing Herb Mistress of the Privy Chamber, managed. She worked it with her husband, Ben Wilton, once a bargeman who now lorded it over the shop, the lazy lout. Through Ned Topside, the queen's fool and principal player, and two other sources of town gossip, Bett and Gil Sharpe, Elizabeth knew Meg's fate. But Meg had misled her queen about being wed. Worse, she had dared to pass herself off as the queen without permission and had even forged her royal signature.

Her Majesty always looked straight ahead as she passed, even when she knew Meg stood in her door, because she could not bear to look into her eyes or admit she had sent the girl away too hastily. God forgive her, she'd far rather trust Meg then her own treason-tainted cousins, Katherine Grey and Margaret Douglas, who coveted her throne.

Katherine was currently confined to the Tower on the other side of town that also housed Margaret's dangerous Scottish husband, Matthew Stewart, Earl of Lennox. Margaret, who favored Mary, Queen of Scots for the English throne, was herself under house arrest with her son Lord Darnley at Sir Richard Sackville's home at Sheen. Her Royal Majesty was not backing down from dealing with anyone who challenged or defied her.

"Don't see Meg—I mean Sarah—today, Your Majesty," Jenks called to her. "She's always hanging out the door or window when you go by. Seen her on boats in the Thames when the royal barge passes too. But look, there's Bett waving!"

"Leave off," Elizabeth said without letting her gaze waver. "I don't give a fig if you and Ned visit the shop, but do not try to cozen me into taking her back."

"But I din't mean—"

"Ride ahead and tell the eminent doctors that their queen is on her way and she has much to say."

HER STOMACH KNOTTED WITH CHURNING EMOTIONS, SARAH Wilton watched and waited. Cocking her head, she listened too. Ah, there was the distant clatter of a goodly number of horses' hooves. Huzzahs came closer, echoing in the narrow, crooked streets of the City, the heart of London within the old walls and gates. She tugged her hood closer about her face, then gripped her hands tightly under her russet cloak. The queen was coming.

As the entourage and its crowd slipped into the end of Knightrider Street, Sarah stepped back into the narrow mouth of an alley so she would not be seen by the palace folk or the robed and flat-capped physicians who were slowly filing outside their ornately facaded guildhall. Their large, four-storied, black-and-white framed building was a place the barber-surgeons and apothecaries of London knew all too well, but she wondered exactly why the queen was visiting today.

Sarah, who still always thought of herself as Meg Milligrew no matter what her husband or the others called her, reckoned she knew most things about the queen, even those that had happened the last two years since she'd been sent away in disgrace from royal service. And one thing Meg Milligrew knew was that Elizabeth of England seldom made purely social visits, not that clever queen.

Pressing herself against the plaster wall, Meg peeked around the corner as the noisy rabble filled the street. She picked out the queen's one-time favorite, Lord Robin Dudley, and skimmed the queen's retainers for Her Grace's Secretary of State, the wily William Cecil. Fortunately, he wasn't here, because not much escaped his eyes. Then Meg saw, in the center of it all, Elizabeth.

Meg's skin prickled, and her mouth went dry. Her Grace looked fine as ever—maybe a bit thinner, if that were possible—but Meg could read vexation in the clenched set of the high, pale brow and purse of the narrow lips. Aye, Bess Tudor was here apurpose for more than reveling in public adoration or a pleasant chat with the chief doctors of her realm. Meg could see her dark eyes assessing the small cluster of cloaked and befurred master physicians before she intentionally turned away from their set smiles to wave again with a slender, gloved hand to the crowd. The people responded as if she'd caressed them, the dolts, for Meg, like Lord Robin, knew well that royal affection lavished one day could languish the next.

Under her dark blue riding cloak, the queen wore another new gown Meg hadn't seen, a dark green brocade edged with sable that set off the gleam of her red-gold hair peeking out from her feathered hat. Her Grace's detested summer freckles still looked faded. Mayhap she was yet using the tansy and buttermilk face wash Meg had suggested when Elizabeth was but a princess and lived in exile.

"But four short years ago," Meg whispered as a shiver raced up her spine. She clasped her hands and glared as those blackguards who were Fellows of the Royal College bowed to the queen and gestured for her to come inside. They were always trying to rule Meg's—and all apothecaries' lives—with their dictums and pronouncements. An apothecary could even go to prison for hinting a particular medicinal cure would work, for they wanted every farthing for their own purses for giving prescriptions.

*Physician's cooks*, the carping, complaining jackanapes were fond of calling those of her profession, and they treated women the worst of all. And neither the Company of Barber-Surgeons nor the guild of Grocers, Apothecaries, and Spicers were getting visits from the queen!

"But then, I'll never get to visit with her again," Meg spit out the words, suddenly more angry than sorry for herself as the queen dismounted and went inside. "Tender and terrible, the worst, cold, cruel and unforgiving . . ."

"Eh, you talking 'bout our queen?" a blue-coated apprentice behind her demanded so loud she jumped. He had come down the alley but now rounded on her. "Who you be, darin' talk 'bout our queen?"

Lest the lout make a scene and wishing that she had the brilliant thespian Ned Topside here to bail her out with some fantastical tale, she lied. "I'm talking about my husband, and if I have to call him over here, you'll be sorry. He's one of the queen's guards."

"Go on then!" the simpleton said, gaping. "God's truth? Eh, you," he went on, leaning closer to peer into her hood, "you know you look a wee bit like the queen, I mean coloring and all?"

Without answering, Meg ducked away into the press of people. Standing on her tiptoes to catch another glimpse of the woman she once would have died for—and now could kill for—Meg scurried between two other tight buildings, cross-cutting into the same alley where she'd hidden her goods. She had a lot to do before Her Majesty came back out.

"ALL OF YOU HAVE A LOFTY HERITAGE TO LIVE UP TO IN this fine edifice and historic site," the queen remarked as she completed her escorted tour and was led into the large front chamber of the College. As the twenty Fellows filed to their seats at the long, dark oak table, she surmised this served as their council room. She decided to forgo the plates of suckets, comfits, and an elaborate marchpane castle—bribes, all of it, she thought—they had laid out for her. But she took the proffered goblet of wine because she expected this to be thirsty work.

Before anyone could answer her subtle challenge about their guildhall, a fuss fomented outside. People on the street peeked in the front windows set ajar and began to cheer again; the royal guards evidently shoved them away. During the moment's respite, Elizabeth surreptitiously studied the assembled physicians, especially Pascal and Caius on either side of her at the head of the table. The two men were physical opposites, she noted, however much they had seemed to covertly conspire with silent, unreadable glances during her tour of their sprawling building and gardens.

The forty-eight-year-old Peter Pascal was as severely dressed as if he were a cleric. Or as if he were still in mourning for, no doubt, his illustrious mentor, whom he managed to mention incessantly. Pascal was plump, to put it nicely, as rosy-cheeked as a milkmaid, and quite effeminate-looking depsite his total baldness. The man obviously shaved what hair he had for its outline was a faint shadow above his ears and on the nape of his neck. Beards and mustaches, trimmed or long, were the fashion of the day, which he seemed to be directly flaunting in favor of older, clean-cut styles. His blue eyes bulged slightly the way her father's had, and that made her even more edgy around him.

Unlike his black-garbed friend, John Caius, aged fifty-two, was ornately attired to show his status with a scarlet and gray taffeta cassock buttoned to his chin and his wide sleeves trimmed with fur. The current president of the College was, in contrast to Pascal, rake-thin with sallow skin and a long, gaunt face, accented by a salt-and-pepper beard and long mustache. Wisps of gray hair peeked from beneath his traditional physician's circular cap. He moved deliberately and spoke portentously. His dark eyes darted, even when he addressed her, as if his mind were flitting elsewhere or he was afraid to look her in the eye.

"Indeed, your observations about our hall are precisely correct, Your Most Gracious Majesty, *Maxima Regina*," John Caius said, grandly addressing the entire assembly. "This building was donated to the College in perpetuity by the brilliant Medieval physician Thomas Linacre after his death. I sometimes feel his spirit still lurks *inter nos* within these walls.

"Erecting edifices and libraries is a worthy goal," the queen agreed. "But above all, we must work together to find new cures and elevate English medicinal practices to rival those on the continent. My people stagger under the burden of too dear a price for some of the new remedies to which they should have access."

"Bread and circuses, *panem et circenses ad infinitum*, that's what they'd like, Your Majesty," Caius muttered with a shake of his head. "Give them one step and they will want a mile, to wit that raucous crowd out there."

"I do not fear my people, but say on," Elizabeth commanded.

"Life is naturally unhealthsome," Pascal put in with a sharp sniff. "No utopias exist, as Sir Thomas More's great book made eminently clear. Besides, it is not just the fees for our learned services that cause the prices to rise but the outrageous reckonings of the apothecaries."

"Who," Caius said, rolling his eyes in feigned disbelief, "are ever clamoring for more freedom, when what they need is a firmer hand."

"But you already hold the power to place apothecaries who sell faulty stuffs in any prison but the Tower," she protested. "And you can legally enter their shops and search for defective and corrupted wares, which you can then destroy. I should think that would not only be enough to keep the herbalists in line but, sadly, to keep you from doing your duty to spend time learning and perfecting cures. I will not have my Royal College of Physicians waste their days being constables or bailiffs and not healers!"

"But, Gracious Majesty," Caius argued with a nervous, ever-shifting smile, "we must keep control of not only the barber-surgeons and apothecaries but other quacksalvers, mountebanks, and runnagates which—"

"Do you mean to say," the queen cut in, "that the shops in town which import and supply your cures are in the same category as quacks?"

"Indeed not," Pascal took up the discussion, steepling his fingers before his broad face as if to hide his expression. "But, just as in the days of your father, Your Grace, each area of mankind's expertise must be left to the experts and not encroached on by those who know not whereof they speak."

She stared him down, unsure if he dared such a direct affront at her, to the apothecaries, or if he was throwing Thomas More's so-called martyrdom in her face again. As the other fellows up and down the long table gaped and leaned out to listen raptly, Caius jumped into the moment's silence.

"*Id est*, there are certain apothecaries who are hardly trained as we by years of study and time abroad, et cetera. Why, madam, some who cannot even read or speak Latin and Greek but only cling to simple herbs dare to question the medical truths of humors within the body."

"Truths, you say, and not theories?" she challenged. "Of a certain we all rely on the wisdom of great men of past ages, but did they not make errors too? We have learned the world is hardly flat."

"Ah, but we do continually re-examine the old ways, though one out-of-town doctor, we've heard," Pascal said, shaking his head, "has been spreading the heretical belief that disease is caused not by warring humors, governed by the planets, nor by bad air. He—and he is not alone," his voice rang out and he pressed fingers fat as sausages on the tabletop as if to prop himself up, "claims that the airborne seeds of disease fall upon open pores of the skin and infect the person. Such a one claims that a man must be most careful shaving or his open pores will allow in certain harmful vapors! So much for new-fledged ideas!"

There was general nodding, head-shaking, or smothered sniggering down the length of the table. Elizabeth's ire rose, and she did too, partly to make everyone stand. Men scrambled to their feet, and she heard her two ladies' skirts rustle as they stood behind her.

"But like all my people," Elizabeth said, "I am plagued by worry that I or those I love, God forbid, may be one of the persons who needs your expertise and wisdom someday, gentlemen. Ergo," she added, staring now directly at the Latin-spewing John Caius, "the next time I send for help, I would expect some of you to be in London healing and not wandering hither and yon to attend meetings or chasing down apothecaries like a wayward constable-of-the-watch or harassing someone who has a new theory which you choose to mock without testing its good first. Never say something cannot be done without trying it, learned and yet-learning doctors. *I* am a new theory, a queen ruling alone, and it can be done, indeed!"

"But, Majesty," Peter Pascal dared to rattle on, after that speech with which she had hoped to make her exit, "about your Lady Katherine Ashley's recent illness. We all know disease is a gift from God to gild a martyr's crown, so each must suffer some in his or her turn in this life."

"And I say"—here she switched to speaking Latin with an occasional phrase in Greek—"that I hate to be ill, and I think illness is a personal affront which a kingdom's doctors must and will spend their precious time to battle. We have yet the small pox and the great pox and the Black Death and numerous other maladies, and there must be something, some way we can discover what the Lord God has given us to fight such. The status quo is not acceptable, and I expect occasional and detailed explanations of how you will strive to improve upon your past performance. Good day to you, Fellows of the Royal College of Physicians."

She smacked her goblet down for effect and started for the door. Caius—even the portly Pascal—raced to keep up.

"Your Grace," Caius cried, "you have put our *credo* so perfectly, has she not, Doctor Pascal?"

"Ah—indeed. We care deeply for all ill persons in our charge and care."

"As I care for and keep a good eye on all, even physicians, in my kingdom," the queen concluded and strode down the escutcheon-hung hall toward the street door. She wanted the final word, the fine exit, and these doctors clung like their own blood-letting leeches.

"Then, Your Gracious Majesty," Caius went on as he reached the door with her, "there is one request that would help us to fulfill your every desire for our work."

"Which is?" she snapped.

"I—we humbly request that we might have bodies," Caius said, "corpses here for dissection to learn the things you would have us to do."

"Corpses?" she cried, her hand flying to her bodice when she tried never to show dismay in public. "Corpses to dissect? I'll not have bodies so abused. Whose?"

The man dared to shrug. "I know not, Your Gracious

Majesty, as the human body is all the same. The poor found dead in the streets. Prisoners or executed felons. Country rabble. Whoever."

"I shall think on it," she declared, raising her voice to its ringing tone, "for quite a long while. You may shrug, Fellows of the College, at the earthly remains of your fellow human beings so abused, but I do not. And now," she concluded again, irked she had to find yet another closing line, "I shall take my leave and, next time I want to see you in the palace or here or anywhere, I warrant you will not be so busy."

Her guard on the front door barely pulled it open before she got to it. On the stoop, watching the crowd, Robin saw her and swirled open her cloak he'd evidently been holding. He offered his arm to escort her out, but she kept going on her own. Furiously blushing and wanting no one to see so in the light, she made for her coach. It waited for her but one house away, behind the line of unmounted horses, as they had obviously expected her to ride back. Coachmen and grooms alike scrambled from their lolling stances and grabbed for reins and bridles. Boonen, the burly coachman, swept open the door for her and banged down the folding, metal steps.

Robin haphazardly settled her cloak about her shoulders, and Mary and Anne tried to help control her voluminous skirts for her climb up and in. But she was too quick even for them. Though her cloak spilled back into Robin's hands, she felt him give her a hoist up, one hand on her waist and one under her left elbow.

And then she nearly stepped on the horrid thing lying on the floor of the dim coach. Gaping at it, despite her long-tended command of herself, the queen screamed.